D0914366

INVITATION FROM MINERVA

BOOKS BY MARCH COST

INVITATION FROM MINERVA

THE HOUR AWAITS

THE BESPOKEN MILE

RACHEL

THE DARK STAR

THE DARK GLASS

A MAN NAMED LUKE

Invitation FROM MINERVA

BY MARCH COST

J. B. LIPPINCOTT COMPANY

Philadelphia and New York

Printed in the
United States of America

First Edition

Library of Congress Catalog Card Number 54-5602

TO

MARY AND NANCY MORRISON

in remembrance of

The First Muse

sometimes shown with the Style, or Pen

Whitsuntide, 1953

"I shake not the earth only,
but also heaven. . . .
That those things which cannot be shaken
may remain."

CONTENTS

CHARACTERS IN ORDER OF REFERENCE:

THE HOSTESS:

Her Serene Highness
the Princess Victoria Babenberg of Austria
daughter of
Frederick, Prince Babenberg of Austria
and his wife
Beatrice Beauharnais of France.

Louise, Mrs. Dobra-Portheim	elderly relative of Princess Victoria
Stephen Abbey	younger, surviving partner of Guerini & Abbey, antique dealers, Florence
Clio Tubbs	seventeen-year-old orphan, ward of Stephen Abbey
François, Comte de Talloires et d'Annecy	fiancé of Princess Victoria
Princess Sophia Babenberg (Tante Sophia)	aunt of Princess Victoria
Frau Alma Winkwurth	Babenberg family hanger-on
Prince Augustus, later Conte Della Rocca	only brother of Princess Victoria
Dominic Gerontius Colonna, Prince Perugia	elderly cousin of Princess Victoria
Estella Storm	musical-comedy star, former mistress of François, Comte de Talloires
Professor Oliver Drury	former lover of Princess Victoria

Mr. Garett Phelps, botanist	Intelligence agent in the service of the British Government
Albert, a child	orphan, and nephew of Louise Dobra-Portheim's housekeeper
George Herriot, M.D.	London doctor who has attended Albert, also Princess Victoria in England
Lord Brompton	influential British subject, one-time admirer of Princess Victoria's mother

THE SERVANTS:

Charlotte, a Viennese	one-time lady's maid, now cook at the Château Maria Sophia
Hans, an elderly Austrian	caretaker at the Château Maria Sophia

SERVANTS WHO LIVE OUT:

Barolyi, a Magyar	steward of the small Babenberg estate
Old Anna	Hans' mother
Young Detta	servant from the village of Springbrunnen

INVITATION FROM MINERVA

INVITATION TO MEMORY . . .

The heat-wave of October 1921 found an inland English spa basking sedately in this blazing aftermath. The avenue of lime trees that led to the decorous Assembly Rooms, the classical façade of the Corn Exchange, surmounted by Ceres, the Georgian buildings, the Victorian hotels staidly fronting the wooded hills stood out in breathless clarity—a shadowless hush.

During this phenomenal summer, October midday still found striped awnings flaunting from all southern exposures. Geraniums continued to run riot from balcony and terrace urn. Now in the apricot afterglow, from open windows the elderly watched the young on bicycles spin by at intervals with the whirring of giant insects. Suddenly the street lights came on—needless stars in a golden world still bright as day, becalmed, it seemed, beyond the possibility of change.

Mrs. Dobra-Portheim sat benevolently on the balcony of her hotel, enjoying the teatime music from the winter-garden across the way. An early evening paper lay on the wrought-iron table, together with her opera-glasses which brought the brass band in the brightly-lit pavilion amusingly near. The Conductor and his twenty-four scarlet Guardsmen were now braying their way through *Samson and Delilah*.

It was all quite delightful!

Strictly speaking, of course, she ought not to have taken this suite, but Victoria had encouraged her, and as Victoria was habitually economical, the cost of the *appartement* had infallibly assumed the appearance of reason, of a moral sanction. "After all, Thérèse wants your convalescence to be comfortable." From this angle, the suite had become almost a duty, for there was no one Louise detested as she did Thérèse, her sister-in-law.

Happily she skimmed the paper and scanned the band, by turns. The tidy trees, the trim shrubs, the bright geraniums, the leisurely listeners in the gardens, the buoyancy of the music induced gaiety. Then too she had had a particularly successful henna before leaving London. Her new beige outfit had done wonders for her—taken at least five years off her age. Positively she didn't look a day more than fifty this evening! Victoria was right—this was the place to come to, until the Continent shook itself into shape again. That had been a distinctly attractive elderly man—Colonel Fortescue—with whom she had had that amusing encounter in the lounge after luncheon. She had always had a weakness for the strong, silent type . . . although frankly, as a start, she had not bargained for his wire-haired terrier leaping into her lap. Neither had he apparently. "But then she is a lady, ma'am, and we have it on the best authority that your sex is inaccessible to reason."

With a gurgle she had responded: "Or we wouldn't have anything to do with yours—you heartless man, now would we?"

They were getting on famously by the time Victoria, somewhat astonished, had found them. Victoria was a dear girl. Louise would miss her when she left tomorrow. Not perhaps as much as she might have done earlier. But of course this was a health-resort. Already she felt braced.

A tap on the door of the room beyond! A second evening

paper . . . most attentive! The chambermaid, a cockney recently promoted, was so much impressed by the best suite that Mrs. Dobra-Portheim was invested for her with some of its importance. She could not do enough for her . . . readjusting chairs, tidying the writing-table, rearranging magazines.

"Yes, Madame, the last week for the Irish Guards. No one to touch them on the band-stand. They keep a steady blaze. The Welsh Guards was too erratic. It was a black-out or a bonfire with them. Never went into the George in the interval like the Highland regiments. But stood about dejected, smoking pipes, which wasn't the thing at all in a place like this . . . though they woke up something surprising on their last night—that I will say. No one knew what got into them after the Regimental quick-step. Proper demons. By the end of the programme, the sixpenny seats were dancing in front of the band-stand. It was the talk of the town later—that there had been dancing in an enclosed area without a licence. People died laughing when they thought it over. And you wouldn't have known the Conductor or the bandsmen for the same sticks. Extra after extra regardless. Yet out they went next day, as dreary as undertakers—standing about the station as helpless as the milk-cans."

"Delightfully graphic, Gladys. Now, before you go—please place another chair upon the balcony for Princess Victoria Babenberg. I expect her at any moment."

Princess Victoria Babenberg had a small bedroom at the back of the hotel, next to the service shaft. She had not troubled to unpack her modest case. Gladys had earlier decided that hers was one of those foreign titles that didn't amount to much. Regretfully the chambermaid now took leave of the widowed but apparently opulent Mrs. Dobra-Portheim.

Left alone, Louise dwelt for a moment on her cousin. Victoria was pleased about her engagement to François. What girl wouldn't be—woman rather. Viccy was now in the thirties. Time was passing. But she was not elated, and this puzzled Louise. François, Comte de Talloires et d'Annecy, was a prize long since despaired of by ambitious mothers and hopeful daughters. Viccy was his equal by birth, of course, but the fact remained that she hadn't a penny piece to bless herself with, as an impoverished member of the disrupted Austrian Court. All of which made it rather foolish of Viccy to delay marriage till next year. Years ago Louise had had an idea that Victoria was more than a little in love with François. Her present behaviour just did not make sense. This insistence too that it was an understanding rather than an engagement was alarmingly maladroit. It was Louise's experience that proffered loop-holes had a way of justifying themselves. All this despite François' recent *Times* announcement too!

François wouldn't like Victoria's attitude when he discovered it. There was a grudging element in it that Louise could not fathom. Especially with lovers no longer in their first youth.

Mrs. Dobra-Portheim brought the band into focus as it now dealt with "Old Comrades."

It was, in fact, an engagement that might well have happened years ago. Was that perhaps the explanation of Victoria's coolness?

Swiftly Louise shied from this conclusion.

Of course Viccy was happy. Not perhaps as happy as Louise would have been at that age, but then Viccy's generation always struck Louise as lack-lustre. Those younger still were swinging too far in the other direction. One ought to remember where to draw the line, even if one did not draw it!

But Viccy, she feared, was too thoroughly mapped. François was twelve years older than Viccy, but although courtly to a degree, it was inconceivable that he should conform to rigidity. Fascinating, of course, to see the outcome of this struggle for supremacy. But Viccy must marry him first. It would be the dear girl's salvation. An entire youth passed in the shadow of one of the most beautiful women in Europe probably accounted for Viccy's lack of *élan*. Beatrice, Princess Babenberg, had been, as well, an exquisite personality, but Louise suspected that such a mother could prove a notable discipline. Viccy might well have come to attach an absurd importance now to personal freedom.

Then she had had the war years, 1914 to 1918, cooped up in that uncomfortable castle in the Dolomites—a miniature baroque palace no better than a summer house. A holiday haunt that was now the only roof remaining to the poor girl. Those war years must have stretched dismally for her—and she was still imprisoned there by poverty. Victoria had now done time at the Château Maria Sophia to the tune of seven years. Louise shuddered to think of its dullness since Beatrice's death. Not a marriageable man nearer than Innsbruck, and isolated with Tante Sophia immersed in her Swedenborg, and that tedious Frau Winkwurth who was not even a lady, and whose feelings had to be studied at every turn. And the servants who remained as a favour because elsewhere they would starve! Frightful. No wonder Viccy lacked *joie de vivre*. It was imperative she married François at once. Louise was devoted to him but he must just take his chance. Viccy had been martyred too long.

Another tap on the door and Victoria stood on the threshold —dark, smiling, surprisingly vibrant after all as the Family sacrifice!

For a moment the Princess paused.

Louise, banked by geraniums, sat blandly Edwardian in the afterglow. The music from the band-stand, in Suppé's "Light Cavalry," trotted across the leafy balcony. The scent of freshly-cut grass from lawns earlier mown lent a fictitious moistness to the dry air. The dim room was still fragrant with this.

"But this is gaiety!" exclaimed Victoria. "Louise, I knew this was the place for you—if you can keep your head in the Victorian seclusion of that lounge downstairs." Smiling, she seated herself. "I'm quite convinced, of course, that Colonel Fortescue has trained his dog to jump upon all likely laps."

Louise beamed. "It's still a compliment."

"I see from the letter-rack," added Victoria, "that he's a V.C., D.S.O., and what not—which confirms my suspicions of enterprise. Now that he's gone into action, I feel no time will be lost."

But unaccountably Louise shook her head. Solemnly she said: "Viccy, time is not to be trifled with—at any age. Don't postpone your marriage till spring. Do as François urges. After all, he's offered in the most delicate and delightful way to send both Sophia and Frau Winkwurth to Bordighera, where sooner or later they'll *have* to go. Without you they simply cannot run the Château. It only means—"

"That he'll begin to pay out for them a little sooner. Yes, I know. But by delaying, I hope to be able to help there."

"You? But Viccy how can you?"

"Can I trust you to keep a secret?"

"Darling, of *course!* I'm perfectly safe if I'm warned in advance."

"If I tell you, I must rely on you not to repeat a word of this. I have reason to think, Louise, that one of the pictures at the Château is much more valuable than anyone guessed . . . otherwise it would have gone long ago. So much depends on this sale now that I'm almost afraid to mention which picture it is—as all such things as insurance have long since lapsed. It has taken us all our time to pay for our food, let alone that of Charlotte, Barolyi, Hans and Anna. Now that the Château is in Italian territory, my only hope is to sell through Italy. There is a dealer in Florence, a man called Stephen Abbey whom I've heard might be interested. I daren't ask for advice in Vienna. But I was told in Paris that this man is an expert in the world market, and of unquestioned probity. If I sell this picture successfully I shall not only be able to help with Sophia and Frau Winkwurth—but I shall be able to buy my own trousseau and not arrive penniless."

"But Viccy this attitude is so absurd! As if it would matter to François."

"It matters to me."

"Darling, how *can* you be so bourgeoise?"

"Quite easily. Now, please, no more about it."

"But it's so selfish. François is well off. To keep him waiting like this—for this sale may take time."

"Of course it may. That's the point of next spring."

"Does he know of this prospective sale?"

"Of course not. As my second cousin, he's one of the Family Trust. He might feel it his duty to inform Augustus."

"There I do sympathize, dear. It's almost immoral the way in which executors hang together. Completely oblivious of the human aspect."

The Princess gave that deep little laugh which was so infectious, yet not heard often enough.

"The legal aspect is that the picture is mine. Maman left it to me with everything else of hers at the Château. Augustus got all the really valuable stuff in the Vienna Palast. But I'm determined that no one shall know of the sale until the money is in the bag. That's why I'm going direct to Florence when I leave here tomorrow. It will save explanations when I get back."

"But what if you run into François there? He leaves Rome next week."

"Next week isn't this week, *Liebste!* I shall be safely home by then. Don't look so lugubrious. After all, the deal may come off much more quickly than we think. I understand that this Mr. Abbey already has a client in view for me. In fact, I was to have seen him last week."

"Instead of which you came over to help me first! Viccy, forgive me. I don't know what the Family would do without you. Yet now, when you try to make a little money, here am I criticizing you! Although what money has to do with François and you I cannot understand. But then I'm wholly Austrian—"

"And I'm half French! Admit you think I'm not grateful enough."

"No, my dear—not glad enough, perhaps. It seems a pity to cross François when he has made such a point of your engagement. And done it publicly too. He is the most charming man, but the last I'd care to trifle with."

"I agree, *Liebste*. That's why I'm guarding him against any precipitate step. And myself. Come," she laughed cajolingly, "I assure you that his interests are my interests. I have him at heart."

The telephone rang sharply.

"Shall I?" Victoria had stepped into the sitting-room and lifted the receiver. She spoke, listened, and then spoke again.

Louise, watching her through the french windows, saw her colourless skin flush suddenly.

"What is it, Viccy?"

"A long-distance call from Rome—from François—is coming through in a few minutes. They couldn't find me in my room."

"Close the window quickly then, or you won't hear a word! I'll wait out here. How delightful!"

Delightful indeed, Louise ruminated. And he hadn't waited for the night-rate either! Things were looking much more healthy.

Enlivened she picked up her opera-glasses, and scanned the scarlet bandsmen again, now romping home in the final number: "Floradora." Dusk was rising heavily from the lime trees as these towered above the pavilion. The hanging baskets of flowers, the dark windows of the Georgian houses with their pale, flat façades, the brass instruments on the band-stand were at last vividly splashed by the street lamps. Geraniums smouldered—their odour faintly oppressive now. Sultry enough for thunder. The sombre but elegant tunic of the Conductor with his white sword-belt stood out as distinctly as the black and ivory of piano keys—happily his figure could stand this! Through the opera-glasses she could detect, as he turned his head, sweat beading his brow. She was also fascinated to see the length of the street and the gardens reflected in the brass of the French horn. A minute but blazing vista. Each time the musician turned the horn round, the town stood on its head, and then righted itself with a flourish.

The lights in the French horn grew brighter, the windows of the mirrored houses were shot with fire as the instrument was professionally shaken out. The whole scene became a comet streaking through darkness to a fanfare of "God Save the King." It might have been an earlier era. Festivity itself!

What an interminable call Viccy was having! François must be spending money like water. It did Louise good to think of it!

The window on to the balcony opened. Victoria's smooth dark head, with the classical knot on the nape of her neck, was outlined by the hanging leaves. Louise noted with approval that she seemed a little breathless. *She's madly in love with him,* Louise decided. Why was I uneasy?

"François is so delighted that you've stood the journey well."

"You were able to put him out of suspense?"

"I swear this call was for you, Louise! He always telephones me later. Before I go to bed. I should be disappointed to think that this was the last of him to-night. It was expressly your call."

"*Wunderbar!*" Delightedly Louise sighed: "What it is to be young!"

"Oh, come," said Victoria a trifle explicitly. "Scarcely *young.*"

"My dear, to see you seated there, since François' call on my behalf, not a day more than twenty-five! Ah! if men only knew the happiness that presence-in-absence gives us they would at any distance be wedded to a telephone or pillar-box."

"Yes," admitted the Princess, "there's a peculiar joy in the defeat of distance. Tante Sophia maintains that if each good-bye prepares us for the final farewell, so do such greetings anticipate the ultimate encounter—that heavenly tryst of which she is so certain."

"Dangerous all the same, darling, *terrestrially.* I can remember having a prolonged affair with an impossible man before I met Dobra, simply because he knew how to exploit absence so companionably. His barrage of letters and telegrams which had at first intrigued, then exasperated me, ended by nourishing me. He was as constant as the next day. I assure you that if we had not been reunited, I should have been ruined."

"Talking of reunions, François wishes to know if you will join us for Christmas at Château Maria Sophia. We're having a little party then, and you know how entrancing the Stromberg is at every season."

"Now, Viccy, you've admitted that the house is cold."

"Yes, the house can be cold. But Barolyi the overseer assured me before I left that he had secured a record load of wood at the cheapest possible price. I don't know how he did it. It's some sort of estate secret that he's managed to hide from Hans."

"Are those two servants still at war?"

"A Magyar and an Austrian invariably distrust each other —that's to be expected. But I can promise that the Château will be warmer this winter."

"Viccy, if you find your house cold, it must be unbearable. People can stand cold in their own homes that would kill them elsewhere. No, I don't think I'll come till later. One thousand thanks nevertheless."

The Princess lifted the newspaper. "Anything in this tonight?"

"Yes, I meant to show you. Really the most extraordinary thing! An English girl of sixteen has climbed the face of the Palazzo Toledo in Florence and down again. You remember the Toledo?"

"Of course. Why didn't she take the stairs?"

"It appears the Palazzo was shut up. She made this sensational climb to rescue a cat from the roof. Fantastic of course, but then she is obviously a British tomboy. There's very little in the papers to-night, so they've spread themselves on this. Already she is known throughout Florence as *La Coraggiosa*."

"Louise, do you believe a word of it?"

"Oh, yes, dear. Italy would scarcely give an English girl an unearned laurel in 1921. Mussolini is much too busy organizing his maniples, centuries, cohorts and legions. But the Italians themselves are an agreeable people and this tribute tempts one to think that they welcome the chance of saying something pleasant about the British for a change."

"Well, unless Cousin Colonna's palace has shrunk overnight it certainly seems a tall tale."

"But, darling, the exploit was watched by any number of eye-witnesses."

"Was it?" For the first time Victoria was impressed.

"Yes, indeed. There's another photograph on the inside page showing the route she took. She was first seen chasing the cat round the roof. A valuable animal for which a large reward had been offered. Then she climbed down as she had come up. You can see from the photograph that the eaves of the lower adjoining wing were level with the top-floor balcony parapet. *That* can't have been an easy moment—she must have nerves like whip-cord! From these eaves she stepped with the cat, crossed the balcony, and again gripping the water-pipe descended forty feet. The populace watched the descent, made with the cat slung in a pudding cloth across her shoulder. A pin could have been heard to fall. Twelve feet from the ground she was rescued. Of course, Viccy, remembering the Latin attitude to animals—they must think it mad."

"It *is* mad."

They both laughed, although Louise broke off to say: "We shouldn't laugh. It's a prodigious thing to have done."

"M'yes," said the Princess reflectively. "I wish I could remember the back of the Palazzo better. I only looked out once or twice. There was something a little unusual about it, but I can't remember what."

"Prodigious," reaffirmed Louise. "Now *I* have only to look down six feet to fall. In fact, I've often thought that if I found myself falling from some great height, my terror would be such, I should automatically begin to fly. Can you understand that?"

"No," said Victoria flatly. "What did you say the girl's name was?"

"Clio Tubbs . . . the Tubbs is rather an anti-climax, poor dear. In the later edition her photograph is on the front page. Here it is."

Together they studied it.

"Is her nose rather large?"

"A trifle," Louise admitted. "Of course, she's young. Once she fills out it won't be so noticeable—there will be less of the hungry sea-gull about her." She laughed.

"What's the joke?"

"Then she'll be the sort of woman that a wisp of veiling turns into a siren at sight."

Victoria smiled. "Yes, do you know—she *has* a look of someone. Who is it?"

Louise shook her head humorously. "We've never seen her before. But Eve always recognizes Lilith at first sight."

"She's certainly got something," Victoria agreed. "I don't know what it is, but it's there. This edition says that her neck was badly scratched by the cat. There's gratitude for you! But I'm glad to see that she's not only got the large reward offered by the cat's owner—a film magnate, Rex Steibel, she's even now on her way to Rome for a film test. Apparently the cat escaped when his party left for Rome, but not into the street as was first thought. It was accidentally shut up in the empty house. *'Miss Tubbs lived until recently with her uncle, the late Mr. Edward Tubbs, artist, in the small hotel adjoining the courtyard of the great Palazzo.'* Louise, now I've remembered the unusual feature of the Palazzo's back quarters: the large walnut tree in the courtyard of the Albergo Toscano. A very large walnut tree. It stretched across to the second-floor window of the Palazzo. Interesting. *'No sooner had Mr. Steibel heard that this gallant girl was seventeen and of arresting appearance than he telegraphed his offer of a film test.'* Do listen to this! '. . . *asked if she were elated at the possibility of a part in Mr. Steibel's next production Miss Tubbs replied, "Not particularly. The Cinema is after all only a bastard branch of the theatre proper."* ' "

"Pompous little horror! What *can* her background be?"

But the Princess was surveying the photograph with a touch of tenderness. "Books, I imagine. Books first and last, with possibly a smattering of man! Yes, I'm certain that this young lady is the only woman in her own world—up to the moment of going to press! The wisp of veiling has not yet occurred to her."

"A film magnate seems rather an incongruous tenant for the Toledo today—unless, of course, he gave a lot of gay parties. But didn't Colonna tell us that half of it was shut up? Viccy, will you ever forget the Palazzo when it was open to the *beau monde?* Those marvellous balls given by the old Prince—the blaze of colour against the white Carrara marble; those suppers in the long arcade of fountains—a feast of Lucullus; and the music—the Austrian orchestras, the Russian Gypsies! And yet the flowers predominated. I don't know how they managed it, but they did! What a lavish host—tragic he had no children. But rather mean, really, the way in which he kept Dominic short of money. After all, he couldn't help being his nephew—the inevitable heir. Yet the old gentleman quite openly admitted he clung to life to delay that happy day!"

"And yet," said the Princess slowly, "with all his faults he seemed so much more admirable than Dominic. He had warmth. Dominic Stefano Gerontius Colonna, Prince of Perugia—what a proud title it is—is flawless but frigid."

"Viccy, how can you call him flawless, with that tiresome lisp which I'm certain is simply an affectation. I find him positively disconcerting, for not only does he look like a monk when one knows he is nothing of the sort, but there's something static about him—he never ages. Yet he must be sixty-six if he's a day. Very odd, looking back—he was the only man at that last ball *not* in fancy-dress. Yet any number of people mistook him for this or that historical character. Your mother insisted that this proved he really *was* the Devil! You know how she loved to laugh."

"I had forgotten. I was twenty-one that night and very full of myself."

"Of course, of course . . . the party was given for you. You went as a Neapolitan Violet—perfectly sweet. And François—most striking as Dante . . . such a superb profile."

"Maman chose his costume, but I believe he found it all rather preposterous."

"François has been too long at the Embassy in London! The English have made him self-conscious. How clearly it all comes back now! Your mother went as an English rose, which Dominic applauded as provocative but unpatriotic in a French woman with a perfectly good Austrian husband! However, as Frederick wasn't present, I don't suppose it gave rise to any international incident. But didn't something happen at the Cotillion?"

The Princess' smile was sprightly. "Yes, François forgot to lead off with me. Augustus deputized. But one's brother is scarcely the hero of the hour."

"My dear, I'd forgotten that. It's so unlike François. What could have happened?"

"A mere nothing, I do assure you! He was later run to earth in the library, with the Belgian ambassador . . . over a little matter of priority in the wine market that was exciting them both. François being irresistible, I understand that Burgundy carried the day."

And the Princess in the warm dusk was thinking: *The Neapolitan Violet costume was exquisite. It was the only time that I have ever looked beautiful, yet it was not such a happy ball after all. That was the night when I finally realized that François did not love me.*

Aloud Louise said: "But you and François danced together later, for I remember an enchanting incident as I came downstairs. Your mother, bountiful as summer itself, was standing in the gallery watching the ballroom from one of the arched alcoves, and I overheard her exclaim with such triumph to the man beside her: 'There she is! You'll see her in a second—as she turns.' The orchestra was playing a sweet, wistful trifle—that waltz of Waldteufel's 'Tres Jolie,' and you know how sentimental I am. That night you outshone everyone! Cherish the memory of that Burgundy. It might have been another woman. François, of course, has never been much interested in women—and so they've left him alone. But now that he's alive to one of them, it's remarkable how this news will spread. Be careful!"

"Perhaps," said the Princess, "that's why *I* came into his

picture at the eleventh hour! Come, Louise, you must have heard all about Estella Storm. Everyone knows about that belated love affair."

"The musical-comedy actress?" It was Louise's turn to be airy. "My dear, I never for a moment imagined that François wasn't human. Any normal man— And that's all over and done with."

"Last month," said the Princess with precision.

"All I can say," retorted Louise, "is that few eligible men have led such blameless lives. When you consider that François is now over forty and that this is the first—er, authenticated—story."

"Exactly!" Viccy's smile gleamed again. "That makes it more impressive, doesn't it?"

For a second Louise hesitated. Viccy was obviously become an unappeasable Rachel mourning for that uncherished child —her own lost youth. The fact that François was now in love with her no longer weighed, apparently. The situation was indeed serious.

"Tell me, Louise," Victoria pursued, "have you ever seen Miss Storm? You've been in London now for years. Like François I am but human. What is she like—this lovely lady?"

"Fair," said Louise firmly. "As perfect as a wax peach. She must inevitably put on weight by the time she's thirty."

"You loyal darling! I believe that she's also wealthy?"

"Well, she must have made a fortune in the last ten years, and she hasn't flung it away like so many in the theatre. Undoubtedly it was not François' money but his title that appealed."

"François himself may have done that."

"Viccy, this *ingénue* attitude is beyond me! Not only are you unfair to François, you are unfair to yourself. And when a woman ceases to be fair to herself, it amounts to suicide. Now, let us go inside to the light and be cheerful. Or I shall suspect that I've no longer patience with your generation—which would be an admission of age that I simply will not entertain. No, no, dear girl, take it from me, you're remembering the wrong things. In memory, at least, one is free to make a happier choice always. . . . Why, that's the invitation to destiny itself, now I come to think of it!"

INVITATION TO MINERVA . . .

It was 3 a.m. The Princess lay in the heat-wave gloom of the narrow back bedroom—Victoria Antoinette Camena Egeria Caroline Augusta, kinswoman of Franz Joseph, one-time Emperor of Austria—and resisted an impulse to turn impatiently.

The thin mattress was too short for the bed; there was a smell of soot from the small, black fireplace; (could it be going to thunder?) and the bed-side lamp did not function. But mercifully the service shaft had also ceased to work. About midnight this so-called dumb-waiter had shot up on its pulley for the last time and its doors had been defiantly slammed shut.

Late-comers had by now paid their ultimate visit to the bath-and-toilet rooms opposite. *They* had not troubled to slam doors, and on each occasion the plumbing system had audibly declared its searching efficiency. For over an hour her room had alternately rushed, wailed and died in sympathy with this cistern. A god-send that Louise was safe in that suite. *She* would long since have rung the bell, firm in the faith that no management could reasonably expect her to excuse the inexcusable. What a generation that was—in its refusal to endure trifles and its ability to see calamity through as a matter of course!

About 1 a.m. someone next door (sans bed-lamp also, apparently) had fallen over a chair, and then got into bed with a groan. The last sound had come from the attic above round about two—when a servant had kicked off his shoes. But still she could not sleep.

Lost love had her at his mercy, and the name was Oliver, not François. A dangerous man who could exploit absence companionably! How aptly Louise's frivolous words had hit off Victoria's love affair with Professor Drury. That unofficial honeymoon in Holland ten years ago had failed to knit them body and soul as had done those years of correspondence since, while Oliver struggled for the Chair that would make marriage possible. Then the compulsory silence of the war-years, so miraculously informed by a sense of deepening communion that, only last month, had proved completely bogus! Her first visit to London after a decade had disclosed the truth. Oliver had achieved his Chair only to resign it for a *chaise-longue!* On the strength of a small fortune, a bequest hitherto concealed, he had, in fact, been idle for years.

But of course Oliver was scarcely to blame. Tolerance, replacing respect, admitted this. Had she and François married years ago, Oliver could never have happened.

No, she would not readily forget Michaelmas this year. That François, belatedly caught on the rebound, should then discover his own affection for her had proved a climax—but not one that added conviction to the present engagement.

She would believe in her marriage once it had come to pass!

François was fond of her of course—a feeling very different from the passion he must have felt for the lovely Miss Storm. That was only to be expected.

In the small hot room, with its oppressive smell of soot,

the Princess suddenly began to laugh noiselessly. Why, she thought, I'm so jealous I won't even compete!

Then as suddenly she paused. She had just remembered something else. The despatch with which François had terminated his affair with the singer once he discovered how exigent she could be!

But had not Victoria been quite as ruthless with Oliver? Unlike the possessive Miss Storm, Oliver had not been possessive enough, and, lethargy once discovered, she had let him pass as promptly as a passer-by with whom she had temporarily collided. Treatment that had since galvanized Oliver into unwelcome ardour—to her exasperation. She herself recognized so conclusively their experience as finished, once its illusion was declared, that patience failed her.

Yet nothing would induce her to commit her heart in advance to François. She had had too many shocks. Once married, she would dedicate herself to him as she had always longed to do. Not before. As *châtelaine* of Vermontaine she would begin to live where she had left off in girlhood, years ago.

The Château d'Annecy had never appealed to her in the same way as his mother's home. She found the formality of the Talloires' seat slightly intimidating. It had something of the curious stillness, the inscrutability of François himself. The combination of both might prove overpowering.

But Vermontaine held a patriarchal peace, a tranquil dignity that stemmed from the country rather than the court—Burgundy itself, with the pastoral landscape of the Plateau de Langres rolling around it. *Vermontaine!* As a child she had first fallen in love with its picture on a wine-bottle. In gold-leaf its graceful chimneys outlined a Renaissance sky; there was the winged court with its shallow centre fountain, stone balustrades, smooth sward that ran surprisingly into hayfields east and west, and a sloping vineyard due south! Minutely the white label had indicated one of the statuesque sycamores which earned the Château its ancient name *Feuilles Vermontaine*. Above this sycamore, half-way between heaven and earth, but quite at home there, was the coat of arms of Tante Geneviève's House, showing shield and crested helm—with a powdering of dots that Viccy had then believed must be snow in summer.

Her own rococo little Schloss in the Stromberg might be sanctuary today, but Vermontaine, with her youth behind her, held a vitality that no other place possessed. Vermontaine was that region where an ideal alternative still presented itself as possibility, where possibility might yet gloriously vindicate itself as certainty. And where the severance of death itself, after fulfilment, would mean no grudging acceptance of the inevitable empty glass, but an escaping *bouquet*—noble Burgundy!

The cloudiness of such an end, this vague apotheosis, satisfied the Princess well enough at her present stage of bodily sufficiency. Brought up as a Protestant in a household dominated by a Roman Catholic mother, and tutored by an English spinster with a passion for Greek antiquity, she had emerged from these mixed influences with a distinctly pagan bias! In the sphere of the eternal values, the Good, the True, the Beautiful, the last came first with Victoria—but sensuously, as revealed in nature and art. Although destiny had not yet pressed home the spiritual issue, her paradise was a classical one.

At the Château Maria Sophia, her favourite point of vantage was still a small temple to Minerva, a charming classical conceit built to salute the Italian vista. Here as a girl, Victoria in spring or summer had winged her romantic wishes to Minerva. In childhood an offering of Alpine heath had marked the first of the holidays—or the purple of the vernal windflower. A handful of wheat the last. It was her shrine and she kept it as gaily furnished florally as did the villagers of Springbrunnen the shrines to the Madonna in the Stromberg. During the winter months the marble figure of Minerva was taken into the Château where it presided from a pedestal in the hall. The country servants, devout Roman Catholics, scrupulously kept its handful of wheat in place there, to ensure next year's harvest. Minerva was one of Viccy's earliest memories. It was a somewhat florid sculpture, but had the suavity and grandiloquence that delight any child. She had first been beguiled by some words read by her father, Frederick Prince Babenberg, in which Minerva of the flashing eyes, out of the West, had called for a following wind and sent it singing over the wine-dark sea! Fascinated, the child would stand before the blind orbs of the statue waiting for the flash and the scene to change. Delay merely heightened expectancy —it never disappointed. Early she had found wonder a food in itself.

But now in the stuffy hotel bedroom, the Princess' head had begun to throb. Again she resisted the temptation to toss. . . . On such a day as this had been, *there* to the open south and Italy, from the depths of a purple-blue horizon, a thunder-cloud of this Tyrrhenian tone would sluggishly unfurl, until midway it spanned the sky—when, with incredible speed, spirals like smoke would issue from it to fly in advance. Minerva's torches, her father had called them.

Oh, for that following wind— Impatiently she flung back the coverlet, Daughter of Zeus, Lady of the Gleaming Eyes!

Suddenly across the hot dark room, there shot a fierce

crackle. Lightning flashed. Thunder broke in judgment, then in deluge.

Rejoicing the Princess lay behind this rushing curtain of rain, breathing afresh its chill, completely at one with its elemental uproar.

Soon Florence would be over, and she be safely home! It would, of course, be unfortunate if François discovered she had been there. She must just pass it off as a whim, a flying visit—and why not? She did not mean to tell him the truth at this stage. But emphatically neither would she tell him an untruth. The less said the better, if occasion arose. And, after all, why should it arise?

At Château Maria Sophia confidence would reclaim her.

Again in the distance she saw the tiny temple of Minerva, its two ancient oaks golden like thinning bubbles upon that vast horizon, the blue autumnal sky.

What a downpour outside. . . . She could listen all night—

But she did not. Almost at once she slept. . . .

Waking in the stricken silence of the first daylight, she found that the heat-haze had again gathered in the small back-garden of the hotel, breaking here and there among the trees. Isolated raindrops fell at intervals from muffled branches, and a flushed light suffused the mist as if the sun were rising through the ground. The commonplace patch was transformed—it loomed, steaming and gigantic as a jungle!

Beauty! she breathed, oh, if there be nothing less than this in life—come what may, it is enough!

A vow, less a challenge than a prayer! Yet gratitude is inevitably spiritual communication. It is of course a platitude that any ambitious spirit making headway in their direction draws the attention of the gods. At that moment the Princess, who had no patience with platitudes, had forgotten her tutelary deity. She had overlooked Minerva whose single-minded aim, regardless of cost, is to preserve integrity in her votaries. Indeed, as far as cost and the Lady of Athens are concerned, expense is no object. Never has been. Never will be.

Irrevocably the invitation to Minerva had been issued. . . .

INVITATION TO COMMERCE . . .

Beneath the banner of "Guerini & Abbey," the Princess stared around, impressed by the vast interior, dismayed by the dust and confusion in which the antiques were displayed. How could anyone distinguish the genuine from junk in this conglomeration? Of course Signor Guerini's death was fairly recent. Some disorder might be expected, yet that furniture looked as if it had been stacked there for generations! Still, she must remember that the place had a notable reputation. The English, too, were invariably honest—as individuals. And this Stephen Abbey, she understood, was the son of a Sussex vicar.

The Princess opened the door, and advanced among the ecclesiastical booty of four centuries. Not a sign of a picture anywhere! Yet Mr. Abbey had been described as one of Duveen's agents. It was enough!

Reinforced by this reminder, she presented Jacob Gaddi with her card, although he suggested a goods-porter in a hurry rather than a major-domo at her service.

The most disconcerting experience of all now occurred: Mr. Abbey, in his shirt-sleeves, emerged rather irritably from sawdust.

Not a day more than thirty, she noted instantly—pale, wiry —although he walked with a slight limp, yet his whole personality suggested nothing weightier than nonchalance. Her misgiving mounted.

"Come along," he said kindly enough, and ushered her into a small but comparatively clean room. Still not a frame, not a canvas to be seen! It might have been the office of a grain merchant. In this sanctum he assumed his jacket as simply as if she had been his wife. A northern roof-light revealed them to each other with such precision that she did, in fact, begin to suspect that she had known him always.

An empty easel stood beside their chairs. A magnifying glass lay on his empty desk. Slowly the idea of a picture was again imposing itself as Mr. Abbey absently pushed back this glass and turned a critical eye upon herself. She saw that he had thin, strenuous hands, and remembered the ease with which he had swung a packing-case aside. His slender appearance now struck her as deceptive. That boyish lock of hair fell over an inflexible brow. A cold, rather querulous face, had it not been for the humorous mouth.

"How surprising," she said graciously, "to find an expert unaged in that process!"

"Instinct is ageless," he retorted dryly. "What is more important at the moment is that I have found a responsible purchaser willing to give your price. And this without quibbling."

Delight warmed her face. "The full price?"

"The full price."

"But this is splendid!"

"Fortunate undoubtedly—when you consider the present state of the market. My client will take the picture subject to one condition—"

"Its being the original, of course."

"No, subject to its being in good condition."

Puzzled, she hesitated. "It is in perfect condition. He can easily satisfy himself as to that. But I'm afraid that he must do so by personal inspection at my house. I simply cannot undertake the responsibility of insurance and despatch for purpose of inspection elsewhere."

"I explained that."

"Once the picture is purchased, Mr. Abbey, its removal must be the buyer's problem. That is part of my bargain."

"Quite. My client fully appreciates the rules you have laid down. But you understand, I'm sure, that it is only reasonable that he satisfy himself as to its condition first."

"Naturally. What astonishes me is that he does not wish preliminary proof that it is an original."

"I showed him the photograph you sent. As a collector he told me he was conversant with the picture's provenance."

"Indeed?"

"Tell me, Princess Victoria, how did you first come to believe that that picture was a copy?"

"My father believed it to be a copy on the opinion of a relative who is a connoisseur—in fact an authority."

"And how did you eventually discover it to be the original?"

She hesitated for a second. "More by intuition than anything, I'm afraid. The picture hangs in the Banner Hall at Château Maria Sophia. At a certain hour of the day, the light is exceptionally favourable for it. I have studied the picture a great deal. In fact I'm going to miss it more than I care to think."

"Quite. But surely some detail pinned perception to the point of certainty. Otherwise you would not have troubled to trace the picture's history, to discover its provenance and importance."

"That was not much trouble. We have an unusually fine library at the Château. I was able to trace its history quite easily."

"But not able to define the detail that originally put you on the right track?"

"Mr. Abbey, you must remember I am not an expert. My impression might appear childish to you, although my researches did satisfactorily supplement this later. What happened was this: one day as I looked at the picture in a peculiarly revealing light, it seemed to me that, without seeing any fresh outline, I was now aware of the original cartoon—and that this was of such complexity as to give almost a stereoscopic effect. As you know it is a landscape with figures. Well, I can only say that all at once I was conscious of the anatomy of each creature and object. I imagine that a copy would follow outer rather than inner indications—so instantly I was convinced that no copy could produce this sense of depths, which was yet so ethereally revealed. Both the letter and the spirit were satisfactorily present! And, if I may say so—in painting the letter is extremely important. These at least it killeth not!"

Briefly Mr. Abbey nodded.

"I'm quite prepared, of course, for your client to subject the canvas to any expert he cares to bring with him. In fact, I'm surprised that its condition is the only thing that seems to weigh with him."

"But, Princess Victoria, I thought I had made it plain that he knows the picture?"

"You said he knew its provenance—its history. Do you mean that he has already seen my picture?"

"I do. He knows it well. He saw it on many occasions years ago, and remembers it perfectly. I understand that he is distantly related to you—which probably explains this familiarity. He is Il Principe di Perugia."

The Princess stared at Mr. Abbey. "But that's impossible!" she said sharply. A painful line had grooved itself between her brows. She looked suddenly formidable. "Prince Colonna is my cousin."

"I hoped that this would make the transaction pleasanter . . . the knowledge that this heirloom was still within the family—" he paused rather at a loss. "And the Prince is, of course, a connoisseur, in fact an authority. I must remind you again that few people today can give such a price. Without demur also."

To his surprise the Princess gave a short laugh. "That of course clinches it! But your news has certainly surprised me."

"I explained to His Highness that your time was short and he has suggested that you drive to his villa this afternoon. The Palazzo Toledo is closed when not let nowadays. Unless he hears to the contrary by telephone, he will await you between three and four o'clock today—when he hopes that the final arrangements for viewing the picture may be made."

"Then the sooner this call is made," said the Princess, "the sooner it will be over. Thank you again, Mr. Abbey, for the trouble you have taken. This I appreciate very much. Perhaps your man would now call a *carrozzella*."

As the Princess drove off into the glare of the afternoon, Jacob Gaddi winked irreverently at his employer. "Quickest deal on record, I should say! I hope the noble lady was grateful?"

"I'm not so sure," said Mr. Abbey. "For some reason she hates her exalted relative's guts. And I've begun to suspect why. . . ."

INVITATION TO BEAUTY . . .

Among funereal cypress, in a solid block of shadow, the gates to the villa lay back from the road to Fiesole. In blinding light Florence lay far below—towers and river emerging at visionary intervals from this white fume of light—seen distantly through feathery groves of olive.

A sharp scent of autumn rose from the dark gateway, but ahead scarlet vine leaves rioted along the marble balustrade, in summer heat.

As she climbed the three-tiered marble stairway to the Doric portico, the silence was so profound that the trickle from the fountain below held the persistence of a stream, as it emerged from the stone lion's snarl. Cicadas clicked like castanets, and a lizard released its weight, with the precision of a spring trap, from the nearest urn, thick-set with fleshy gloxinias.

It was the Princess' first visit to the Villa Leonardo, and the monumental Palladian windows, closely shuttered in the sun-blaze, gave her an immediate sense of remoteness. The portico, with its attendant statuary, appeared to be gazing blankly into another century and an Olympian scene.

A man-servant led her from the entrance into the great hall, a spectacular interior with a marble floor, and walls cool and white as milk, its coffered ceiling bordered with Greek honeysuckles. Massive wall mouldings framed colourless reliefs of classical figures. At the far end an apse, coffered like the ceiling, enshrined a statue of the Hermes of Praxiteles, epitome of eloquence in marble. God of each roadway, guardian of every door, herald of heaven, guide of the dead, all communication was in that solitary form calmly resolved, serenely declared. The child Dionysos, born of flame and daemon of the artist, lay at peace upon his arm, gazing devoutly into that divine face—distant as heaven, yet familiar as Arcady.

Spell-bound, the Princess paused. Felicity rose like a fountain from this threshold, mediating its ethers in tranquil benediction.

Then turning she followed the servant through another recess, up some steps into an ante-room, where, in startling contrast, between pillars of *verde antico,* maize linen covered the walls, and crimson curtains shone in the polished scagliola floor. Gilt trophies overpowered the mantel, but were off-set by the elegance of Directoire furniture. In the centre of the room a gold *jardinière* upon a green marble pedestal was thickly massed with cardinal begonias. The room was an assault of colour after the Greek hall, yet such was its vigour that no trace of excess weakened the effect.

Smiling, the Prince came forward, pale as parchment against his gilt and velvet household gods, but lean, leathery, agile—and very much aware.

"My *very* dear Victoria!" Bowing piously upon her hands, he barely brushed them with his lips. "Extortioner, how are you?" His outrageous statements were discounted always by a slight lisp. This sibilance lent a disconcerting effeminacy to his forthright utterance. Strangers never knew where they were with this soft-voiced predatory newcomer, who suggested some dedicated Order, and yet was, emphatically, not a priest.

By the time onlookers had decided, they were usually in his pocket. "Yes, how are you, my Extortioner?"

"Adamant," retorted Victoria.

"And angry—so angry! But iced coffee awaits you. . . . Come, confess now as you drink it!"

"I confess to curiosity only, Cousin Colonna. At what date did you change your opinion on the Del Abbate picture?"

"I have never altered it. Shall we say that earlier I reserved my views? And had I not done so—today you would have no picture to sell!"

"May I ask why you showed such consideration for my interests?"

"Because they were bound up with my own, dear lady. Frederick, your father, had just sold the Admont reliquary and a number of other treasures that I was then in no position to buy. I was a poor man until my unlamented uncle's death. Shall we say that I permitted your father to nurse his own conviction that the 'Landscape with the Death of Eurydice' was a copy. In this way I deferred its entrance into the arena until I was ready for it. But my agents have been waiting ever since. Now that the Château Maria Sophia stands on Italian soil—it was clear that its sale would be more likely to take place in this market. Nevertheless, my scouts have been watching in Austria also. I rather wondered, my dear Victoria, why you did not think of Rauchnitz of Vienna. He has done so much business with Augustus in happier days."

The Princess stiffened. "This picture does not concern my brother. It is my property."

"Indeed? Most interesting. This must, of course, simplify the position for you. No Family red-tape to trip you up."

Coldly the Princess said: "I understood that Mr. Abbey,

the dealer, had explained that this is a private transaction, not a Family affair."

"Mr. Abbey has explained. He was explicit to the point of tedium. My discretion will equal your own. I merely wondered if you were acting on Augustus' behalf—remembering your sisterly affection for him. But your ownership of the picture explains the situation. Has the iced coffee cooled you?"

"It is refreshing me, Cousin Colonna. When do you wish to see the picture?"

"I hope to be in the Stromberg in December. Would it be possible to view it then?"

"December?" She hesitated for an instant. "Next month would suit me better."

"Alas, I am desolated to admit it—November does not suit me."

"December then. Perhaps you will be kind enough to advise me in advance. Life at the Château is very much changed. I should like you to be as comfortable as possible."

"Victoria, your solicitude touches me! But my address on this occasion will be the hotel at Springbrunnen. I shall be one of a party of three. It would, of course, be delightful to dine with you—once the picture is mine, and, naturally, the cheque yours!"

Despite herself she smiled. "That is arranged then. And I must tell you frankly how glad I am that you propose to meet my price so generously."

"It is a stiff price. You would not get it in the open market. But," he bowed with undeniable grace, "the picture is worth that to me. Now, come, I shall show you where I hope to hang it."

He led her through a long vestibule, up a small, curving

flight of stairs, to a faded green and gold gallery, above a garden arcade which occupied the entire south frontage. At intervals, between the pictures in small recessed chambers, marquetry chairs were grouped, and books housed in restful bays—commanding a wide view of the olive-grove beyond the formal ilex and cedars of the grounds.

Victoria gave an involuntary exclamation of pleasure, but already the Prince was regretfully announcing: "I *had* hoped to show my collection to François on his arrival from Rome this week."

"This week? François does not arrive in Florence till next week."

"Next week? Of course! In any case I shall miss him, as I leave tonight for Naples. An assignation with an enchanting terracotta which I have reason to believe is Ghilberti's own."

Relieved, she exclaimed, "Indeed! Now *that* is a remarkable picture," and paused in tribute.

"A very remarkable picture," he corrected her.

Silently they gazed. A painting of the modern school, the canvas showed the head and shoulders of a woman, after the classical tradition, against a blue sky, but a sky of such intensity that it gave an immediate effect of storm. In the background, a small riderless white horse was seen at a gallop on a smooth, pale shore. Yet the woman in her archaic stillness suggested a force more fundamental than either storm or speed.

"As a rule," said the Princess, "I do not care for that particular school. These moderns seem to be perpetually at the transition stage."

"Any serious artist," lisped the Prince, "is perpetually at that point. How else does he achieve his frontier?"

"You are quite right," said the Princess quickly. "My observation was superficial. It is indeed a remarkable picture."

" 'Neptune's Venus' pleases you then?"

"Indeed she does. An unforgettable face."

"The portrait is of an Irish lady, a Miss Gallacher, a friend of mine. I am fortunate to have secured it."

"An odd name, surely, for the picture? 'Neptune's Venus.' "

"Not at all. When Neptune and Minerva contended for Athens, Neptune struck the ground and a horse appeared—emblem of war and misery, yet a noble animal. Minerva's less strenuous olive-tree, you remember, earned the day with the gods, but it is obvious that this artist's muse sprang from Neptune's kingdom. Nevertheless, a noble animal!"

Did he now refer to the lady or the horse? Victoria could not determine. Smoothly the Prince continued: "Hitherto I have regarded you as I might Minerva herself. Last month's announcement of your engagement in the London *Times* came as the proverbial bolt from the blue."

His tone was caressing, but she was instantly alert. "Minerva? I wonder why."

"That inaccessible heart! It was in his reply to my congratulations that I learnt of François' arrival in Florence this —er, next week. Lamentable to miss him! This now is the bay that I have reserved for—our masterpiece, shall I say?"

"Perfection," said the Princess crisply. All too well could she see the superb landscape by Del Abbate hanging there.

"And now, my dear, my costly Victoria, I am about to throw myself on your mercy, and ask you a favour."

Surprised she turned. He was quite sincere.

"You have at the Château Maria Sophia a small canvas that I covet. It is not an original, but a charming copy. I shall, however, give you your own price for that picture too. I have long wanted this."

Touched despite herself she said: "No, Cousin Colonna, you shall give me *your* price for that one—if I can sell it. Which is it?"

"A landscape by Domenichino, with Tobias and the Angel. Unhappily the original hangs in the National Gallery, London. But yours is a delectable copy."

"Oh, *no!*" she exclaimed with something like a note of anguish in her voice. "I can't sell that—it's bad enough having to sell the other. But the Tobias is linked with my whole life in—in a peculiar way. I've planned to give it to François as my wedding gift. He always said it was a miracle it achieved such serenity when he considered its contents: Gothic landscape, classical Angel, and an almost modern Tobias. Such a tiny Tobias too, though the Fish is gratifyingly large. I've promised myself that François shall have it. It's the last picture that I should have picked for you. The Fish is doing everything but wink."

Playfully he shook his head. "You plan to add this picture to the Talloires collection at d'Annecy or to that august gallery at Vermontaine? Come, my dear Viccy, be reasonable! Had it been the Del Abbate landscape, that would have been a fitting addition to Monsieur le Comte's treasures, but this trifle—"

She gave a half-hearted little laugh. "I'm sorry to seem ungracious, for you have indeed been generous about the Del Abbate. But it's impossible to explain all that that little picture means to me."

"And to me." Again he bowed. "Think it over, and give me your answer once the other transaction is completed."

"Cousin Colonna, I prefer to tell you frankly now."

"No, no," he said pleasantly. "You may change your mind. Do not bolt and bar the door upon us both like this. Have you not changed your mind before? Why, only last month you decided against celibacy."

She laughed good-naturedly, as they turned to go. "I suppose my engagement does seem rather late in the day. I remember the Grand Duchess Marie Alexandrovna insisting to Maman: 'Princesses must marry young. When they are over twenty, they begin to think too much, and to have too many ideas of their own, which complicates matters.' "

"But that complication," once more he bent over her hand, "starts in the cradle with Minerva's own. And I congratulate you on the malady."

Side by side, in the rich afterglow, beneath idly drifting scarlet leaves, they went down the marble steps to the waiting *carrozzella.*

As the Prince opened the door, he remarked calmly: "Your aunt's death during the war was unexpected. I did not hear of it till later. I trust she did not suffer?"

Surprised, the Princess said, "I scarcely think so. It was so sudden that one does not know what to say. She died in her sleep."

"In her sleep?" For the first time the mask was startled into life—it looked alarmed.

"Many think it is the best way to go."

"She did not," he said shortly.

"There was no illness," said Victoria. "We found her dead next morning. So we like to believe she died in her sleep."

"Ah!" He smiled. "You like to believe . . ." the mask had again closed down. "Felicitations—*addio!*"

Driving downhill into the deepening dusk of cypress, "What an extraordinary remark!" she decided uneasily.

Astonishing to think that Tante Elise should have confided her views on such a subject to that flippant personality, whom none of the Family had ever trusted.

All at once, her attention quickened. She had suddenly remembered some gossip of Louise's—that Colonna and Tante Sophia had earlier been in love. Surely a fantastic tale! His erudition would be all that could appeal to Sophia, and erudition scarcely suggested the basis of a grand passion! In fact, it was almost sacrilege to think of Tante Sophia, so complete and perfect in herself, the Family's especial saint, as in any way involved with that subtle individual.

But was it possible that in the chaos of the war years he had been misinformed?

Did he actually believe that Tante Sophia was dead?

Instantly she signalled the driver.

He looked around.

But a lifetime of diplomacy prevailed on second thought. This was news that Sophia herself might wish to break. There were swift, stealthy undercurrents here that might engulf the unwary.

"I have changed my mind," said the Princess. "Please drive on. . . ."

INVITATION TO HAZARD . . .

The Hôtel Visconti in the narrow, somewhat secretive Via Tribolo, was not one of the largest hotels in Florence, but neither was it one of the smallest. It was certainly one of the quietest. The Princess had, in fact, chosen it carefully.

Between thinning chestnut-trees, which had spent their strength achieving height in the struggle for light, it now stood silent in a twilight drift of leaves, its baroque façade plastered with the same staring greens and yellows, as these fell or faltered through the lifeless air. From her window, a copy of Tribolo's fountain lent charm to the hotel garden, although at present the goddess shook leaves as well as water from her hair. An October scene that suggested solitude. Enticed by its privacy the Princess had decided to dine downstairs. The house seemed fairly full, but there would be no one likely to recognize her. Most of the visitors appeared to be elderly persons. There was a sedate tranquility about the place as if mild autumn perpetually prevailed here.

At eight o'clock that night, Victoria stepped out of the elevator on her way to the restaurant. She wore an afternoon frock by Worth, years old, but its cut still unassailable—of a mushroom brown that defied imitation, and which exactly matched her small Mercury cap. The identical outfit that she had worn for her visit to London—for the simple reason that it was now her best. To-night she had added a bunch of violets which she had been unable to resist earlier in the street. A sense of festivity brightened her eyes, and lent a touch of carmine to her lips. The picture was as good as sold, her visit here successfully closed.

Passing across the vestibule, she was startled to hear a remembered voice addressing the hall-porter—in business-like French with a British accent.

Her heart missed a beat, but coolly she proceeded across the dining-room to the secluded table, earlier chosen. It was just possible that she would not be seen in this alcove.

Calmly she ordered her meal. Coolly she surveyed the room. It was undoubtedly full. Nor could she see the entrance from this table. Her luck might hold. With deliberation she began to eat, but her appetite had fled.

For the second time in a lifetime, for the second time in a month, she had just seen her own father—she, the supposed daughter of the late Frederick, Prince Babenberg . . . the idolized parent who had meant far more to her than her mother ever had.

Mechanically she worked her way through three courses. When the waiter returned with coffee, she would ask if it were possible to leave the restaurant from this end of the room. That door on the right there—was it available?

As if in answer, the *maître d'hôtel* himself made an appearance by it, bearing, surprisingly enough, a small salver. Bowing he presented a card to her.

Coldly she lifted it. It bore the address of The Athenaeum, London, and the name: Mr. Garett Phelps.

Turning it over she read: *"I should greatly value a few words with you."*

Without any appreciable pause she said levelly: "Has Mr. Phelps dined?"

"Yes, Serene Highness."

"Tell him, please, that I shall be glad if he will take coffee with me now."

Two minutes later, a thin, slight man with the crooked, nimble walk of a horseman, was following the *maître d'hôtel* across the room. His fair skin had for years been burnt black from exposure to sun and wind. He might have been sixty, he might have been seventy. His manner was dry, professional, as he greeted her.

"I was about to write you, Princess. I hope you will forgive this intrusion."

"But of course. I'm just as surprised to see you."

"A coincidence—but a fortunate one for me, as I have two important matters to relate." There was no mistaking his growing pleasure—indeed it amounted to relief—and she smiled in response. The encounter was working out less embarrassingly, after all.

"First of all," he said, "thank you for the letter you sent through General Maitland. It was extremely nice of you."

"No," she said swiftly, "it was the least I could do. That our first meeting last month in London should have been so —so—"

"Unpleasant?" he cocked a wry eyebrow.

"So painful, was entirely my fault. My mother only broke the news of . . . of your relationship as she was dying, ten days earlier. I was still—"

"Smarting," he supplemented briskly. "Naturally. You may rest assured that she would never have disturbed you, any more than I should have done, had it not been for that letter that involved us both. You only could secure it, but I only could vouch for its destruction later. All that is now over and done with. Let us finally dismiss it."

But with a touch of hardihood that closely resembled his own, she retorted: "Life is not lived to order in the heart. Mine is still disquieted to discover that my mother supplied certain information to you—not only as her lover, but as a British Intelligence Agent."

His pale eyes snapped at her behind bleached lashes. "Your mother, a patriotic Frenchwoman, married to an Austrian Prince, only afforded me certain information at a time of crisis, in the hope that war might yet be averted. As I told you during our last interview, Austria never had a better friend than in your mother."

"Nor I'm sure had England," Victoria added ironically.

"As I previously reminded you: the two are not incompatible, and history may yet confirm this."

Intractably they faced each other, and for the first time a resemblance in the line of their profile could be seen—as of a coin reversed.

"Nevertheless," said the Princess shortly, "you must forgive me if I am a trifle slow with my act of oblivion. I find Maman's predicament with you perplexing in the extreme."

"Ah!" He smiled sourly. "But have you not just explained that life is not lived to order in the heart."

Her expression softened. *"Touché!"* she said softly, and held out her hand.

He held it lightly for a second. "From that recent announcement in the *Times,* I gather that your own has not been unaffected. I am glad to know that François de Talloires is the happy man."

"Thank you," she said simply.

"Does he, by any chance, know of our relationship?"

"Yes. I told him at once. He and Augustus, my half brother, alone know the truth. Both had heard of you, of course, as Garett Phelps, naturalist, the authority on Alpine flora. But of Maman's patriotic preoccupations, and your other—er . . . line of country, I have, of course, said nothing."

"Admirable," he said briefly. "Now, before I follow our act of oblivion into final limbo, I wish to ask you a favour. You were good enough to tell me in your letter that if you could at any time do anything for me, you would be pleased. Reading this, I had no idea that I should so soon avail myself of your offer. But the unforeseen has occurred—hence my arrival in Florence. To be frank, I need a woman's help."

Her eyes sparkled. With amusement she replied: "I imagine this to be unusual for you!"

"It is. It's more than that, it's a confounded nuisance. Through the death of a colleague and friend here—colleague rather than friend—I, an elderly bachelor, find myself with his child on my hands. Actually the girl is his niece and an orphan. He and this child lived at the Albergo Toscano. There was very little money, but he kept going by painting old master reproductions. I am in a dilemma about the girl, until some permanent arrangement can be made for her. General Maitland earlier told me of your situation at the Château Maria Sophia. Had it not been for the announcement of your engagement to the Comte de Talloires, I should have felt less embarrassment in suggesting that the girl come to you as a paying guest for a month or two."

"Now, come," she said kindly, "why should my happiness prove your stumbling-block? I'm sure something can still be arranged, if you will give me a few more details. There is already one child at the Château, a little cockney who arrived from London recently—the nephew of my Cousin Louise's housekeeper. He has a slight chest weakness, but we hope that the pure air of the Stromberg will soon put that to rights.

The two children could no doubt amuse one another. But as regards this friend who was more a colleague than a friend, there is one point I'd like to be clear upon: was he connected with what I described as your other line of country?"

He gave a noiseless little laugh. All his movements were singularly quiet.

"Yes and no. His brother, a newspaper correspondent, one of the ablest of his day, was directly connected. This brother was killed during the war. But I have continued to use his Florentine address from time to time. Correspondence arriving there is of considerable importance to me."

"This newspaper correspondent was perhaps the father of this little girl?"

"Precisely."

"And her mother? Mothers are rather important."

For the first time Mr. Garett Phelps twinkled. "Her mother was a *force-majeure*. There is no other way to describe that lady but as an act of God. Gusto unenlivened by a single spark of humour! The miraculous was her *milieu*. She would probably have lived for ever had not this natural accident of a human birth surprised her. In England she was a household word as the romance writer Sybil Chatterton. But her chief claim to fame was a series of Sunday books: *It Shall Come Right. Best Foot Foremost,* and *Halt Here for Hope*. Her marriage to Clayton Tubbs is completely inexplicable, except on your own showing: life is not lived to order in the heart."

The Princess smiled. "Perhaps destiny will leave the answer with the child. With journalism on one side, and romance on the other, she ought to be eloquent. How old is the little thing?"

"Seventeen, I believe."

"*Seventeen?*" the Princess drew back.

"Or sixteen," he amended. "No age at all. Although I have not seen her yet, I understand from Stephen Abbey, a family friend, that she's still a schoolgirl running wild."

"Seventeen!" protested the Princess. "I'm afraid the Château Maria Sophia would have no attraction nowadays for a young lady of that age."

"A schoolgirl, I assure you, Princess. And something of a hoyden at that. Two months with you would work wonders there. It is of the utmost importance to me that she should be out of her present address by the end of November, when I intend to occupy her uncle's room at the Toscano. By January I hope to arrange a permanent home for her in England. That is the situation in a nutshell. . . . Can you not help me?" The note of uncertainty in his voice gave it an odd humility.

There was an awkward silence.

"Very well," she answered. "But we must remember that she may not wish to come."

"Not wish to visit the Princess Victoria Antoinette Camena Egeria Caroline Augusta Babenberg? My dear lady!"

On impulse she again held out her hand, "My dear Victoria," she amended.

"My dear Victoria," he repeated slowly, as if listening to his own voice. Then abruptly he arose. "I shall write you," he said. "May I ask when you are leaving Florence?"

"Tomorrow was my original intention. But Florence fascinates. I'm half-tempted to cancel my reservations and spend another day here."

"Don't," he said abruptly. "Don't cancel your reservations. Postponement sometimes means delay. At the moment I would rather think of you in the calm of the Stromberg."

Genially she laughed. "I can see you are determined to have Florence for yourself! Well, I shall probably follow your wishes in this too. Good night. I prefer that to goodbye, don't you?"

Her mother's blue, bewildering eyes were smiling at him from another face.

"I do indeed. Good night, Victoria."

For a few minutes she lingered alone at the table, feeling oddly bereft. Like most solitaries, she was only conscious of loneliness after association. Then she too left the room.

As she crossed the hall, green with flowering plants, the front door stood wide on the warm evening, and she went down the shallow steps for a breath of air.

She knew now why she was restless. No telephone call from François tonight! Dismaying to realize how lost she felt without it. Nor could there be another for weeks. The telephone at Springbrunnen was hopelessly erratic. It was the rarest thing for a long-distance call to get through to the Château Maria Sophia successfully.

Suddenly, she paused.

What if the unforeseen occurred, and, in her absence François attempted a call, and got through? If Sophia, or one of the servants blandly explained that she had not yet arrived—was indeed not yet expected?

Pacing the pavement hastily now, among the fallen leaves, she turned back at the corner.

To her astonishment, she saw a newspaper lad from the nearest kiosk come running down the street, shouting in Italian as he dashed up the Visconti steps.

By the time she re-entered the hall, the staid interior was seething. People had flocked from lounges and stairs. Everyone talked vehemently, in the Italian way. Nobody paused to listen. The uproar was continuous.

In the general confusion, she had difficulty in making herself heard.

"What has happened?" she urged the night-porter. "What has happened? I cannot understand!"

"The ex-Emperor of Austria, Madame! King Karl has attempted another *coup d'état*. He has just been arrested in Hungary by Admiral Horthy."

Horrified, she repeated: "Admiral Horthy!"

"Yes, Madame, the White Terror . . ."

Like a sleep-walker, she stepped into the crowd, buffeted this way and that in an attempt to reach the stairs and her bedroom. The elevator gate was blocked. Where had all these people come from on one bad moment's notice?

As she gained the first step of the stairs, she heard a woman shrilly demanding: "But what does it *mean?*" And her escort's reply: "If they don't murder him first, he'll be turned out of his own country like a criminal."

"But how did it happen? Where was he caught?"

"Can't you hear what they're shouting? Komoru, of course. This is the end of the Habsburgs."

Someone else gave a cynical laugh: "Seven centuries down the drain!"

Abstractedly she mounted the stairs. This computation thrust the Babenbergs further still into the abyss. Did not each history book record: *the year 976 is celebrated by tradition as marking the birth of Austria, for it was under the Babenbergs that it began its long and steady rise to power?* Almost a thousand years were vanishing with her own House.

Her fingers shook slightly as she fitted the key into her bedroom door, for by this time her alarm was not solely on behalf of Karl at Komoru. She came of a circle that had for centuries known the danger of giving a false impression.

That she should be remote from home, her whereabouts unknown to her relatives, at such a time was simply the wildest contretemps, neither more nor less. But by her seniors, it would be held inexcusable. François' chill astonishment she simply dare not now envisage.

Absurd fetish! Born in bonds, need her physical reactions be quite so abject?

But her fingers still trembled as she unpinned her violets. She would certainly catch her connection for the Stromberg tomorrow. . . .

INVITATION TO ROMANCE . . .

That same evening François, Comte de Talloires et d'Annecy, boarding the Rome express one week earlier than anticipated, considered this satisfactory as far as it went. It would expedite his return to London and routine. His empty first-class carriage was also welcome.

He was, however, faintly annoyed, although no hint of this appeared in the statuesque profile turned on the flying landscape.

Tonight, Monday the 24th October, for the first time in history he had achieved a perfectly clear line to the Château Maria Sophia and, to his surprise, had heard Sophia Babenberg state that she had no idea when her niece might be expected. Another call of equal clarity to Louise Dobra-Portheim had not resulted in Sophia's praiseworthy brevity. Louise had spent a full sixty seconds congratulating him on his audibility, and his superiority in this respect to any local call of her experience. But on the subject of Victoria's departure he received only the most chaotic rejoinders. That Victoria had not yet reached home, that she was, in fact, twenty-four hours overdue left Louise, apparently, unconcerned. Her suggestions were playful rather than plausible. Victoria might have dropped off the train—at Paris or Innsbruck.

"For what purpose?"

"Now, François, how should I know? Perhaps her trousseau? Oh, dear, they're cutting us off—" And he had been left with an unfortunate impression that Louise had deliberately anticipated the Exchange.

But this selfishness, this indifference was, he reflected, typical of the Family's attitude to Victoria. They used her right and left.

All that would shortly cease, however—on marriage.

His present impatience, he realized, was largely due to the fact that he had been out of London during this visit of Victoria's.

He felt a sense of frustration not known since youth. He only hoped that this unruly emotion would not complicate that deeper feeling she had awakened in him last month. Then he had finally realized that his response to her was something in time and yet out of it—that the fervour she now aroused was such that the rest of his life would scarcely be long enough to enjoy it in.

He recalled her sceptical look as he told her this.

"And I must warn you," he had smiled, "that you can do nothing to spoil it—nor can I. I am at a loss to understand all I now feel. But I am enchanted by it."

Enchanted . . . but chagrined also by the way in which some reminder could wipe out her growing pleasure in him. Perpetually she escaped him in laughter or a smile.

Was it possible that his past brief association with Estella Storm could trouble her? Fantastic! As had so often been said: there is nothing so dead as a dead love affair.

There had been, of course, Victoria's own affair with Professor Drury—a relationship now ended.

How dead was that?

He did not know, but earlier he had come to a clear-cut

decision on the subject of Professor Drury. Professor Drury was finished. Did any feeling for Professor Drury still remain, that would be unfortunate for all three of them. The important point was that Victoria would shortly become Comtesse de Talloires et d'Annecy, and that her prospective husband felt himself quite capable of dealing with any lover, alive or moribund.

He glanced towards the door. Some sort of altercation was going on in the corridor. The next moment the door opened, and an English voice announced in Italian: "There's plenty of room here. I have a first-class ticket. You've no right to stop me."

A young woman had taken possession of his carriage.

"But there are other seats," the *contrôleur* was expostulating. "Further along . . ."

Wrathfully the young woman turned upon the Comte. "Is this carriage reserved?"

"On the contrary, Madame."

"There you are!" The *contrôleur,* however, had shut her in and beaten a retreat.

"Sorry for the fuss," said the young person, "but I saw from the cut of your clothes that you were English, and air I've got to have or die. Not one window open in the entire coach. Frightful."

He was mystified by her appearance. There was enough veiling on her hat to drape a widow, and she was dressed in unrelieved black, yet her high-heeled shoes, transparent stockings and patent-leather bag were those of the casual promenader. Her accent, nevertheless, was educated.

Before he could help her, she had slung her luggage on to the rack like a schoolboy.

Seating herself opposite him, she straightened her hat, after which she submitted him to a stare that became steadily more incredulous. Then, delightedly, she smiled.

"What an amazing thing!" she exclaimed. "Your face I mean—I've never seen such a likeness. Bone for bone. You're Dante's double."

Imperturbably he replied: "You flatter me."

"Why should I? No, this is really weird, for it might quite easily have been anyone else sitting in your place. But Dante of all people! You must often have been told this before."

"Never," he lied equably. "Would you like the window wide open?"

"Thank you—this is sheer heaven. D'you mind if I take off my hat?"

"Why not?" he said cautiously.

"With this heat," she explained, "my fringe has come out of curl. It is now longer than my nose."

As she removed her hat and eye-veil, he saw that this was only too true. Calmly she divided these red locks, sticking them through the heavier hair, in which they stood up like two horns.

He now perceived that he was dealing with a schoolgirl.

With some severity she said: "I'm only travelling first because the Company bought the ticket. If they'd given me the money for it, I could have gone third. However, they had to give me the needful for dinner—and I've saved on that by bringing sandwiches and fruit. It was all a complete washout."

Courteously he replied, "I'm sorry to hear that."

"But not the blow it would have been if it had been a theatrical engagement."

"There are," he observed, "always compensations."

She frowned. "I could have had the part—but at a price. You'll never guess what."

Impassively he agreed: "It is indeed beyond me."

"*And* me. That man—the casting director—told Mr. Steibel in front of me that a film test would be money wasted unless I first had my nose changed. By plastic surgery. The man wanted to alter the shape of my face."

"A sobering suggestion certainly."

"They told me to think it over, but I simply said: '*My* nose does not call for thought, but thanksgiving—*good* afternoon!' "

"A conclusive rejoinder!"

"They were electrified. Seriously, I ask you: what would I be without my own nose?"

Monsieur de Talloires adjusted his eye-glass. "Very different, I imagine."

"Of course. It would be fatal. I'd be insipid. My nose may be a little prominent, but at least it gives me presence."

Judicially he said: "I congratulate you on your decision. In all such experiments there is bound to be an element of risk."

"And besides what can be better than one's own nose. You've only to look at mine to see it's just me."

Calmly he looked into her candid eyes, and reflected that seldom had he been confronted by such self-satisfaction.

"You've been very kind," she added handsomely. "I feel better now I've got it off my chest. It's a mistake to consume one's own smoke indefinitely. And of course I've still got the reward."

"The reward?"

"For rescuing Mr. Steibel's prize cat from the roof of the Toledo—less what I paid for these clothes."

"Indeed!" the Comte's astonishment was genuine. "Then

you must be that nine days' wonder—Miss Tubbs herself?"

"Please!" She closed her eyes again, in a minor agony. "Not that name. It's a humiliation. *Tubbs* . . . I ask you!"

"Come," cordially he reminded her, "you may change it sooner than you think."

Sombrely she replied: "Or there again destiny may step in. One of my dreads is that I shall meet my fate, only to discover that his name is Potts. And my first name is so beautiful too. Clio—Goddess of History, or Legend."

Gravely he bowed. "I am delighted to meet you."

"She was also the first of the Muses, you remember. Usually shown in statuary with a scroll, or a chest of books. Sometimes with a pen—an anachronism for the style, of course."

As she rattled on, De Talloires wondered what kind of environment had produced this voluble yet explicit creature. He shuddered to think what he would have suffered had she been five years older. Mercifully the journey would end before she aged appreciably. Youth saved the situation—for the moment.

Aloud he said: "Florence has already renamed you, I believe. La Coraggiosa, according to my newspaper. A remarkable exploit. I know Prince Colonna's palazzo well."

"Is he a friend of yours?"

"It would be more accurate to say he is a distant relative."

Swiftly she said, "I don't want to talk about it. To tell you the truth, I don't know how I did it. It makes me quite sick when I remember. A hideous experience— So if you'll excuse me. . . . You did say that you were English, didn't you?"

"I think the observation was yours."

She stared at him for a second, and again smiled appreciatively. "You *are* apt," she told him. "It isn't often I feel I am conversing. I never get enough of it."

"It is my own complaint. A lack of listeners is the defect of this planet."

With a hearty laugh she flung back her head, and her rather wide mouth took a bewitching scarlet curve, revealing flawless teeth. He was somewhat startled by the rapidity with which the schoolgirl had become a siren—albeit an unconscious one.

At that moment, an attendant announced dinner.

Smiling, De Talloires arose: "With your permission, Mademoiselle. . . . We may meet on my return."

Significantly she replied: "We may—or we may not."

Not a nuance was lost on him, she noted. He sighed imperceptibly, then formally bowed. He was sheer perfection. And his eyes, she decided, were definitely a little sad as he withdrew.

What an experience—breathlessly she hugged it to herself. An Englishman with the finish of a Frenchman!

Alone in the carriage, she realized that he had been still more remarkable standing. He was, in fact, unique.

To disappear at once would be her most telling gesture. To remain could only mean an anti-climax. But to vanish was confounding, mysterious. He would wonder ever after. . . .

Instantly she arose. She owed it to herself that her exit at least be memorable.

Wide-eyed she stared at her papier-mâché case. Can this be love? she wondered, and blushed furiously.

There was her new hat! She had almost forgotten it. It would never do to lose her head.

Breathlessly, she slung down her luggage, and almost ran along the train, in the opposite direction from the dining car. Her heart was thudding like the drum-fire that heralds infantry attack. This was life at last!

INVITATION TO DECEPTION . . .

Regaining his compartment, De Talloires found it empty—the charming but preposterous child had gone. It was now close on midnight, and he hoped that some appropriate parent would meet her on arrival. She then passed completely from his mind.

The train reached Florence on time, and he was surprised to find an unusual crowd beyond the booking-hall.

"What's happened?" he asked sharply as his luggage was lifted into the waiting automobile.

"*Coup d'état,* Signor. The ex-Emperor of Austria has made another attempt in Hungary."

"Are you certain?"

"*Si,* Signor. And he has failed. His arrest has been announced by Admiral Horthy."

"Hotel first; then the French Embassy."

But the hotel entrance was blocked by another car, in the act of being loaded for a departing guest.

As De Talloires advanced into the hall itself, he was again obliged to stop short on the threshold.

A handsome man, quite as powerfully built as himself but with a pale, rather heavy jowl collided with him. Muttering an apology, this visitor also stopped short, but in recognition of the Comte . . . bowed, and hurried out.

Curtly De Talloires acknowledged the salute and passed

through. This, his second surprise since arrival, left him for once with a cold rather than calm expression.

Professor Drury, although so lately in his thoughts of Victoria, was certainly the last man he had expected to find here. On his doorstep. Blocking the way.

An odd coincidence.

His luggage deposited, he went straight to the Embassy. There the chauffeur's story was not only confirmed but amplified. He put through a call to Paris and one to London, and was preparing to return to his hotel when Captain Dubost, military attaché, remarked in farewell: "My wife was delighted to see Princess Victoria looking so well yesterday."

De Talloires paused in the hall. "Indeed? Where did Madame Dubost see Princess Victoria?"

"In the street, I believe, on foot. Unfortunately, my wife was driving. There was no chance to greet the Princess, but my wife remarked that she had never seen her look better. Heat-wave and all!"

"Ah," the Comte de Talloires smiled slightly, "the town is just possible in the early morning."

"This was late afternoon, I understand. Happily tonight is cooler. Good night, Monsieur de Talloires."

Cooler indeed the Comte decided, compressing his lips.

Regaining the hotel, he at once requested the register.

It confirmed that Professor Drury had spent two nights there. Of Victoria's name there was no sign. Yet this had always been her hotel: that wretched Madame Dubost might have been mistaken.

Or she might not?

If Madame Dubost were not mistaken, Victoria had deliberately concealed from him the fact that she intended to visit Florence. That was incontrovertible fact.

Professor Drury was, of course, a coincidence, but a remarkable one.

The Comte remained awake an unusually long time, absorbed by reflections on the nature of coincidence. The peculiar difficulty of applying the law of average to govern its possibilities was in his case, as a Frenchman, increased by the liveliness of his sense of probability. Among his philosophical deductions, intuition persisted in taking its disastrous short-cut. His night was spent chiefly in contemplation of Professor Drury.

Awaking unusually early, he found another heat-wave dawn flushing the sky with sultry colour. In the east, the morning star shone like a hot cinder, paling as light grew, from multiple to single splendour.

Whatever the explanation might be, Victoria's behaviour had been invidious, if not indiscreet. And in her position the two were synonymous. He was unpleasantly surprised. Once she was Madame la Comtesse de Talloires, this sort of nonsense must stop.

Frowning, he opened his pocket-book and consulted his diary. Outlining a date in early January, he replaced the book, and exasperated, lay back.

Without consultation of the bride-to-be, he had just decided on his wedding-day. . . .

INVITATION TO RECRIMINATION . . .

"And where," inquired Stephen Abbey two nights later, "did we purchase these widow's weeds?"

With hauteur Clio returned his gaze. "Rome."

"My eternal aunt!" he murmured.

"If Uncle Edward's recent death doesn't entitle me to wear black, I'd like to know what does . . . my last surviving relative gone."

And Clio began to eat. It was not advisable to quarrel at this stage. Not only was she Abbey's guest for dinner, but he had chosen the Pompeii, and she doted on the Pompeii. In addition, he had for once ordered Asti Spumante, as she had urged, instead of that ever-lasting Chianti.

Seated on the balcony of this marble and gold caravanserai, in the red plush alcove designated "Naples," she had a commanding view of the plashing fountain in the garden, and every other table—without being deafened by the orchestra. The only shadows in this bewilderment of gaiety and baroque were the black-coated figures of the waiters scurrying assiduously to and fro. The only deterrent to felicity, her host. Why couldn't Uncle Edward have chosen dear old Sir Teddy Glossop who was so fond of her as his executor? Or that polite Mr. Erskine at the Embassy, whom she only saw once in a blue moon. But Abbey of all people—

"Since when," he enquired next, "have you grown old enough to put your hair up?"

"I beg your pardon?" she said coldly.

Mr. Abbey repeated his question with such clarity that "Palermo," the next alcove, must have heard every word.

With a look of active dislike, she retaliated: "Since when have you become my nurse?"

It was Mr. Abbey's turn to take refuge in his meal. No use having a rumpus at this stage. Too much to settle first.

Instead he said briskly: "What do you think of your uncle's old friend—Mr. Garett Phelps?"

"I think he's a nervous little man."

"Nervous?" Mr. Abbey stopped eating in his astonishment.

"Fussy, then. It's the same thing. But I think he means well. And there's no doubt his publishers must think highly of him. All those coloured plates of the plants in his books. The cost must be enormous. Signora Perotti is all over him, of course, now that she's captured him for two months."

"And the invitation that he's got for you from Princess Victoria Babenberg, at the Château Maria Sophia?"

"Out of the question of course."

"You prefer to remain under the fussy eye of Mr. Phelps?"

"I do. Men can't interfere in the way that women do. They don't get so near you. They daren't."

"More wine?" suggested Mr. Abbey.

"Yes, please. I like it very much. It was nice of you to order it," she conceded.

"Not at all," said Mr. Abbey benevolently. "I think you're mistaken about Princess Victoria, you know. I've met her in my own gallery, and she gave me an impression of complete detachment. Most people would give a great deal for the chance of such an invitation."

For the first time Clio smiled into space, with calculated superiority, and his hopes sank at the sight.

"May I have some more Chicken Maryland? I'm hungry to-night."

Mr. Abbey signalled the waiter. "Your cinema career was short-lived anyway."

"Puss-puss," she warned. "I told you that *I* rejected them."

"On the subject of puss-puss," he said, "I yearn to hear more of that heroic episode. This is, after all, our first meeting since your memorable exploit. Why not make a clean breast?"

Aloofly she said, "You're quite unspeakable."

"Come along—out with the truth."

"What d'you mean?" Indignantly she turned upon him.

"Exactly what I say."

"The truth is: it's been providential—the money, the reward, coming when it did—with Uncle's will still unproven."

"No, no," he shook his head. "It's the courage I'm interested in. I find such courage (you'll excuse me I hope) almost incredible. Such craziness!" amended Mr. Abbey smoothly. "Even allowing for the fact that it's always easier going down than up."

"I tell you, I never stopped to think. Everybody present *saw*."

"Ah, yes, your Public! My dear Clio, I don't deny for a moment that there was a sensation. I now hope to have the facts."

"You've had them. I saw that cat on the roof, and I brought it down. Nothing you can say or do in your grudging way can alter that. It was a horrible experience. I don't intend to discuss it further. It makes me quite sick to relive it."

He glanced at her grimly. "I can well believe that. You

must have had the escape of your life—even allowing for the fact that the devil looks after his own. You see, I don't credit one word of this tall tale. I remember that before Mr. Steibel took up residence on the first floors, you and Rosa took food from the Albergo Toscano to the house cleaners. You looked over the Palazzo then, and were much impressed by a glimpse of the Prince's library. Remember? It's my belief that you've been secretly in and out of those top floors ever since. You probably got in by a second-floor window with the help of the Toscano walnut tree, having thoughtfully left that particular window unfastened. From the street, you and the cat were first seen on the roof. In fact, a section of the populace hallooed you—cat-conscious also because of the reward. And you waved back. That must have been damned inconvenient, when you thought you had the place to yourself! Little Clio had forgotten the Square loiterers. But how did this missing animal get through a locked door in the house itself? I think I can explain that mystery, too. During the months you used the Prince's library, you daren't open any windows. Except perhaps the roof one. Those top floors grow hot. *You* opened that locked door between the upper and the lower floors. You opened it for air. The key? The key in Prince Colonna's pocket? You probably found another in the upper corridor that fitted. Lost in the Prince's library, you did not notice till too late that the cat had fled upwards. So far the story is of a simplicity. It's your heroic descent in full view of the multitude—the seven or eight street-corner habituées that defeats me. Yet there you hung fifteen feet from the ground as they rounded the back of the building after they'd previously lost time racing to the front door! Sixty seconds sooner, would they have found you slipping out of the house by the second-floor window ledge, heaving yourself on to the rain-pipe, with the kindly help of the Toscano walnut tree? Successful housebreakers have one golden rule if they wish to avoid imprisonment: they must not be caught. You're terrific," he acknowledged ironically, "whichever way it was."

"I don't think I'll have cheese," she said coldly. "You've spoiled this dinner for me. And you are my host. I'll finish with an ice tonight."

"Too bad." Despite himself he smiled. "Pêche Melba?"

Distantly she agreed, "Pêche Melba."

Not until dessert was before them, did she unbend again. Then airily she announced: "Rosa and I visited a friend of hers this afternoon—a Madame Bondini, who is a fortune-teller. It's a case of genuine second sight with her. She says I am a medium. If I were to develop my possibilities, she thinks I would go far."

"What an understatement!"

"Now, you're flippant. And I thought you might be interested. After all, it's not as if you were an intellectual—though I've the greatest respect for your aesthetic judgment."

"So I'm not an intellectual!" unfeignedly he threw back his head in laughter, but it was at her expense. "You presumptuous puppy!"

Clio's cheek flushed. "Abbey," she said, "that was abominably rude of me. I'm sorry. I thought I'd conquered impetuosity since—since my ordeal. Something I read about the Musae seemed direct guidance."

"Out with the oracle then . . . what was it?"

"I felt convinced I'd never fail again. According to Hesiod the Musae were originally three in number: Melete, the practising one, Mneme, the remembering one, and Aoide, the singing one. Now my weakness is in remembering. As soon as I remember, I'm saved. Mneme is not with me faithfully enough."

"No, no, Clio," to her chagrin, he was still laughing softly, but irrepressibly, "Melete, the practising one, is the girl for you. Aoide, the lyrical, has you running round in circles."

A solitary guest was advancing along the balcony—a meagre man, with iron-grey hair *en brosse* and a penetrating eye.

Clio forgot discomfiture. "That's Hediger of the *Intelletto,* isn't it?"

"Yes. As a literary aspirant you ought to meet him." Abbey had risen.

A second later the famous editor was bowing over her hand. It was indeed a moment, to be followed by another yet more startling.

"Your article will be out next week," genially this lion was addressing Abbey. "Held it over for premier position then. Don't forget I want one also on Renaissance painting shortly—preferably the Venetian School," and Signor Hediger passed on to his own alcove.

"Oh, Abbey!" deflated, she sank back. Her face had paled. She looked quite ill. "My humiliation is complete."

"Poor dear," he lifted the hand next him, and kissed it lightly.

"Sometimes things I've said come over me in bed afterwards and I writhe. It's worse if I remember them in the street. But to have this happen with you, of all people—and in such a confined space!"

"Well, no more penitence. You're absolved. Have a liqueur?"

But it was a moment before she looked elated. "A Grand Marnier. I've never had a Grand Marnier."

"Certainly not. A Star-Board Light. Be your age."

"Abbey," she hesitated, and then almost hungrily said: "What was your article upon?"

Wickedly he winked. "The occult."

"You're not serious?"

"But I am. It was a re-examination of Myers' theory that in the spiritual world telepathy amounts to a force analogous to that of gravity."

"Abbey, how marvellous—"

"I said my article was a re-examination. I did not say I subscribed to the claim."

"It doesn't matter. For my purpose, you'll do. You're the very person for the experiment. Madame Bondini said I only needed a little practice. And you usually keep your word —if you promise."

"In this case, I haven't given it."

"No, but you must. You will. It's the simplest thing, the merest trifle." She paused, and with calculated seduction said: "After all, we ought to be kind to each other, we're both orphans."

"Well, get on with it—what do you want?"

"Madame Bondini says that if one arranges to think of anyone—but it must always be the same person, at a set hour each day for five minutes—in the course of time, one can communicate with them, mind to mind, at any distance."

"That might be a misfortune."

"Don't be tiresome, Abbey. I mean to try this, and you're the only person I know who might keep it up. We'll make it eleven each night. There's something much more potent about the eleventh hour than midnight."

"Wouldn't remember, that's flat."

"Yes, you will. You're reliable. It's your greatest asset."

"But what is there to be said between us that can't be said in person?"

"Stop jeering! This is serious."

"Talk sense then, instead of Madame Bondini and Rosa. You're coming out of that albergo kitchen, if I have to get a crane to lever you into the drawing-room."

"Please, Abbey, meet me in this matter. It's hopeless getting Rosa to do it with me. She's willing. But she falls asleep as soon as she starts to think. Do the experiment with me for the next three months. It's nothing."

"All right. I'll do it for two months. But for three minutes only each night."

"Madame Bondini said five."

"I've said three."

"Well, word of honour?"

"Word of honour."

Jocularly he shook hands with her.

"And of course, Abbey," she said critically, "you must do it properly. That's understood. Madame Bondini warned us of that. You can't cheat in the spiritual world. It's not like cards. It's serious."

"Quite. Now perhaps you'll do me a favour—by accepting that invitation of Princess Victoria's."

"I've told you I can't."

"Why?"

"I decline to stoop to charity."

"Charity—didn't Mr. Phelps explain that the Princess will be paid?"

"He did. But I don't intend to spend my money in this way, when I can live more cheaply in Florence."

"Your money?" said Mr. Abbey acidly. "Where did you

get those large ideas? What makes you think that you have money?"

Calmly she said: "People don't make a will unless they've something to *will*. I know there must be money. Uncle and I couldn't have lived as we did off his pictures alone."

"That may be. But let me disabuse your mind of the idea that he left anything behind him. I think it is too bad of Phelps not to have put this bluntly himself. The fact is, Clio," Mr. Abbey paused, then added brusquely, "wherever you live now, until you're old enough to earn your living, Mr. Phelps will have to pay the piper—or I shall, as . . . as executor. Therefore, I think the least you can do to repay him is to go where he wishes his money spent."

He had been prepared for tears, heroics, mutiny. He was not prepared for what actually happened.

Like a flash she turned on him. Disdainfully she inquired: "Is this your murderous way of telling me I'm destitute?"

"I'm afraid it is. You have a choice of remaining in Florence at my expense, or at the Château Maria Sophia at Mr. Phelps'. It's up to you."

Distastefully she surveyed him, and he had to admit that had she been thirty she could not have done it better. "There *is* no choice," she said aloofly. "I prefer Mr. Phelps' charity."

"Splendid," he applauded.

Side by side, they stared at each other.

Then stiffening with rage she arose. Her flight to the heights was over. "Mark my words," she said between her teeth, "you'll live to regret this!"

Cautiously Mr. Abbey replied: "As long as you don't—I'll bear up."

get these large ideas? What makes you think that you have money?"

Calmly she said: "People don't make a will unless they've something to leave. I know there must be money. Uncle and I couldn't have lived as we did off his pictures alone."

"That may be. But let me disabuse your mind of the idea that he left anything behind him. I think it is too late in [illegible] to [illegible] this [illegible] himself. The fact is, Cleo," Mr. Abbey paused, then added brusquely, "wherever you live now, until you're old enough to earn your living, Mr. Phelps will have to pay the piper—and I think as [illegible] for the piece. I think the least you can do is repay him by [illegible] he wishes his money spent."

He had been prepared for tears, hysterics, mutiny. He was not prepared for what actually happened.

[illegible] "Is this your roundabout way of telling me I'm destitute?"

"I'm afraid it is. You have a choice of remaining in Florence at my expense, or at the Château Marie-Sophia at Mr. Phelps'. It's up to you."

Disdainfully she surveyed him, and he had to admit that had she been thirty she could not have done it better. "There is no choice," she said acidly. "I prefer Mr. Phelps' charity."

"Splendid!" he applauded.

Side by side, they stared at each other.

[illegible] "Make my excuses," she said between her teeth. "You'll like to collect this."

[illegible] Mr. Abbey replied. [illegible]

[illegible]

INVITATION TO DESTINATION . .

Her journey was over. She was safely home. And the Princess smiled, for the October evening was still golden, and she could distinctly see her beloved domain.

As usual she had got down at the avenue gates to save the hired horse the last lap. It was a long drive along the plateau from the triple pinnacles of the old frontier, dominated by the Cima Tregua. Behind her, the Garten-Girlande flowed to the open south and was precipitously lost in thickening dusk. In the west the monster mass of the Madchenbrüste was hollowed to a shallow cup by the immensity of a sunset now spent, but still dazzling.

Ahead of her the Château Maria Sophia in its green grounds stood silent. The mighty parapet of the Stromberg behind it was gently familiar in this level radiance, a bedrock boundary at present luminous. Acacia leaves glinted as they fell. The three grass parterres had been freshly cut, and the house beyond them looked shabbier than ever—like an untidy bird's nest now that the vine had fallen from the top storey across the balcony. Hans ought to put it up.

Still—he had cut the grass. In the autumn he cut it faithfully enough, as each mowing might prove the last before frost set in.

What cynic, with an eye on perpetual change, had said one could never return? Here she was back again, and the sight and scent of the little estate made her feel as mild as milk, as strong as a boy!

From the centre turret of the Château, the Apostle Clock struck the hour. Her frets and fears fell away. She had regained her sanctuary: Beauty.

Deliberately she took the long way round.

Beneath the stone-pines, the giant needles lay thick as hay! Yet a few yards farther on, and grass grew mossily beneath the turkey-oaks, and she could feel acorns crunching under her feet. There were the Japanese cedars with prancing boughs and fluffy monkey hands! And on her right, the Mammoth-trees, their tall, feathery branches sweeping the ground in waves, their bark tawny red, as if an inner fire consumed them. And dotting a rounded knoll, as neatly as on a sampler, were Noah's Ark treelets of silver green cypress, with a blue tinge, as if they had risen from the sea. What a contrast to the monkey-puzzle beyond, juggling with the last of the light. . . . To her it was the finest arboretum outside Eden!

With a sigh of happiness, she emerged upon the lower terrace, and began climbing the steps between the last of the rock roses. The lighter soil here, and a sunny situation always produced a spendthrift crop. . . .

At the top of the steps, she paused and looked due south, beyond Minerva's distant temple, and the bland, open spaces of the Garten-Girlande—to Italy, dim as a dream in the dusk.

There was no frost, and the odour of dead leaves smote her with the chill of an open well. The silence was intense. In it, the drowsy crooning of the house pigeons sounded like a bubbling pot. The sky shone with a white light now. The garden alone caught the rich afterglow, as if the time it took light to travel was for once defined by a radiance in which earth held that triumphant last word.

Suddenly, the quiet so near the open door struck her as unnatural; yet through the hall window she could see Sophia's lamp.

Odd that the front door should be open! The draught would strike through the entrance and ante-room into the Banner Hall, which when summer was gone, they used instead of the drawing-room.

In the dark ante-room, she again paused, mystified. Cold as a grave usually, tonight warm air reached her in a sustained wave of heat. Was the place on fire?

"Tante Sophia!" she called. "This heat—what's happened?"

"My dear child, the workmen from Innsbruck left this morning. François, in your absence, has had central heating electrically installed."

Hurriedly Victoria pushed the next door wider still.

The Banner Hall, vaulted like a church, leapt to life before her in all its loveliness. Against ivory walls the carved limewood staircase, with its rich stairheads, swirled in that triumphant circular movement to the long gallery above, where massive doors, brilliant as mirrors, were crowned by mouldings of the seasons' fruits and flowers. From the musicians' balcony, hanging like a bird-cage from the west end, the black and gold banner of the Babenbergs wavered now in tropical heat. The perfume from the white and magenta cyclamen that were her labour and delight rose headily.

Yet the Utrecht hangings of scarlet velvet and gold which so festively festooned the lower-floor windows (as if a stage-box framed the Dolomites) were undrawn. These tall windows were actually open. At the east end of the hall, the modest fire burning below the Venetian-glass overmantel was almost out.

Bewildered, Victoria gazed around. To the right of the fireplace, and below the gallery—another feature of this striking interior—a charming bay enshrined the large Del Abbate picture. Every object in the state room was in order, but its rococo yet harmonious display of Italian paintings, Spanish leather, Russian icons, and faded gilt saints shimmered in this jungle temperature.

An elderly woman looked up calmly from the book she was reading by lamplight at the open window. "Equatorial, isn't it? But the silence is welcome again. The place has been an inferno of noise for a week."

"*Liebste,* I'm so sorry! And, of course, we're not accustomed to comfort. There must be some way of controlling the heating. I expect the servants are terrified to adjust it. I'll see to it at once."

"Victoria," her aunt regarded her with a pale, inquiring eye, "where have you come from?"

"Didn't you get my telegram?"

"No—it will probably arrive to-morrow at breakfast time."

"That wretched Springbrunnen telephone—"

"I assure you, Viccy, that it operated with the greatest clarity on Monday night. A long-distance call from François in which every syllable of his disquiet registered."

"What did you tell him?"

"The truth, my dear. It was quite unanswerable, I had no idea where you were."

Victoria sat down suddenly. "Most unfortunate," she muttered. "I went to Florence. A little business matter I hope to bring off privately. I won't embarrass you with details yet—in case of leading questions from Augustus. Actually, of course, it's none of the Family's business. Everything in the Château belongs to me, after all."

"What an amusing coincidence," said her aunt. "I've just been reading from a new translation of Homer this very passage—Minerva speaks: 'You know what a woman's disposition is. She likes to bring riches to the house of the man she is about to marry.'"

"I don't think that's particularly apropos—in view of the riches I'm likely to hand over for that purpose. Besides, I thought Swedenborg was your bed-side book."

"Scarcely time for bed yet," said Sophia pleasantly. "Won't you have some supper?"

"Later, thank you." She looked round half-ruefully. "How cold the bedrooms will seem after this."

"The bedrooms, or most of them, are also heated. Yours being small is like an oven."

"Dear heaven!" Victoria stared at her. "What this must have cost! It almost looks as if François didn't expcct me to leave after all."

"My dear," said the other slowly, "how drugged you are with sorrow."

"*Sorrow?*" Victoria was startled.

"Yes, you're like a patient, forever tossing off François instead of the illness. Surely it is obvious that when you come to leave this house, it will now be a business proposition, if you sell it—instead of an incubus."

Swiftly Victoria glanced away. "How's Albert?"

"Albert, I'm sorry to say, has been a perfect fiend."

"But, Sophia, it just isn't possible. The poor little thing's so anaemic he can't say boo to a goose."

"He's certainly said it to Frau Winkwurth—almost hourly."

"I suppose he's in bed now?"

"I'm thankful to say he is," said Sophia, and proceeded to give chapter and verse. . . .

"Well," said Victoria defensively, "you surprise me very much."

"Albert has surprised us quite as much. Barolyi and Hans have both whipped him."

"Sophia! how could you allow it? A delicate child of eight."

"The servants did not consult me. Frankly, I too had grown a little tired of Albert. I rather sympathized with them."

"You amaze me. Albert was as good as gold during his first fortnight. Dr. Herriot will think it absurd that we can't control a child of his age without corporal punishment."

"By the way, Viccy, does François clearly understand that Albert is simply here for a month or so to oblige Louise's housekeeper?"

"But of course. How could Albert possibly affect François? As soon as Dr. Herriot thinks Albert is fit to go home, back he'll go."

"And how is this doctor in London to come to such a welcome conclusion?"

"Didn't I tell you? Dr. Herriot expects to come out himself this winter. A busman's holiday which includes some professional consultations at Bergers Sanatorium. He hopes to drop in here for a few days—to see how Albert is getting on."

"He hopes to *what?*"

"To come to Château Maria Sophia for a night or two next month. No chance of his visit coinciding with the Christmas gathering. Don't worry."

"How old is this man?"

"Forty, I imagine," she hesitated. "Now that we're on the subject of visitors: did you ever meet a Mr. Garett Phelps in the old days, a friend of Maman's?"

"I believe," said her aunt carefully, "that I did. Once."

"I had rather an odd experience in Florence. I met him by accident, and he asked me to do him a favour. General Maitland had earlier explained our financial position, and he wondered if we would allow a young girl of sixteen to come here as a paying guest for a few weeks. She is the niece of an old friend of his who died recently, and is not yet old enough to earn her living. Would you mind if she came for a month or so?"

"Of course not, Viccy. You will explain to François naturally."

Laughing, the Princess arose. "Of course! By the way, I called on Cousin Colonna when I was in Florence."

"Did you, my dear? I hope you found him well."

"Yes, but it's a little embarrassing. From something he said as he bade me goodbye, I have an idea that he thinks that you are dead–not Tante Elise."

"Indeed? Did you not correct this?"

"No, *Liebste*. I blame myself that I did not. But I was on my way back to Florence when it dawned on me. He's to be in this neighbourhood in December, and having said he'd dine here one night, I felt it might be better for you to readjust this."

"Of course, darling. Much better." Her aunt resumed her reading.

Again her niece hesitated. "If I'm right about this–we must remember that your survival may be rather–rather a surprise to him."

Sophia Babenberg glanced up from her book with a smile. "Let us hope a pleasant one."

"Of course!" Victoria continued to look dubious. "But it might be kinder to prepare him. You may think it advisable to write him beforehand."

"I hardly think so," again her aunt picked up her book. "It is so long since I astonished anyone, that this may have its charm."

Victoria stopped short on her way to the stairs. "Do you know—that sounds as heartless as you were about Albert! You've shocked me."

"Bless you," said her aunt mildly.

But as the younger woman turned away, the other's pale blue eyes looked up with a blinding flash in the still face—revealing a personality withdrawn rather than muted. In the light her hair shone white—in the shadow, grey. As a wood-fire, banked in its own ash does not disclose life till stirred, unobserved now that flash displayed a vitality beside which Victoria's bodily vigour seemed slender as summer grass. . . .

INVITATION TO BED . . .

As the Princess passed from the gallery to the next floor, she noticed that Albert's door was ajar, but she resisted the temptation to peep in. Foolish to awaken or unsettle him.

At the foot of the turret stairs, he rose like a Jack-in-the-box from behind a dower-chest. She was absurdly pleased to see him.

"You ought to be in bed," she expostulated.

"Let me come up to the turret?"

"Fasten your dressing-gown then, and put your shoes on properly. Five minutes only. I'm sorry to hear you've been troublesome in my absence."

"It's a lie," said Albert flatly.

"It's nothing of the sort."

Albert scowled, but the effect registered by honey-coloured brows on transparent skin was a pained perplexity. Quickly he preceded the Princess upstairs.

In the bedroom, "Have you brought me anything?" he asked anxiously.

Unlovely but natural! At his age she too would have wondered, but never would have dared to ask. Albert was completely uninhibited.

"Tomorrow," she said firmly. "Tonight I am astonished to hear that you climbed onto the glass roof of the greenhouse. Most dangerous. And that you have been rude to Frau Winkwurth. Very unkind. Also that you hid her *toupet,* and made a tent of the Emperor's bed-spread. This means that you have gone into two bedrooms other than your own—a thing that must not happen again."

Albert looked mortally offended.

"When the statue of Minerva was moved into the Banner Hall some days ago, did you also remove the little sheaf of wheat that the servants left for her?"

"Yes," said Albert sullenly. His eyes in the fairness of his skin slid to and fro as dark as sloes. His colourless eyebrows were arched in perpetual surprise. But the hair was too fine and the skin was too fine for the strenuous arch of that brow. He had a toothy smile that spoiled him, yet she longed to see him smile again.

"It has annoyed the servants very much that you have tampered with the sheaf. What did you do with the wheat?"

"I gave it to the Virgin Mary—in her little open-air church along the road. The dear little church without a door, and all the presents."

Victoria looked at him uneasily. It was the first time that she had heard this affectionate diminutive from him.

"I give her things quite often," challenged Albert.

"Albert," again she paused, oddly defeated. "You are a Protestant, and so am I. It is very right to be respectful to the shrine. But Dr. Herriot made a special point of the fact that your thoughts belong to your own church at present. The servants will probably put another sheaf beside Minerva. You are not to touch it. And before breakfast tomorrow you will apologize to Hans and Anna."

"They don't speak my language."

"Yes they do, if you speak slowly and politely," and the

Princess proceeded to open the window. The room was indeed as hot as an oven.

"Why is she called Minerva?"

"It's the Latin for her Greek name Athena."

"Does she belong to heaven, too?"

Victoria hesitated. "To a kind of paradise—on the outskirts."

"The suburbs?"

"Well, perhaps . . ." the Princess was unpacking her dressing-case.

"Can you pray to her too?"

"No, of course not. Minerva is only a myth."

"What's that?"

"An idea."

"Do you mean she's a notion?"

Not for the first time, Victoria was startled by Albert's appositeness. She ventured a little further:

"A dream of sorts."

Albert frowned. "Is she a ghost?"

"In a way, yes. But a pleasant ghost. You can see that. Calm and earnest, almost smiling."

"She's got a spear," said Albert argumentatively, "—a long pointed spear to stab."

"That's enough!"

"Well, why do they give her the wheat?"

"Just a little compliment."

Albert looked interested. "They're trying to please her with a little present?"

"Yes . . . yes, I suppose so. Now. I'm going into the bathroom to wash my hands."

"Don't be long."

Weakly she obeyed him.

On her return the turret bedroom, facing east, south, and west, held the last light of the evening, in a saffron stillness that lay like a bloom on the growing dark of its interior. Round the circular balcony, the ancient vine, knotted like a rope, hung into space like a tipsy wreath.

"Put on the light," said Albert, "so I can see the man with the helmet."

"Please," said the Princess mechanically, and obliged.

Albert stood rooted below a large photograph on the wall. The portrait revealed Monsieur le Comte de Talloires et d'Annecy in all the hauteur of military youth and the white tunic and silver helmet of Russia's *Chevaliers Gardes*.

"Crikey!" said Albert, as usual torn between admiration and protest. "When's he coming?"

"I must have told you twenty times—Christmas," but she was not ill-pleased. Repetition was a form of affirmation, and although François knew nothing of that trifling deception in Florence, already it had separated them in a ludicrous way.

"Who's that?" Albert pointed to a much smaller photograph, a little in the background—the photograph of a classically lovely woman.

"That's my mother's picture—she's dead," said Victoria abruptly.

Again Albert looked interested. "Who killed her?"

"I ought not to have put it like that. She has died—passed from this life."

"You mean she's gone to heaven?"

Victoria glanced at the bland beauty, and hesitated for an instant. "Yes."

"With the angels?" he insisted.

"Yes, I'm sure she's among angels," Victoria agreed.

"Are there angels in the suburbs too—with Minerva?"

"Albert—it's time you went to bed."

"But the angels know their way about, don't they," persisted Albert. "Even in the dark?"

"Of course. Now go to bed, Albert. I mean this."

And because she did, Albert went.

INVITATION TO DECEMBER . . .

"Another month of this accursed snow," groaned Clio, "and not a blink of sun! I warn you, Princess Sophia, that if it doesn't stop today, I shall die of depression. Nothing to do at nights, either, except play planchette with Frau Winkwurth. Or listen to her raving about what she calls my Florentine Exploit. And still it snows!"

The older woman laughed indulgently. "It has certainly gone on rather long, but we must sometimes expect that here. Once the sky clears, you will be entranced by the beauty of the scene. Meantime, you're warm and well."

"Warm, warm—what does my wretched body matter? My mind is shrivelled without sun—churning endlessly in this nebulous grey vacuum."

Cordially the other said: "Your wretched body looks very agreeable in that Viennese frock."

On the opposite side of a leaping fire Clio was, in fact, another creature, in a sage-green woollen dress belonging to Victoria, its colour opulent, its style severe, her red-gold hair neatly snooded on her neck.

For four weeks now Clio had daily unburdened herself to the woman beside her. The entire household, with varying degrees of patience, had also shared these confidences which extended as far back as Clio could remember, and as far forward as she dared hope. But Princess Sophia had remained longer, and more attentively, in the confessional.

"If it hadn't been for you," Clio was now admitting, "I should have committed suicide on Sunday. It isn't even like ordinary snow. There's no heart in it. The last time I tried to go out, a fortnight ago, it ran off me like air, floating around without resistance. A nightmare fluff! The laziest stuff—yet the servants call it wild-snow. Today when Princess Victoria opened the side-door, we couldn't see the conservatory. I put down the pail outside, and instantly it disappeared. That somehow finished me."

"What about your work on the Scaligers—your uncle's book? Weren't you editing that?"

"I seem to have lost all interest in it since you mesmerized me into doing the honourable thing, yet to finish his book successfully I'd have to alter it. It's a ghastly problem really, for if I don't finish it—the book will be lost, and he put a great deal of work into it. It was his only original creation. Yet if I do liven it up, Uncle Edward would hate it. Remorse might haunt me. And of course I mightn't find a publisher, after all my trouble."

"Then why not start a book of your own?"

"As a matter of fact, I *did* get a brilliant idea the other day —when Princess Victoria got those four letters by the same post saying that her guests were coming together, instead of separately as she had hoped."

"Now, Clio, that was a secret."

"Of course, and I won't breathe a word of it to any of them. But it certainly gave me an inspiration for a play. You know, Princess, that each of us is supposed to have an affinity —the person we pine for, the dream companion of our soul. Well, Abbey, who is a hideous debunker told me once that according to the law of averages, we must each of us have several affinities—which I just don't believe. But it struck me when those letters came that it might be most dramatic to stage an unexpected gathering of such affinities in a private house, and see what happened. Hell might boil up."

"Why not heaven?"

"No, no," said Clio briefly. "Not on *earth*, Princess. The conflict would be terrific. The adored and adoring wouldn't know where to turn in this embarrassment of riches. In the end, the one disagreeable intruder might steal everyone's thunder."

The Princess laughed. "Clio, you must write this play."

The girl frowned. "Technically, it presents difficulties."

"But isn't that stimulating?"

"Yes, but I don't want to resort to fantasy. So *fin de siècle*. No, I must get a fresh angle. You wait. I'll do it yet—" She broke off. "How old are the guests who come tonight?"

"I think Dr. Herriot is about the same age as Monsieur de Talloires—forty six perhaps."

"Pretty ancient. But if a personality is powerful, I don't object to maturity. *He* might have been thirty-five."

The Princess sighed sympathetically, "Ah, yes—your once-met hero."

"Is Dr. Herriot married?"

"I believe not."

"But it is the Comte de Talloires that Princess Victoria is going to marry?"

"I hope so."

"Do these two come from London together?"

"No. I believe Dr. Herriot will arrive first, by a local train from Bergers. He has been visiting the sanatorium there."

"What age is Lord Brompton who comes tomorrow?"

"Sixty at least."

"Deadly, isn't it?"

"I gather he doesn't think so. And Clio, we are most anxious that he enjoys his brief stay here. A great deal will depend on his visit to the district. It may mean the redirection of the English tourist traffic to the Stromberg."

"And Il Principe di Perugia?"

"Sixty-six."

"Sixty-six! That's the end. I can see nothing's going to happen here—ever."

"The Prince will not be staying here. He and his two friends are remaining at Springbrunnen. You will only have to bear the weight of his years at dinner tomorrow!"

"Now you're laughing at me! Sometimes I despair—"

A bell clanged from the entrance. Anna's answering feet could be heard in the vestibule.

Princess Victoria appeared on the gallery in a frock that Clio had not seen before, Parma-violet colour with a line that lent importance to her slim figure. Quickly she came downstairs, sleek dark head bent, and lips a bewitching carmine in her pale face.

"This must be Dr. Herriot!" She smiled, and disappeared into the ante-room.

Princess Sophia studied the flames reflectively, and Clio's head was turned alertly to the door.

It opened. An exceptionally tall man was following the Princess, a man whose deceptively indolent air, charming manner, cold eye and chiselled features were already set like a seal on the girl's impressionable heart.

Her hero of the Rome-Florence train was advancing upon her, as if he fully expected to see her! It was magical, it was mystical!

With a little cry she arose.

"Ah!" he declared, "I thought it must be the same Muse! There can be only one Goddess of Legend!" This time he kissed her hand, his greeting as always part of the perfection of his address.

Trembling with delight, she exclaimed: "Dr. Herriot!"

"No," said Princess Victoria with fatal precision, "this is my cousin, François de Talloires."

Clio's face stiffened.

"Clio and I have met before." He smiled. "A charming encounter on the train from Rome. . . . Sophia, how are you?" he was bowing now over the Princess' hand. Gaily they were greeting each other.

For a moment Victoria and Clio exchanged a glance—of compassion on the part of the Princess, of panic on the girl's.

Then haughtily Clio subsided onto her chair. . . .

INVITATION TO LOVE . . .

The clock struck one in the morning, but Victoria decided to wait a minute or two longer in the housemaid's pantry.

Dinner had passed off well enough. Clio had recovered herself—surprisingly quickly.

Dr. Herriot had failed to arrive—storm-bound at Bergers, no doubt.

Everyone had now retired to bed—an hour later than usual, unfortunately. The coast would be clear enough, though the fires might not yet be dead.

But she dare not delay resetting them till seven. François was an early riser. She might be caught before breakfast.

The Princess who had changed her frock for a morning wrapper with an old baize apron, impatiently seized the empty pail for the ashes, and the housemaid's basket.

One-five a.m.!

Passing from the deserted back corridor into the Banner Hall, its decorum soothed her at sight. Cheered, she set down the pail, and proceeded to clean out the fire.

Charlotte, one-time lady's maid, now crippled with rheumatism, could only manage to cook the midday meal and dinner. Old Anna was responsible for the washing-up. These were the admitted tasks. But there were others never openly acknowledged. Ashes emptied, stove-chimneys swept, flues freed, logs split, fowls plucked, game and fish gutted. Anna also controlled the dairy, and hen-house; the Princess the vegetable and flower garden; Hans, the farm animals; Barolyi, the estate and orchards. Each had his own province, jealously preserved. The only bond between the servants was a common detestation of Frau Winkwurth. Between these warring factions, Victoria might be said to occupy the uneasy situation of a buffer-state.

Kneeling at the open hearth now, she worked briskly, completely at home with her undertaking.

The Banner Hall was the heart of the house for her. At all seasons, it had charm, but perhaps its best moment was on early mornings in late May, as she came downstairs to prepare breakfast. Then the sleepy house had the summer warmth of fresh rooms shut in upon themselves by night . . . redolent of clean linen, flowers and fruit. The ghost of yesterday's baking surprised one in a whiff of vanilla near the still-room, till she opened that window upon hay and clover. But on the Banner stairway itself, from her flowering plants, a honeyed odour hung, curiously compounded too, of bygone port wine and vanished cigars! A heady moment till the great door was opened and these drowsy but pleasant phantoms were dispersed by a draught of air, cold as spring water, but aromatic with pine, and already brilliant with sunshine. . . .

One-twenty a.m.!

Swiftly she swept the last of the ash from the freshly prepared hearth, her entire performance so competent that she almost struck a match automatically and set the whole ablaze. Hours later, attired as a Princess should be for breakfast and her guests, she would deftly apply its light—and none be any the wiser!

Suddenly she stiffened. Without turning, she was aware, as she knelt there with blackened hands, and the kerchief that protected her hair white with dust, that she was under observation.

The Comte de Talloires, fully dressed, was coming downstairs.

"Good God, Victoria, what on earth are you doing?"

Her eyes snapped with a mixture of merriment and annoyance.

"Cleaning out the grate, François. Why aren't you in bed? This is trespass, you know. Midnight is a frontier here."

Coldly he surveyed her. There was a fair powdering of ash on her head, and a smudge on one cheek. "How long has this sort of thing been going on?"

"Seven years, or so. I can't leave everything till morning."

Stiffly he said: "I find it quite incredible."

Crisply she replied: "You wouldn't—if you knew what we've had to live on."

"As I told you in London last September, your brother ought to be shot."

"Augustus has his own problems. We have not been favoured with visitors for years. You, yourself, although the Family senior have been otherwise engaged. One must wear the shoe to know where it pinches."

"I had no idea that you were doing the work of a servant."

Her teeth glinted, her singularly melodious laugh mocked them both. "The work of three servants. Don't underestimate me! As Dr. Herriot may arrive before breakfast, it is important that he does not find his hostess on her knees. Besides, as I told you, I prefer to get the rough work over first. I am a conscientious creature."

Abruptly he stopped in his pacing. "Are you?" he challenged.

Arrested by his tone, she hesitated—and then added brightly:

"Trustworthy to a fault. Loyalty itself." She stripped the handkerchief from her head, bowing as she knelt. "Don't you recognize me in the rôle?"

"As the oppressively faithful?" he gave a short laugh. "Frankly I do not—unless it be to the past."

"I don't understand you."

Ironically he said: "Let me enlighten you. I understood from you in September that your love affair with Professor Drury had lasted ten years till then—and that during all but the first six months of that decade you had not seen each other."

"Yes. That is so."

"I find myself in the absurd position, then, of being jealous of a dream. Yet a dream like this can be very powerful, for its strength resides in the fact that it has never been put to the acid test of reality."

She stared up at him from the floor, and her voice shook slightly as she said: "But, François, I thought you understood about those first six months. I saw a great deal of Oliver then. I made that quite plain."

"Perhaps you did not make it plain enough."

Her face paled slightly, but in a steadier voice she said: "I had to get away from the Family to avoid scandal. I met him in Holland. I lived with him there."

"Indeed!" aloofly he surveyed her. "A pity," he said dryly.

Astonished, she gazed. "You didn't guess?"

"Not precisely."

"I'm sorry," she hesitated. "I thought your own love affair would have enlightened you."

"How long did this—this idyll last?"

"Three days and two nights."

He gave an exclamation of displeasure.

"You seemed annoyed," said Victoria somewhat defiantly, "at its brevity."

Formally he regarded her. "Not at its brevity—its waste. It should never have happened."

Rather uncertainly she arose.

Politely he held out his hand to help her. "I shall never forgive you," he said quietly.

Her face flushed as suddenly as it had paled. "Perhaps you should not forgive yourself," she retorted.

He gave, unexpectedly, an impatient sigh. "We are one and the same," he answered almost absently.

For a second she smiled into his expressionless face. "Then be kinder to me," she said. "Or is it a case of whom the Lord loveth He chastiseth? You do love me, I suppose, François? Otherwise the chastisement is inexcusable."

"My dear Victoria, you represent for me the poetry of existence—and other things as well. It is those other things that make *my* chastisement."

"The poetry of existence?" she repeated on a note of wonder. "How lovely, and how unlikely from you—of me."

"Unlikely?"

"Well, belated. The lyric terminates at twenty for the lady, doesn't it?"

"Have you never heard of a sonnet?"

Fleetingly she glanced away, and flippantly said: "Which had you in mind? *That time of year thou mayst in me behold When yellow leaves, or none, or few, do hang upon those boughs . . .*"

"No," he replied. "Turn the page of that copy I once gave you. The one hundred and ninth: *O! never say that I was false of heart, Though absence seem'd my flame to qualify.*

As easy might I from myself depart As from my soul, which in thy breast doth lie—"

Why doesn't he kiss me, she wondered. As he did in September? After all my face is quite clean. This is the time for it. Everything calls for it now. He should. He *must!*

But De Talloires' arms remained folded calmly on himself, his eyes at gaze across the room.

The Princess glanced in the same direction.

Between the long windows which ran the length of the hall, opposite the gallery and stairs, and in front of a tall pier glass, the marble Minerva caught the light—pure, radiant, celestial. The reflection in the mirror was shadowed as if daily life had passed over the figure. This dual cxistence, one in loveliness, leapt to the eye with revelation.

Beauty; smiled the Princess, staring at the goddess.

Turning he saw her eyes shining in the perfect oval of her dusty face, and swiftly caught her to him.

At that instant there came a resounding peal from the front door.

Involuntarily they started.

"At this hour—" she said. "What an extraordinary thing!"

"Who the devil . . . ?" he began.

And she exclaimed, "We would not hear the sleigh! It must be Dr. Herriot after all. How very strange. . . ."

INVITATION TO ZEPHYRUS . . .

Dr. Herriot awoke after his belated arrival to find the first sunshine in a month dazzling him.

His first impression was that the endless sleigh-drive from Bergers in a thinning snow-storm to this miniature baroque palace, white as a wedding-cake in drifting moonlight, had been a dream. Fantasy had quickened with the sight of its luxurious interior and a Princess who greeted him attired as a housemaid at two in the morning! Her blue eyes were black with merriment at his plight—instead of her own—and her fascination had again worked its conclusive spell on his reluctant heart.

The villain of the piece was, of course, the statuesque fiancé in his immaculate dinner jacket!

It had been like a charade, and the Doctor couldn't guess for the life of him what that incongruous scene might represent!

The Comte was so completely the haughty stick that his confounded courtesy hit one like a blow below the belt. They had unequivocally disliked each other at first sight. The boredom to which the exalted are subject, had instantly been diagnosed by the Doctor, yet with this particular patient it was not so easy to venture on prognosis. That stiff neck had a supple bow! The Comte, in fact, evaded the pigeon-hole to which he officially belonged. . . .

Dourly Dr. Herriot wondered why he had been fool enough to come. The answer was certainly not Albert!

The bedroom was stiflingly hot from its central-heating radiator. This no doubt accounted for his splitting head.

Glumly he looked around. A dull-green and a dull-gold room! The mahogany bed was draped with Pekin, like a blessed bride. Upon the rosewood furniture there were lacquer baskets bright with cyclamen. In the corner his Presbyterian eye detected a *prie-dieu* with a terracotta statue of the Virgin and Child. These early fifteenth-century Florentine figures held his grudging attention. Tender, expressive yet only half-opened faces! Suspiciously he sniffed. A faint odour of incense still persisted. The silence was profound as prayer . . . and for a moment or two, vaguely he mused. Despite himself, he found tension easing in these unsuitable surroundings.

A tap on the door! Anna bore down on him with the gargantuan breakfast that mid-Europeans think appropriate for the Britisher.

If there was one thing he detested it was breakfast in bed!

His German, which had known active-service during the occupation of Vienna, was fluent. The old servant was delighted with his thanks and brusque pleasantries, as she adjusted the radiator, opened the window, and lingered for more.

Ten men were now out from Springbrunnen, she informed him, making the road to the Château possible for the carriage. Tonight the Princess was holding a dinner-party. Il Principe di Perugia was already in the hotel there, with two ladies. Another guest was also expected. Lord Brompton. Did the Herr Doktor, by any chance, know this English nobleman?

Briefly Dr. Herriot admitted to a committee acquaintance. How was Albert?

Anna shook her head.

The Princess spoiled him. That was inevitable. However, he had been twice spanked in her absence, and some improvement since had been noticed. The child was waiting in the corridor. Was Anna to send him in, as she went downstairs?

Albert, small and slightly knock-kneed, walked with the delicacy of a tight-rope performer across the floor. His fair hair, fine as floss-silk, was less closely clipped than in London, but his head still looked nimbly winged by the coral curves of his ears. His toothy smile did more than spoil him now. One missing incisor had changed a cherub into a goblin.

He greeted the Doctor without enthusiasm.

"Well," inquired his medical adviser, "how are you?"

Albert looked up with that admixture of guilt and resentment peculiar to the out-patient. With Anglo-Saxon brevity he announced, "My belly's bad."

Dr. Herriot grimaced. "Put out your tongue."

Albert complied.

"Rubbish," said the Doctor. "You're as healthy as a haddock. What's the bright idea?"

Sullenly Albert rejoined, "I'm not coming back—ever."

"Who said so?"

"Me—and the Princess."

"The Princess said so?"

Albert looked him stonily in the eye. "Two times," he lied.

"Clear out," said the Doctor. . . .

Dressing as speedily as if he were en route for hospital, instead of the sun-lit courtyard below, he watched the Princess from the window.

There he had seen her, hooded in scarlet like a mediaeval page, passing to and fro between the out-houses, where Hans had beaten out a foothold in the snow.

Clio and Albert, muffled to the ears, were floundering on and off this path, with snowballs, shouting.

Two or three people, who looked like farm-workers, were grouped beside the stable, pointing jocularly to the weather-vane, glittering in the sun. In this white void their squat figures were vivid, startling—human beings ankle deep in a white cloud, their closest link with vanished earth, the castle turret now shining in the deep blue sky.

Once outside, he found the startling cold of the air freshened by sightless currents of ozone, like some invading mirage of the sea. Then once again his nostrils would be assailed by numbness—he could simply feel each hair icily singled out, and knew himself imprisoned in his own rebuffing body. Sound carried here only within immediate proximity—beyond, an invisible barrier hung upon it as a glass bell encloses a bright specimen for closer inspection.

The Princess hailed him cheerfully. "The servants are reading the omens. An old custom. This is the twenty-first—St. Thomas' Day—and for the next quarter they believe the wind will stick in the direction of this hour. Look! you can see for yourself—it has veered due south."

But Dr. Herriot found himself absorbed by the snow-bound spectacle around him. The obliteration of background served to bring those present upon his notice with the urgency of fate. It amounted to a confrontation. And although its significance was one he could not gauge, he was suddenly aware of some increased momentum—as if his whole experience were converging in crisis.

"Due south!" cried Clio. "Hurrah, hurrah, hurrah! When I think of the past month, I could scream: I've been cut off, clamped down, frozen. I can't live unless I *flow—*" and she plunged off after Albert.

Sceptically the Doctor noted this exuberance. An affected monkey!

Amused, the Princess said: "Clio has certainly not the patience of Job! For thirty days on end she's vociferated against the treasures of the snow!"

"You duped me too," he retorted. "I understood your garden was one of the wonders of the world, outrivalling Semiramis'. Instead I find the vacuum abhorred by man and beast!"

"What a challenge—" swiftly she rolled back the sleeve of her coat, and thrust her arm, naked to the elbow, into the thick snow of the wall. Her skin glowed golden against this dead-white mass, the contour of her arm delicate as a peeled almond. In triumph she retrieved a spray of flowering jasmine. "A *boutonnière* from Château Maria Sophia!"

For a second he saw her head and the long line of her throat turned against the sky, her profile secretive as a cameo against its quivering blue—

Then the next moment, the Comte stalked into the courtyard. He carried binoculars and, although he inquired politely as to Dr. Herriot's well-being, it was apparent that another problem more closely exercised him.

"Victoria," he said, "I can scarcely believe the evidence of my eyes. What has happened to the Teplitz Ridge?"

"I forgot to tell you. A surprise this summer. Barolyi cut down the trees. We have enough wood now to burn for years. Hans was furious. You know how he hates the Magyar. But it didn't cost us a pfennig in labour. Barolyi paid the villagers in timber."

Again De Talloires adjusted his glasses, and scanned the Stromberg behind the Château.

"They have certainly made a wholesale job of it."

"But, François, I think it looks so much better now without that ragged screen of trees, and the bluff still shelters us."

"True," said the Comte shortly. "And in neither case have the villagers, two miles off, been affected. They have simply secured firewood for their pains."

"Princess!" shouted Clio. "Don't go for a moment please! Tonight after dinner, may we dance in the Banner Hall?"

"Dance? It's too small a party."

"No, no—just perfect. Princess Sophia will play—I've asked her. And there will be four men and only you and me—what could be better?"

"Four ladies," corrected Victoria. "Frau Winkwurth, and the Prince is bringing one of his guests with him."

"Oh, she's bound to be old!" said Clio. "She will quite enjoy looking on—with Frau Winkwurth."

De Talloires who had turned away, stopped short. "Who is the other guest?"

"An Irish lady who's going on to Bergers with him and the Baroness tomorrow."

"An Irish lady?"

"I know as little of her as you do. Clio, we must first see how our other guests feel tonight. I have arranged to have the *apéritif* in the Banner Hall—dinner in the state dining-room as the servants have set their hearts on this. Then cards or music in the drawing-room."

"But if the Prince and the other lady like to dance?"

"I think it most unlikely. Lord Brompton I know would prefer Bridge."

"Monsieur de Talloires," urged Clio, "please, *please* ask the Princess to relent. Just one dance, or perhaps two. Why can't we all be pleased?"

He smiled. "I've yet to learn that compromise satisfies anyone. Besides, Clio, you and I are tonight accepting an invitation—not issuing one."

The young girl stared at him for a second. "You're quite right. . . . Princess, I'm sorry. Forget it!"

To Dr. Herriot's embarrassment, she next addressed him. Nodding in the direction of the Comte's retreating back, she exclaimed:

"Isn't he sheer perfection? Couldn't you just lie down and die for him?"

"I think," said the Doctor shortly, "I must first try to live for him."

The Princess flashed him a glance. "Perhaps not such an easy task!" . . . and oddly appeased he followed her into the Château.

Clio had not stopped to listen. Already she was speeding in the opposite direction, after her hero.

INVITATION TO ENCOUNTER . . .

Victoria stood alone in the candle-lit Banner Hall. *L'heure attendue!* On the telephone the Prince had stated he would arrive early to view the picture.

"And your guest?"

"She will be absorbed by your other treasures. One glance is all I shall require to fall under the old spell. But if I am in any doubt—perhaps you will allow a further examination to-morrow?"

"I should prefer a daylight decision."

She could still hear his purring laugh as she stood waiting now by the bright welcome of the fire.

Her black lace frock by Paquin was ten years old, but dateless, flawless even now. Her only ornament was a four-row pearl necklet, with a pendant pearl drop—the fabulous Vallorbe collar which the Family entail safeguarded from sale. Its lustrous beauty lent bewitchment to her poise, warmth to her distinction. The heirloom answered her as intimately as an echo. The Princess was very much at home in the superb setting in which she stood. The Babenberg coat of arms which blazed from the west end of the hall was reflected in the Venetian glass panelling of the fireplace—its Austrian eagle towering above her small, sleek head like some grotesque dark angel, its shield charged with the ancient symbol of her House, the Mark or Boundary, Crowned.

Outwardly an epitome of assurance, her glance into the flames was dubious.

The hostess in her deplored the fact that Hans must be major-domo tonight. His detestation of Barolyi made it impossible to substitute the Magyar. The estate-steward was much more presentable, but she had no choice in the teeth of Hans's seniority. It was her custom still to issue orders much as her father once had done, but Hans, one-time country caretaker at the Château, and now general factotum, responded to ten years of petticoat rule and a nominal wage with a surly nod, and the solitary admission: "*Durchlaucht.*" On this concession, which amounted to a grunt, their relationship was based. But she recognized that when this word went, together with the perfunctory nod, her tribal votary must go. This catastrophe, however, must not be precipitated by any fleeting extravagance such as dinner guests!

Hans had received his instructions in the potting-shed.

"And you will, of course," said the Princess, "announce that dinner is served in Italian—in compliment to his Serene Highness."

"Italian!" Briefly Hans turned aside and spat.

Horrified, the Princess made a lightning decision in favour of oblivion. Sternly she said: "Tonight we forget that it is 1921. We remember that the Prince is not only a connection of this House, but our guest. Attend to this."

There was a pause—an abyss, above which the Babenberg eagle appeared to hover, or was it to tremble?

"*Durchlaucht,*" agreed Hans, with greater clarity than usual.

But at what a cost had she bought civility! As she turned decisively away, Victoria wondered if the knees of Hans's sergeant-major had also failed him after issuing commands to this inimical recruit? And his borrowed uniform tonight, an outsize, would prove a further humiliation for both of them!

Yet it was typical of her that she immediately tackled Charlotte, that disgruntled Viennese, former lady's maid, but now cook at the Château, and its inflexible dictator.

"Charlotte, today you will have to bury the hatchet with old Anna and young Detta. They must help you to cook, as it's essential you wait at table tonight."

"*Durchlaucht!*" acknowledged the six-foot spinster wryly, then added with ferocity: "Be it understood that both these women are out of my kitchen, and on their way back to the village as soon as the banquet is served."

"But don't you want them to wash the dishes?"

"*Durchlaucht,* I do not wish these reptiles at all. One is a serpent, the other a scorpion. Hans will wash up."

Charlotte was, apparently, at the moment, on speaking terms with Hans, whom she was wont to describe, with elaborate irony, as "*yokel-and-bachelor, if you please!*" But on a warning note, the Princess said:

"Hans must, of course, serve the wine throughout."

"To my instructions, *Altesse.*"

Coldly the Princess said: "Arrange it between yourselves."

"*Altesse,* I have already done so. A banquet such as tonight's cannot be arranged in a couple of hours. These persons had their orders two days ago."

Yet contentious as her servants were, all had desired the larger, laborious dining-room for this evening . . . had, indeed, insisted upon it. And upon a much more elaborate meal than Victoria wished. She could only hope for the best. To do the Prince justice, such petty contretemps as might tonight befall, would scarcely trouble him, but she deplored the possibility for his guest's sake. It was a blessing that the Baroness, a stickler for punctilio, was not coming with them. Lord Brompton could be under no illusion as to the state of affairs at the Château. She had already ascertained by telephone to Springbrunnen that he would not arrive with the Prince:

"No, no, my dear Victoria—I find that Prince Colonna is here with a party. I shall come under by own steam!"

There remained the perturbing problem of Frau Winkwurth. That persistent toady had been anything but polite to Dr. Herriot at luncheon. He had taken it surprisingly well, for an impatient man. Alma, of course, like many born on the border-line of aristocracy, was an arrant snob. Her frontier had to be secured at all costs! A guest was sacred, but François had not rallied to the defence as Victoria had hoped. He had done what courtesy demanded and no more. Both men had later returned from skiing on the lower slopes, at an inconveniently early hour. It had—they were at least agreed on this—begun to snow again.

Glancing earlier from the turret window, she had seen a sulphur west quaking between bars of cloud, and noticed that already the snow mantling the wild landscape lent a spurious brightness to a leaden evening. Even as she looked, the low light on the horizon had appeared to shudder—in a slow, but sustained way. She knew the signs. More snow.

Now, she could only hope that Colonna would keep his promise, and arrive before Lord Brompton.

Swiftly she glanced to the right, where, in the bay below the noble arch of the stairway, the Del Abbate picture commanded its own vista. Impossible that he should not be recaptured by it, for in this gracious hall, which presented so many delightful distractions, the landscape quite effortlessly imposed its own sanctuary.

By this time tomorrow that place on the wall would be

blank. Instead she would hold a huge cheque on the Bank of Milan.

Doubtfully she gazed at this treasure from Fontainebleau. Oddly enough, now that she envisaged its absence, the picture rather than the hearth appeared to be the focal centre of the Banner Hall.

Sharply she raised her head. The tower-bell tolled. Cousin Colonna had been as good as his word.

A few minutes later, Hans flung open the door. So grim was his expression that the ludicrous roominess of his uniform scarcely occurred even on second thoughts. Hospitality-in-earnest had become with him an embodied threat!

As one herdsman hails another across the valley, he announced in Italian: "His Illustrious Highness, Il Principe di Perugia."

The Prince, slim as a skeleton, sleek as a shadow, advanced smiling. But the Princess had eyes only for the woman beside him . . . the most startling beauty she had ever beheld.

"Mees Gallacher," bayed Hans.

Neptune's Venus in oyster-coloured velvet and pearls, her fair hair severely knotted and spread like a shell behind one sculptured ear, sailed notably forward—the lady of the portrait in the Villa Leonardo.

But, no, she did not sail! This was no legendary swan such as Victoria's mother, the Princess Babenberg, had been. As she drew nearer, the goddess did not bewitch, bewilder—setting the distance of enchantment, stirring imagination. This was reality robustly overtaking Victoria, with eyes green as the sea, a voluptuous but unsmiling mouth, dignity without distinction—yet Helen herself in loveliness.

"I am delighted to see you," said Victoria untruthfully but

with the winning simplicity that is the prerogative of Royalty at home.

"Frightful weather," said Venus, unimpressed, and on a note of reproof. "How d'you do. . . ." No heartening trace of an Irish brogue. The voice was brisk, the enunciation clear —Bow-bells might just be discerned, if the ear were critical. That of the Princess was.

"My enchanting companion," said the Prince, "comes from an island that boasts the worse weather in Europe—and now she rails at snow in a winter-sports resort. In this she emulates her late ally Foch: *We are defeated— Attack!* And who would not be defeated, my dear cousin, by you—so exquisitely at home in the blizzard."

"It's certainly a remarkable interior," agreed Miss Gallacher. Her patronage was not intentional. She was quite sincere. Not a vestige of humour, the Princess realized. "In fact," admitted Miss Gallacher casting a business-like glance around, "I've only once seen one that resembled it. In the second act of *Sunshades at San Remo* . . . the state salon of Prince Max's palace."

For a second the blood drained from Victoria's heart, but not a tremor crossed her face. Her smile still glinted on eyes and lips.

"I think you recognize Miss Gallacher?" suggested the Prince. "Neptune's Venus—you saw the portrait at my villa."

But the Princess' smile did not waver. It became, if anything, more explicit—narrowing her eyes. With precision she inquired:

"Do I also recognize Miss Gallacher, from hearsay, as Estella Storm of this comedy—" the pause was infinitesimal but devastating—*"Sunshades at San Remo?"*

The Prince bowed. Miss Storm merely stood. Smoothly

he said: "You do indeed, but it is, naturally, in a private capacity she is with us tonight. As our guest, dear cousin. And now, ladies, forgive me if I too prove but human, and return to a first love."

He crossed directly to the Del Abbate picture. Unseen by the other two, he took out a small pocket torch and flashed it to and fro across the canvas.

"Miss Storm," said the Princess, "are you aware that my cousin, Monsieur de Talloires, is here tonight?"

Unperturbed, Miss Storm replied. "So the newspapers said. It's some time since we met. Only recently I discovered that he and Prince Colonna are related."

"Distantly," said the Princess frigidly, but, although her dignity set its gulf between them, the woman opposite continued stolidly to return her gaze.

"Felicity itself," commented the Prince, returning to them, "but that of course is simply another name for Fontainebleau!"

Feverishly the Princess thought: *Why has he done this?* He is on good enough terms with François. He must know what François and this woman have been to each other. What is the meaning of it? He must hate me. . . . But why?

The door opened and Clio entered.

Despite the present predicament, Clio's appearance was such that Victoria almost laughed in dismay. The girl looked preposterous in a crimson brocade house-coat, which the Princess had not seen before, with leg-of-mutton sleeves, and with her red hair dressed high, Edwardian fashion. She was wearing far too much make-up, and suggested a tousy edition of Lucretia Borgia, modern version. Clio, whose taste was excellent in literature, assured in the arts—to have made such an error, and in her own, the feminine field! Alas, for rash youth! Beside her the sophisticated Miss Storm looked like a Lenten lily!

Watchfully, the Princess' guests were presented to each other.

"We are contemplating the 'Death of Eurydice'," the Prince raised a languid hand toward the picture. "The timeless quality in any work of art, of course, obscures the activity with which it is compact . . . but one recalls that the Musae were first known as three in number—"

"That's so," interrupted Clio. "Melete, the Practising One, Mneme, the Remembering One, and Aoide, the Singing One. Go on!"

Expressionlessly, Dominic Stefano Gerontius Colonna surveyed her. "I was about to suggest that the splendour of Renaissance work has a suavity that implies Aoide alone, but it is, in fact, the spontaneity of the fully instructed."

"That's good," said Clio heartily, "that's very good. I follow you fully. He means," she turned to the older women, "that the integrity of the Practising One, the fortitude of the Remembering One, are here a secret sacrifice. And don't I know it! The agony of Mneme is nothing to the agony of Melete."

Miss Storm shrugged: "It's Greek to me."

Clio smiled indulgently. "You needn't bother—you're the Greek embodiment. The Renaissance is bogus beside you."

"That is charming, Clio." The Princess smiled. Miss Storm merely continued to look bored.

Shrewdly Clio exclaimed: "You hear this too often!"

For the first time Venus laughed. Apparently she reacted best to bluntness. "Oh, I'm not such a success with my fellowman as you might imagine. I have a temper. I lose patience before I lose interest!"

"Why not?" lisped the Prince, adroitly diverting these personal revelations. "Time, like history, is a modern imposition. The classical world leapt to life in its own *tempo,* from its own legends. But, Victoria, why, oh why, do you permit that marble Minerva here? Now had it been a bronze—"

"No, no!" cried Clio, "it's perfect—like everything else here. Of course the finish is rather florid, and certainly not of the best period. I mean, you can tell at a glance it's not even from a first-rate hand! But on second thought, it fits with this rococo interior marvellously. Look at those plump velvet curtains, and the Biedermeyer sofas! All the splendour here is suspended with the banners in mid-air. The flowering plants and that swirling stairway are the cunning links. The Princess' taste is impeccable—" she rapped out the word again like a bird tapping a shell, "impeccable!"

The two women regarded her with momentary amusement, but the Prince's smile was feline, and as Victoria proceeded to hand them sherry, she feared for Clio, as she heard him inquire:

"An authority on the Arts?"

"Not on sculpture," said Clio. "Thank you, Princess, a cocktail would be much more thrilling than sherry. May I have one? But on painting, definitely, yes."

"Now," purred the Prince, "this interests me very much. Which school is favoured by your attention?"

Clio took a greedy sip of her gin-and-orange, and then replied: "I have a serviceable knowledge of *all* the Italian schools. But my own period is the fifteenth century, the schools of Padua and Parma."

The Princess restrained a desire to laugh. "Clio, I had no idea of this."

But the young girl was observing the Prince. "Do you paint?"

"Unfortunately, no."

"A pity," she agreed. "That's where I have the advantage of you. Stephen Abbey, of Guerini and Abbey, Florence, is the best judge of painting I know, and he always admits that technical ability is an asset."

"You are an artist then?"

"No. I said technical ability. For years I helped my uncle with his work, which was the reproduction of old masters. His specialty was those Renaissance frames with hand-carved doors. Diptych or triptych, take your choice. There's precious little I don't know about the preparation of those wooden panels, their coats of lacquer, sanding, etcetera. *And* the tedious job of painting the chosen composition in miniature on them. With my eyes shut, I can smell a fake!"

"What would you say, Signorina, of this delectable Tobias and the Angel?"

"That's not fair!" she retorted. "One day, when I was alone, I took it out of the frame to see the back."

"Clio!"

"Well, Princess, as you've probably suspected yourself—it *is* after Domenichino, but pretty good too."

"Yes, Signorina, both the Princess and I were aware of that —but not so alive to the fact of a connoisseur in our midst."

Once more the Princess trembled for her, but need not have done.

Indulgently Clio shook her head. "Wrong again! Actually I'm a writer, by profession."

"Indeed? And what may we ask are you writing at present? A novel, inevitably!"

This time insolence lifted his lip. For a moment the young

girl stared at him astonished. Then she dropped her gaze, but doggedly replied: "Wrong still. At present I'm editing a life of the Scaligers!"

Behind them the door opened.

"*Eh bien,* Colonna?" said De Talloires cheerfully . . . and paused. He had seen the intruder.

Quietly the Princess said: "François, I believe you know Miss Gallacher. . . ."

Easily the Prince interposed: "Everyone in London knows Miss Storm—or should."

Very much her serene highness now, the Princess replied: "It is as Miss Gallacher we welcome her tonight. It was as Miss Gallacher you introduced her."

"Hello, François!" For the first time, Miss Storm smiled broadly, and a devil of defiance danced across her face. Thus kindled she looked dangerous, but aloofly the Comte stood his ground. How well Victoria knew that impassive air, the cold eye—every clue to his secretive nature. Despite a slight stoop, he moved with a tall man's elegance.

Briefly he bowed. He did not appear to see the singer's tentative hand. Swiftly the Princess said:

"Ah, Lord Brompton . . . and Dr. Herriot!"

"*Wunderbar!*" boomed Lord Brompton. Abroad he was invariably more native than the natives. It warmed him to give satisfaction. He had been out to bless since birth.

Benign as a bishop, he advanced, familiar as the daily paper—his massive face better known than that of the stage-star opposite him. Photographs of Lord Brompton were recurrent as the popular press itself: presenting prizes; laying foundation stones; opening old people's homes; closing slums; launching youth clubs; accepting donations on behalf of one charity or another; awarding this; bestowing that . . . a universal provider. Organized benevolence. "Dear and gracious lady, I hope we are not late? Good evening, Prince! *And* the fabulous Miss Storm . . . no, it cannot be! Dr. Herriot, I dare you confirm my illusion: the one and only Estella!"

Briskly Dr. Herriot shook hands with Venus. "Miss Storm it is! But my idol has feet of clay. I can't forgive anyone with as fine a voice as hers wasting it! Why aren't you in Grand Opera?"

She laughed as she had done at Clio's challenge. "Because I wasn't prepared to give the additional years demanded at the start. Singers have to eat like the rest of you, and impatience is my malady, Dr. Herriot. But as I'm incurable, spare me professional advice!"

She did not even trouble to speak pleasantly. Lovely as Lilith, she could afford to say exactly what she thought or felt. The policy of Victoria's mother, the Princess Babenberg, another reigning beauty, had been charm—her daughter remembered. The present lady's was, apparently, the straight punch. Clever really, for no man could deal with her without seeming a brute. It would take a woman—

"Good evening," said the Princess Sophia from the stairway.

All turned. Sheathed in grey lace to the chin, the most elegant figure in the room was descending, Babenberg diamonds sparkling at her throat, and catching the light in drop ear-rings on either side of her suave face. Fragile, elderly, she achieved the minor miracle of being as evocative as restraint itself.

Involuntarily the Prince stepped forward.

"Ah, Colonna . . ." she smiled, "what a lot of water has run under the bridge since last we met!"

Kissing her hand, mechanically he found words. "You always confound me. Is it possible we are still on the same side of Jordan?"

But she hardly heard him, for as he stepped back, she and Miss Storm were confronted. To the astonishment of those present, both women exclaimed with delight.

"Of all people–" Miss Storm's face was transformed.

"My dear child, this is amazing!"

Holding each other's hands, they continued to express incredulity, oblivious of observers.

"I have so often thought of you!"

"And I of you!"

"So stupid that I did not have your name."

"Nor I yours!"

The statuesque Miss Storm, now flushed with pleasure, still held the other's hands. "For months I put an advertisement in the *Times*, hoping to catch your eye."

"But that week I returned to Austria, so I never saw it. It must be quite ten years ago. How well you look!"

"The tide turned the next day, all thanks to you."

"No, no, to your own courage. Your courage was the first thing to impress me, as it must impress all."

"Estella," lisped the Prince, "this encounter confuses me. But I warn you that Princess Sophia is a sorceress who steals souls at sight. No one knows what she does with them afterwards–least of all, she!"

Indulgently Princess Sophia turned to a critical audience. "You must excuse us, Lord Brompton and Dr. Herriot–and perhaps rejoice with us–for this is more than a reunion. It is a celebration!"

De Talloires stiffened. Clio frowned. Victoria remained rigid.

"Although I only met her once," the mild, authoritative

voice continued, "for various reasons I have long looked on this dear child as very much the apple of my eye."

From the background, in stentorian tones, Hans announced:

"Your Serene Highness, dinner is served."

INVITATION TO ELEVEN MASKS . . .

An exclamation of pleasure broke from the guests as they entered the dining-room. A panelled ceiling and Italian tapestries of the sixteenth century brought intimacy to its stately size. The room with its dim green walls was hushed and warm as midsummer night in some mediaeval forest. But the banqueting board blazed with candlestands which dazzlingly displayed the Venetian glass fountain at the table's centre, spraying and tinkling its diminutive waters. Glancing light and sparkling spray shone on the Babenberg silver; the Beauharnais glass; and the Claret-Worcester china. Around the board, tall-backed seventeenth-century chairs, ribbed with resida silk rippled their invitation—those at the top and bottom of the table terminating in carved crowns.

De Talloires, paler than usual, hesitated.

"François," Victoria's smile was adequate, "will you take the head of the table?"

Relieved, he stepped forward, but she indicated the carved chair at the bottom. Victoria had sat so long in Prince Babenberg's chair that the top of the table was now second-nature—a point not lost on each man present. François, amused, walked to the far end.

Victoria, whose obsession tonight was the sideboard behind her, where stood the six-foot Charlotte and a totally inadequate Hans, did not notice these nuances. She was startled by the fact that Charlotte, erect as a guardsman had actually assumed that badge of servitude, an apron—a phenomenon that only Tante Sophia could appreciate. But how loudly Hans was breathing in the background—like a boar in a thicket!

Aloud she said smoothly in English, for in courtesy to the British guests, this was the language spoken throughout: "Miss Gallacher, your chair is on Monsieur de Talloires' right. Lord Brompton, my left."

"Ah, dear lady, next your heart—what could be better!"

"Cousin Colonna, at my right hand, please."

Promptly Clio took the chair on Lord Brompton's left. Automatically Dr. Herriot placed himself between her and Miss Storm—Princess Sophia seating herself opposite on the Prince's right.

"What's this?" queried De Talloires. "An empty chair on my left! Is it Elijah's?"

"Frau Winkwurth!" exclaimed Victoria. "Hans, go upstairs and announce dinner."

"Princess," Clio said quickly, "shall I go? It might be better."

It might indeed! To mislay Hans at this moment was to court disaster. Already he was charging round the table with the *foie gras*. Why had Charlotte given him his head like this? He ought to have been serving the Sauternes.

Precipitately Victoria's thoughts pursued him as, amiably, she assured Lord Brompton that the past month of sunlessness was wholly exceptional for the Stromberg. "Not for another century probably, will such a thing occur!"

Promptly Dr. Herriot bore her out. Yesterday at Bergers

Sanatorium, he had heard the physician-in-chief confirm this.

"Why should the English tourist hesitate?" lisped the Prince. "He will always find himself at home on Italian soil."

Hans, in the act of belatedly bestowing the Sauternes, stopped breathing behind the Prince's chair. He glared.

"Italian *territory,* Cousin Colonna," said the Princess sweetly, but clearly. "The difference between a signpost and a shrub resides in the roots, doesn't it?"

Hans proceeded to pour, but a spurt of general conversation again ceased abruptly.

Frau Winkwurth upholstered in red velvet, with her bloodstone necklet heaving tumultuously, steamed into the room, peremptory with indignation.

The gentlemen stood to attention with the precision of marines saluting a man-of-war.

"Viccy—I apologize. But that infamous child again locked me in my room!"

"Alma, I *am* so sorry! Tomorrow Albert will be punished for this. Now, help us to forget him—as only you can."

In a chorus of condolence, the old lady, mollified, moved to her place. "Well, of course, when I see a badly behaved child or dog, I do not blame the child or animal. I blame those responsible—" she shot a look at Dr. Herriot. Waving a plump hand, she dismissed the soup. "No, thank you, I shall go straight on. I'm sure Clio will too."

Admirable, was the unspoken comment, and Frau Winkworth, conscious of success, bowed cordially to Miss Storm.

Urbanely Victoria could be heard: "Dr. Herriot, Lord Brompton would like to hear about your experiences in post-war Vienna—where we Austrians owe so much to your work in our hospitals."

Lord Brompton beamed. "I have it on final authority that your name, Dr. Herriot, may now be numbered with that of Von Pirquet, Schick, Wenckeback."

Really, Victoria decided, there was much to be said for a fair-weather friend who faithfully followed barometric indications at table!

But Dr. Herriot's smile was sour. "You flatter me. I only did what any medical man would have done to ameliorate the results of the English blockade among innocent children."

Danger signals again hoisted! It was ten years since the Princess had given a dinner-party. What had happened to people since? In the old days, resentment might be rife, but no rancour threatened the amenities in this way. It simply was not civilized!

"I packed up sooner than I intended," ruthlessly the Doctor proceeded with his work of demolition. "As ashamed of one country as the other. To watch a people sicken and die had an unfortunate effect on my own health. Equally disgusted with myself, I went home before I should."

Unexpectedly Prince Colonna effected rescue. "Your attitude was truly philosophical. It is always a mistake to do anything *invita* Minerva—"

Fascinated, Clio interrupted. "*Invita* Minerva—translate please."

"Briefly, 'against the grain,' Signorina. Or more explicitly, as Horace advises us: Beware of attempting anything for which nature has not fitted you."

"I like Horace's nerve!" scoffed Miss Storm. "From birth to death life is a conspiracy to force you to disregard this advice."

"Dear girl," said Princess Sophia, "there are other moments."

The singer's face softened for a second. "One or two."

"But the story is not finished," insisted Sophia, and again they exchanged glances.

"Frightfully interesting," Clio addressed the Prince. "And, of course, I see Horace's point. But what about achievement? I mean to say: wouldn't this caution put an end to development?"

"Not at all," again Princess Sophia, gentle but assured, replied: "One would simply take the precaution of fitting oneself for the enterprise. Every athlete trains."

Said Clio suspiciously, "By changing one's nature?"

"Princess," said Dr. Herriot, "I share this young lady's misgiving. To attempt the impossible may disrupt personality."

"I agree," Sophia Babenberg regarded him directly, "if one does this in one's own strength."

"I'm afraid," said the Doctor stiffly, "that most of us find ourselves pretty much alone these days. Modern psychology stresses the importance of candid admission. One must move with the times."

With charm Princess Sophia suggested: "As long as one doesn't stop short with them. Frankly, Dr. Herriot, don't you find the times date?"

The Doctor stared.

"Less delicately," the Prince declared, "Princess Sophia finds modernity old-fashioned!"

Despite argument, how quickly they were eating! Anxiously Victoria noted that the *Suprême de Sole au vin du Rhin* was already despatched. Would Detta and Anna ever be able to stand up to this speed in dishing?

"Nevertheless," Dr. Herriot's expression was now so grim that the entire table accorded him involuntary attention, "each of us is entirely alone. Custom, or the comfort of the moment," he made an impatient gesture to the luxurious room, "may obscure the fact. But it remains. Proximity is an illusion. Man's recurring neurosis in the midst of this—often as age advances—points to unacknowledged fear."

"But surely, Dr. Herriot," said Princess Sophia amiably, "neurosis is itself a hopeful sign, an indication, after all, that we are running on the wrong lines, when we run alone."

"I agree with the Princess," De Talloires announced. "A symptom has only to be pronounced for it to hypnotize us as *fait accompli.*"

Dear heaven! thought Victoria, what had come over him and Sophia—exploiting such a theme? Where was their resource? The only gaiety and sparkle at her dinner party came from the toy fountain in their midst—beside which they were huddling as introspectively as Russians round a samovar.

Coldly the Doctor returned De Talloires' glance. "You simply confirm my point that each case being individual must be treated on its own."

At this juncture Victoria was swiftly sustained by the fact that the *Wiener Schnitzel* had arrived on time and was being served with despatch! She permitted herself to breathe again. Mercifully, Lord Brompton was bustling into the breach with one breezy anecdote after another. What an evening! Who could have foreseen the day that she would rely on him as sheet-anchor?

Again his voice boomed pleasantly across the table. "And has the Toledo recovered from its recent adventure, Prince Colonna? An account of this reached the London papers you know. What a climb for any woman—and the descent must have been worse! Was it a bet? Or a publicity stunt."

"Neither," pronounced the Prince. "It was a fraud."

"*What!*" Frau Winkwurth was delightedly aghast, her gaze darting towards Clio.

"I naturally made it my business," said the Prince, "to discover the truth. The girl had been in the habit of entering the empty Palazzo secretly, by a second-floor window. She was seen chasing the cat along the roof. After that she simply dived back into the house, ran down several flights of stairs, climbed out of the window, and was caught on the water-pipe fifteen feet from the ground. The end of an odyssey!"

"Kept her head any way," commented Lord Brompton.

Miss Storm laughed. "How on earth did you find out? The newspaper article was quite convincing. I read it myself."

"The cloth in which she slung the cat over her shoulder had been seized off an empty parrot cage in the attic. This linen bore my monogram. The police, who claimed the cat, later returned the cloth, but I decided not to prosecute. I had by that time satisfied myself that the lady was not a thief in the usual sense."

"But what was she doing there?"

"Availing herself of a unique library, dear Estella. I know my shelves as a lover knows his mistress' mouth. It is instantly arresting to find the canines where the incisors should be!"

Dr. Herriot laughed outright, but calmly De Talloires intervened.

"Come, Colonna, logical deductions may be irresistible, but the fact remains that the climb was witnessed by a large and appreciative crowd."

"Of course!" Victoria's accomplished smile imposed finality. "You don't suggest that the lady performed the rope trick on the multitude? That would have been still more of a feat! Forgive me, Clio, but this seems an appropriate moment to reveal that you are La Coraggiosa."

The rouge on Clio's cheeks could be seen as two bright islands on an increasing pallor.

"Ten thousand apologies," said the Prince piously—he was indeed startled.

"One will do," said the girl tartly. "If it's genuine—"

"Now, Miss Tubbs," Miss Storm spoke quite genially, "never tempt a man to elaborate his own downfall. It makes them like us less than ever! That's so, isn't it, François?"

Unperturbed he answered: "I think you must give the reason. Women are invincible, but happily do not know it. Experience has proved how deadly any organized minority can prove in the body politic— But envisage an organized majority! No wonder we tremble."

The Prince laughed. "Fortunately they continue to betray themselves by their absorption in us."

"Except the career-girls," amended the Doctor. The beauty was obviously a bit of a bitch, and had asked for those two delicate snubs, but he himself disliked the way the Comte had earlier ignored that tentative hand. Some past history there? A disdainful merchant, anyway!

Gamely enough Clio turned to the singer. "*You* must have had some wonderful experiences. Which impressed you most?"

Laconically Miss Storm replied: "My first tour abroad. At the age of eighteen, Singapore, Straits Settlements, Penang, Shanghai certainly leave their mark. When business was bad, we put on *The Sign of the Cross* or *Floradora*. These never failed us. That left an impression too."

Where was this unsuitable conversation leading? Yes, the worst had happened verbally. Shanghai and Penang had led to tropical diseases. Victoria could hear Frau Winkwurth launching another broadside at Dr. Herriot. She was, in fact, contradicting him on his own subject—all on the strength of a distant cousin who had recovered from beriberi, *no* thanks to the medical profession! This party was a nightmare. François had barely said a word to that woman. . . . If he didn't cover his traces better, everyone would tumble to the truth. What an agony it all was. Yet gastronomically the evening was being a great success. Each course had been perfection so far. Charlotte was a remarkable person! Once the sorbet arrived, Victoria could relax! Now Frau Winkwurth was dilating to Miss Storm on the boon of central heating. Surely that was safe enough?

"Monsieur de Talloires installed ours within a week."

"On his hands and knees?" queried the singer.

"What I *should* have said," amended Frau Winkwurth, "is that the men were in and out within six days."

"Ah," intoned Miss Storm, "the workers! Now, I follow. . . ."

Victoria in the act of addressing Clio, who had again lapsed into leaden silence, was suddenly deflected by the sound of a scuffle behind her chair. Incredible to relate, Charlotte was snapping audibly at Hans. Hans had now raised his voice as well. He was protesting at the sorbet. Angrily he insisted that it go back to the kitchen. *Ices came at the end of a meal—every idiot knew that. "Imbecile!"* Charlotte barked.

Cousin Colonna's face remained irreproachable, but Lord Brompton's mouth twitched. Hans had thrown down the wine-napkin, and charged from the room.

Charlotte served the sorbet, which was eaten amid innocent acclamation by those at the far end of the table. . . .

Detta, in place of Hans, with crimson cheeks and a spotless apron brought in the roast.

"François," with composure Victoria addressed him, "would you be kind enough to pass the Gevrey-Chambertin for me?"

"But of course" . . . his fine, fastidious hand poured the wine like a silent benefaction into each glass. His every movement had a precision that was grace in him.

Victoria glanced up as he stood at her right hand. Gravely he looked down at her: "That year of grace!" he murmured. It was an old joke between them that she had been three in the heroic year for Burgundy: 1889. For an instant she smiled to him in perfect sympathy.

Miss Storm gave an abrupt laugh. "No butler can beat the Diplomatic Corps on its accomplished round!"

The other guests stiffened. The Prince shuddered. Only Princess Sophia appeared to notice nothing untoward. "After all," she agreed graciously, "the business of both is amelioration!"

With a gasp Clio came to the surface again, "But this is weird," she said, "—watching you all! Earlier I told Princess Sophia of a plot I'd got for a play—a gathering of affinities in a private house, just like this. In the first act, you would be as you are now. Hidden. In the second act, you would be disclosed. And the third act—the third act would be the most gorgeous of all . . . for we'd all be back together, facing what we *then* knew of each other. Why! in some cases it might be simply frightful—" her inquisitorial glance flashed along the board—"or very wonderful." She paused to consider the Comte, and lost vigour.

"May I ask," purred the Prince, "how you remove masks from persons who literally *are* façades, like my unfortunate self? We tend to cling to reticence."

Impatiently Clio nodded. "I know, I know! There will be

difficulties. But I shall think of something. It's an absorbing idea . . ." she bubbled on.

Each man present had earlier been intrigued by the way in which Princess Victoria's distinction had captured attention alternately with Miss Storm's beauty. The Apple of Paris was held first by one woman, then the other. The onlookers, in accepting their own wavering allegiance, had yielded complacently to the varied nature of their entertainment. But as this young girl, unsuitably dressed, badly made up, continued to monopolize the conversation, another element entered the circle with her eagerness. Beauty and distinction took back-seats to vitality. Youth, launched on an idea, held the honours.

The Prince alone was out to kill. "But are you not afraid?"

"Afraid? Of what should I be afraid?"

"Our brightest ideas, Signorina, and the highest flown, are invariably put to the test of personal experience. Artists and writers alike have admitted this. On paper you may prevail, but the gods have a way of taking us, literally, at our word. Why should the scribe escape? Sooner or later you will work out the truth you've snared."

"Great Scott," exclaimed Dr. Herriot, "then many inventors and most artists must invite ordeal?"

The Prince smiled. "And those who take refuge in platitudes, a well-deserved martyrdom sooner or later! I have the greatest respect for Nemesis. Thus integrity is preserved. For this reason, Miss Tubbs, you might fittingly name your drama: Invitation from Minerva. She is, after all, patroness of the arts *and* goddess of storm and thundercloud."

"*Invitation from Minerva*," repeated Clio slowly. "Yes, I think you've got something there. Thank you very much.

I'll use it if I don't think of anything better. *Invitation from Minerva*—it certainly rings a bell."

Hans re-entering at that moment startled Victoria afresh. Curiosity, she suspected, had got the better of his habit of cutting off his nose to spite his face.

With hauteur he bore aloft that crowning achievement of the Viennese table: *Sachertorte.*

In acclamation Lord Brompton raised his glass: "An Englishman can forgive Metternich anything at such a moment! The *gâteau* of the gods!"

"Hear, hear!" applauded Dr. Herriot. "The destiny of Europe must often have been determined at the Hôtel Sacher, but so too have its delights. Princess Victoria, this is a most welcome reappearance!"

Hans, reinstated with full rights of sovereignty, shot Victoria a look of triumph. Anyone would think that he had made the cake!

Armistice declared, the *chef d'oeuvre* was eaten amid general good-will.

Victoria's anxiety, released, flowed now in a deeper channel. There had been ample opportunity for Colonna to confirm his offer. One word would have sufficed. But he had not spoken. Did he, or did he not, mean to buy? Had her confidence on that score been presumptuous? But if she did not get the money—if she failed to sell? After all, the sum demanded was huge.

As if in answer to her thought, instantly he spoke. It was, in fact, uncanny!

"A small fortune," he murmured. "But I have no regrets. I trust that you will have none."

Aloud he added: "This is the address I think you wished," and handed her a thin slip of paper.

"Ah, thank you!" she said lightly, placing the cheque in her *tabatière*. "I am glad to have it."

Glancing down the table she saw that nobody had noticed—except Lord Brompton, who was, of course, none the wiser. François' head was luckily averted—for the moment he was talking to Miss Storm.

Miss Storm, *sotto voce,* was challenging her one-time lover. "Interesting idea that of Miss Tubbs! Don't you think? But why did she settle for affinities? This is more like a board-meeting of hungry creditors. Enemies. Life is so full, isn't it, of people feeling the right thing for the wrong person? And eternal love from the wrong person can be *so* embarrassing! One just can't understand it, even if one is an ambassador . . . until one comes to feel the same thing for someone who is quite indifferent—" her look leapt to Victoria and back—"or as cold as charity. It amounts to the same thing!"

Politely he listened, perfunctorily he replied—exercised by the slip of paper he had just seen pass between the Prince and the Princess.

"Even then, Madame, I imagine one would still be in the dark. . . ."

Sachertorte had vanished. They were still chasing through the courses: in the old days Victoria had never been oppressed by haste like this. Court dinners, state functions, civic banquets, graced by a leisured dignity, revived in her memory . . . Most of her guests were now talking sixteen to the dozen—so how was it done? Yet amiability at last seemed to prevail.

Dessert, however, reintroduced hostility. As the figs were placed on the table in the celebrated Romulus and Remus dishes, which like the Princess' pearls, were also safeguarded from sale by Family entail, Lord Brompton shook his head affectionately:

"Ah, Viccy, how well I remember the Princess Babenberg's fondness for figs! She was surprisingly abstemious at table. In fact, it was a pleasure to discover she had a weakness there."

With icy pleasantry the Prince retorted: "I decline to believe that Princess Babenberg had any weakness. Had your ravishing mother been a man, Victoria—which heaven happily forbade—I should quote Aristotle and describe her as *a political animal.* More gracefully I now hail her as Athene Promachos. . . . Yes, Miss Tubbs, Front-Line Minerva!"

Victoria's face had for the first time paled. What did he know? Tensely she remembered her own recent discovery—the secret known only to Garett Phelps—of her mother's work for the British Intelligence. *How did Colonna know?*

Tante Sophia, instant in thought, was speaking for her: "No, no, I always think of my sister-in-law as that earlier Athene, Goddess of the Dawn—Golden, All-Radiant."

Cordially Lord Brompton added: "Of course, of course! Princess Babenberg's brilliance enlivened the common round for the rest of us quite remarkably. With the poet one *could* exclaim in those days: *Ere Pallas issued from the Thund'rer's head, Dullness o'er all possessed her ancient right!*"

"Gracious!" exclaimed Clio, "you make her sound almost inhuman."

"I prefer the word immortal," once more the Prince had intervened, and swiftly Victoria realized: It's Maman he really hates. . . . He strikes at me because I'm all that's left—but I don't really matter at all.

Inwardly shrinking, she raised her head and, slim and

stately, stared in François' direction. From a long way off, she heard him declare:

"Princess Babenberg was legendary, and so she could afford to stand alone. She not only fared far, she fared successfully. Our sex sometimes finds this hard to forgive."

"How very true," concluded Lord Brompton, with more dignity and less gusto than usual. "But then Princess Babenberg was so cheerful that one constantly forgot her courage."

At this appropriate cue for exit, Victoria in the act of catching the ladies' eyes, remembered the dying flash in her mother's, that unspoken fear that her son might also be considered illegitimate, if the truth about Victoria emerged—Augustus, whose sole support today was the money from his Italian estates as Count Della Rocca.

Her smile a trifle set, the Princess arose.

But as the ladies withdrew, Hans, charging ahead with the port, bumped into a guest!

The disaster haunting every dinner party as contingency occurred, and in no uncertain fashion—

Wine splashed over Miss Estella Storm.

Her hostess, in consternation and humiliation, hurried her from the room.

The singer was laughing. "Launched in port—well, what battle-ship isn't, after all!"

Clio said eagerly: "Princess, let me take Miss Storm upstairs. It won't take more than a few minutes. Most of it went on her arm and the floor."

"Very well, Clio. But don't rub that delicate fabric. The stain must be removed later by an expert cleaner."

"Yes, yes . . . yes, yes!" Frau Winkwurth was bustling after the two younger women. "I'll keep an eye on this!"

Alone in the Banner Hall, Victoria turned to the Princess

and coldly said: "Tante Sophia, do you know who that woman is, this friend of yours?"

"I heard her name for the first time tonight, Victoria."

"She was François' mistress for a year—the affair only ended three months ago. Yet she dared to come here tonight."

Gravely the older woman returned her gaze. "How very painful for you! Well, this is something she will have to work out as she goes along."

Anger against Sophia, fierce as it was unaccountable, welled up in Victoria, to be instantly subdued. Her voice trembling slightly she replied: "Is that all you have to say about her effrontery?"

"Yes, Victoria," and the other sighed as she sat down. "I can see what you do not—how she is suffering. Be generous. Above all to François, for nothing makes one more ruthless at times than having moral support. . . ."

INVITATION TO CALAMITY . . .

Coffee and liqueurs found the guests grouped once more in the centre of the Banner Hall.

Dr. Herriot drank standing. Stirring his coffee he frowned. Here in this brilliant light, Princess Victoria looked older beside the Beauty . . . Clio coltish. The girl only kindled in conversation. Without this she looked hang-dog, he noticed, in spite of her festive make-up!

Oddly enough he felt as uneasy about her as he did about the Princess. Perhaps some unsuitable love affair? Youth was a sensitive, wretched time. Thank God his own was behind him! Was this tempting Providence—or Minerva, according to that pagan gent? Did youth automatically renew its agonies and its ecstasies each time one fell in love? Yes, that was nearer the mark! Paradoxically enough, one grew old as a result of these ill-advised revivals. Age was the sum total of vigour's visitations. *Ergo:* if the spirit were immortal, one might quite easily suffer indefinitely! What an outlook!

How closely Prince Colonna watched Princess Sophia—precious little *he* missed between those half-closed lids! Yet the Doctor rather liked him; perhaps because he suspected that he and the Prince were the two most unpopular guests in the room! That supercilious mandarin of a Comte was making some sort of speech to the maid as she finally set down the coffee tray. Over his liqueur glass he was bowing to the servant:

"Charlotte, your dinner was superb. Our congratulations and your very good health!"

The Prince and Lord Brompton rose and bowed also, the Doctor noticed. . . .

Stiffly Charlotte inclined her head. By this unconventional tribute Monsieur le Comte had ruined the formality she had throughout been at such pains to uphold. Yet some hours later, with the evening safely washed-up, tidied past, it might be possible to review this disconcerting moment with belated pleasure!

At the Doctor's elbow, Clio exclaimed. "Isn't Monsieur de Talloires wonderful? Can't you hear the centuries speaking through him."

"Yes," said Dr. Herriot maliciously, "and all saying the same thing!" but the girl scarcely heard him. She was gazing raptly at her idol, as he listened to Lord Brompton extolling a small bronze Cupid.

"What nonsense, Brompton," lisped the Prince. "Only our vanity suggests that we share an emotion like love with the gods. Most people are incapable of ardour. In jealousy alone we meet the immortals on their own ground, that frontier region where they put on mortality, and share our no-man's-land."

"Jealousy a no-man's-land?" exclaimed Victoria. "Why, its pettiness makes it household province!"

"My delightful cousin, jealousy is not a petty emotion, although petty people may also be ravaged by it. Jealousy is a dynamic experience, a daemonic intoxication under which strong men stagger and virtuous women reel! Both sexes feel it, mutual passion may excite it, but it exists independently of sex, as anyone knows who has studied human beings or animals. Jealousy is the most primordial of all emotions. You disbelieve me? But then you are a woman, and imagination may not be at once your destruction and enlightenment. Make no mistake about it, jealousy is fundamental–" indolently he indicated the Babenberg banner with its Boundary Crowned–"the Mark or March over which every frontier incident precipitates its war in private or in national destiny."

"As usual you are right, Colonna," said De Talloires calmly, "–as far as you go. But you don't go far enough–you never do. You have forgotten that in the end the gods are always merciful. Mortals and demons alone fail there, through fear; for we are subject to time. But the gods have eternity at their disposal. Ladies, let us take the long view and refuse to be ruffled. We are in good hands."

The Prince's eye gleamed. "Yet Holy Writ confirms me: *I shake not the earth only, but also heaven.*"

Amused, Sophia said, "But that is exactly what makes divinity so restful, Dominic. You ought to finish the quotation: . . . *the removing of those things that are shaken . . . that those things which cannot be shaken may remain.*"

"In other words, Princess," and Dr. Herriot again looked grim, "you suggest that calamity protects us from credulity? Well, may I be allowed to remain in a state of superstitious comfort a little longer!"

But Frau Winkwurth had cut him short: "Here's a pretty girl beside me who is longing to dance before we start Bridge. Now, gentlemen, as Princess Sophia has already gone up to the musicians' gallery, what is it to be? Not a schottische, I beg you!"

Before they could answer, Waldteufel's "Très Jolie" swirled from above.

Startled, Victoria raised her head. This souvenir from her twenty-first birthday came with a pang, its wistful sweetness wholly inadequate to express its true burden—that woe-begone ball which had promised so well.

But Lord Brompton, gallantry creaking a trifle, was speaking: "No woman has danced since your mother vanished, but I hope her daughter will try."

Together they drifted off.

Compressing his lips, the Doctor turned to Miss Storm. Without a word they too waltzed away.

Eagerly Clio took a step forward but Monsieur de Talloires was bending over Frau Winkwurth. At her age she couldn't be—but the old lady *was* going to dance! She, Clio, was left as a wallflower, hideously exposed, at the dance that she herself had contrived.

"Miss Tubbs?" the forgotten Prince was bowing, his face expressionless.

Silently they too followed the others. But barely had they spun away than Clio forgot her chagrin. Prince Colonna danced as no partner had ever danced before. This elderly, impervious gentleman waltzed as she imagined an angel would. She felt ashamed of her earlier reluctance.

With the impulsive patronage of youth she said: "You dance beautifully, Prince Colonna."

The eyes so near her own remained opaque as pebbles. He merely bowed, and again politeness and perfunctoriness combined to suggest but not to declare insolence.

Once more, something in the young girl quailed, as, bewildered, she stared at the whirling room across his rigid shoulder.

It was an older woman and her partner who encored the dance. Vigorously Miss Storm and Dr. Herriot applauded.

In the same arms as before each couple now advanced in Strauss' "Thunder and Lightning" gallop.

"*Miracolosa!*" murmured the Prince as it came to an end.

"Thank you . . . thank you . . . thank you!" the other dancers were hailing the musicians' gallery, as Princess Sophia came downstairs.

"How very warm it is!" Victoria turned to the girl and said quickly: "Clio, would you run upstairs and open the small lancet window. You know how to do it—and it will give us air without a draught."

As if she were flying from a blight, Clio leapt up the stairs.

Along the gallery she scampered—free, released, to the musicians' loft. From this, a narrow balcony, no more than a gilt bridge, ran above the great windows below. Half-way was a small aperture with sculptured reliefs of the Horae on either side.

Before opening this lancet window, which was immediately above the statue of Minerva in the hall below, Clio hesitated for a second, arrested by the unusual festivity of the scene downstairs. No doubt about it, men did enliven a group! Seen from above like this, the figures might be puppets belonging to the spectator: Princess Victoria, elegant in her black lace; Princess Sophia, elusive in grey; the sumptuous Miss Storm unfurling like a lily from that oyster-coloured frock; Frau Winkwurth, wrinkled as a crocodile in ruby-red velvet. The women's appearance gained brilliance from the sombre male attire beside them. Monsieur de Talloires' clothes were sheer perfection; the Prince, for all his *bon-ton,* tapered to a shadow beside him. Lord Brompton's face was glistening with heat. He was wearing a waistcoat much too tight for his portly figure—odd to think that men could be as vain as women; and somehow more pathetic! Dr. Herriot was speaking—his voice as usual rasping with nervous energy, his intolerant grey eyes raking Monsieur de Talloires. A man of medium height, he looked shorter than usual beside the Comte, for he was stockily built. Yet he too held his own. Brusque he might be, but sincerity gave him consequence.

Princess Victoria glanced up and smiled, pointing to the window behind the girl.

But Clio did not move. For some reason the Banner Hall suddenly shone brighter than belief, the graceful gallery opposite, the springing stairs, the plump Biedermeyer sofas, the French paintings, Venetian glass, Spanish leather and flowering plants—the whole interior and its gathered guests were held suspended with the faded gilt saints, twisted icons, and electrically lit candles. Mingled with the rising scent of stephanotis, she caught a whiff from the bowls of aromatic thyme along the balcony, and that unmistakable odour of incense that clung like a dye to so many valuable objects here. Sight, sound, scent shimmered with dazzling clarity. The scene surged to her with some overpowering significance that she could not read.

For a split-second that was in time, and yet out of it, she only knew that this was the beginning and the end.

The next instant there came an explosion like the volley of a blast furnace, stunning the ear. Swift as a flash, every light in the Château went out.

Through this tornado of sound, in pitch blackness, Clio tore along the balcony, screaming.

She missed the turn, and in the dark beat senselessly against the wall. Her yells of terror, with the frantic shouting of the others below, and the noise of people falling over furniture were drowned in a vanishing uproar, which yet seemed to endure for untold ages.

Then the Banner Hall, as swiftly drained of thunder as a tunnel once an express train has sped from its desolation, was left to stupor and blackness.

At the initial blast, each guest below reacted automatically. The Prince, flashing his pocket torch, revealed a spasmodic tableau: Miss Storm had flung herself across De Talloires' chest; Frau Winkwurth was crouched on her chair; Lord Brompton lay full length on the floor; Princess Sophia was gazing at the ceiling; Dr. Herriot, one arm around Princess Victoria, stood stiffly to attention with her, both staring at De Talloires.

As the hurricane of sound died, Clio's screams outraged hearing.

"Clio!" shouted Victoria, "we're coming!"

Dr. Herriot, snatching the torch from the Prince, leapt up the stairs.

Mechanically the Princess leant forward, and in the darkness fumbled for the switch of a table-lamp hitherto not lighted with the candelabra and wall-brackets. It sprang into light, as did another solitary light above the Del Abbate picture.

Instantly Frau Winkwurth recovered. Angrily she cried: "What did I tell you? It's that abominable new electric plant! It's almost blown the house up—but *that* lamp belongs to the old installation. Really, Monsieur de Talloires, it's too bad!"

The Comte did not reply. His behaviour was very odd. Rapidly he crossed the floor to the bay by the gallery, and in the light, below the Del Abbate picture, consulted his watch. This he proceeded to wind as if in preparation for bed.

"Damned dangerous!" Lord Brompton was picking himself

up with much less agility than he had flung himself flat. "These old houses should only be rewired by experts."

"What an explosion—terrifying beyond belief!" Princess Sophia held out her hand to aid him.

"Hell!" exclaimed Miss Storm, "now I've lost my cigarettes —" Suddenly she began to cough.

Dr. Herriot, with La Coraggiosa sobbing on his arm, came rapidly downstairs.

De Talloires, reappearing from beneath the gallery, demanded: "Where is Victoria?"

The others glanced round apprehensively in the gloom, but her aunt replied: "Gone to Albert, I imagine—" And she too began to cough.

Across the dim hall it could now be seen that a cloud of smoke was issuing from the fireplace.

"Quick!" shouted Frau Winkwurth, "look at that . . . the house is on fire!"

"Don't be a fool," ordered the Doctor. "The fire's doused. That's why it's smoking."

"Oh, Doctor, what a relief. . . . What a comfort you are! Can you be certain?"

"Of course I can. So can you. Use your eyes."

"Thank the lord for *that!*" Miss Storm had retrieved her cigarettes. Hurriedly she and Lord Brompton proceeded to light up.

Clio, who had subsided on the sofa, had ceased to sob. In the murky light she was watching the Comte as he hurried upstairs.

Half-way he stopped. Victoria had reappeared on the gallery with Albert in his dressing-gown.

Suddenly the Doctor's voice rang out:

"Put those cigarettes out at once."

"My good sir—" began Lord Brompton.

"Put them out."

Lord Brompton hesitated, then bent to stub his, but Miss Storm stood her ground.

"Why the devil should I? The chimney smoke is dying down."

"Put it out."

"I tell you, I need it."

"In a little you're going to need air still more."

"Yes, yes," Princess Sophia interposed. "Look at the hearth, my dear child, and you will see that it's running with water."

"*Water!*" Frau Winkwurth rushed forward. "Does this mean the electrical fault has also affected the plumbing? It really is disgraceful. Criminal negligence."

"Rubbish!" irately Dr. Herriot had rounded on her. "This is no case of criminal negligence, and the sooner you wake up to the fact, the better. This is what is known as an act of God. Come on, snap out of it, all of you! We've got to organize ourselves. You know quite well what's happened—"

"Again I protest—" began Lord Brompton. "Your manner leaves a lot to be desired, I must say. At least have the civility to tell us the worst quickly."

"The worst," said the Doctor disagreeably, "none of us yet can say. But it must be quite obvious to anyone, who isn't an imbecile, that this house has been hit by an avalanche. . . ."

INVITATION TO CRISIS . . .

In a silence that amounted to stupor, Albert, half-way down the stairs could be heard inquiring, crossly, sleepily:

"What's a navalange?"

The question was never answered for, from the far end of the hall, through the door leading from the servants' quarters, two forgotten figures appeared.

Hans was leading Charlotte, and although she was a full head taller, it was at once apparent that she was in some way afflicted—the individual under protection.

Proceeding slowly but steadily there issued from both an indescribable aura of fatality.

The guests stood arrested, but Victoria taking a sudden breath went forward.

"What's happened?" she said sharply.

Hans, shame-faced for the first time in her experience of him, replied: "*Durchlaucht,* it is Charlotte."

"Yes, yes, I see that. Is she blind?"

"No, Serene Highness, she can see, but she cannot shut her eye. You notice one side of her face is twisted."

"Charlotte, speak to me! What has happened?" urgently the Princess put her arms around the tall, ungainly figure.

"*Durchlaucht,* she can speak, but she doesn't want to, because her speech is slurred. One would think she had been drinking—" Hans gave an apologetic cackle—"but," he added, "she has not been drinking."

"Come along, Charlotte!" Dr. Herriot was brisk but reassuring. "Sit down here, and tell me when you first noticed this. These nervous spasms do occur at times. Don't be alarmed."

"I flust floticed it," began Charlotte, then humiliated, turned her head away.

"Herr Doktor," said Hans, "in the afternoon she felt her face stiff. Twice she said to me: 'Is my face straight?' at which I laughed, for her face was as usual. And she had no pain."

"Come," said Dr. Herriot, "this is much more promising! It suggests a neuritis of sorts. You've probably caught cold in the facial nerve, Charlotte."

"No, no, Herr Doktor, she has not caught cold. She has not used a handkerchief. Dropping that *verdammte* Venetian glass when the *Lawine* struck the Schloss has given her a stroke. Such glass cannot be replaced."

Cheerfully the Doctor laughed. "Since when have you qualified, Hans? Princess Victoria, may I have a little sugar, a little salt, and something sour—a teaspoon dipped in the pickle-bottle will do. Right away, please. Now, Charlotte, this is a tiresome experience, and it may prove a tedious one. But I hope not. Anyway, I trust you'll rely on my diagnosis rather than that of Hans."

One half of Charlotte's face twitched with scorn. "Fly should flay so!"

At this witticism Dr. Herriot gave a flattering, indeed a stentorian laugh. He clapped Charlotte approvingly on the shoulder. "Still . . . I can see Jonah has your interest at heart —if not at head!"

"Fla, fla!" dutifully Charlotte laughed, saliva running from her helpless mouth.

Stupefied, but fascinated, the guests drew closer, their own predicament thankfully shelved.

Testily the Doctor turned. "Great Scott! can't you people find something better to do. Sit down, will you? Clio, get an eiderdown for Albert. Can't you see he's falling asleep on that chair. Frau Winkwurth, be good enough to bring the attaché case from my bedroom . . . on a chair, near the door. Thank you. Prince, let me have your torch. I don't know why you took it back. I need it now. Ah, here comes the Princess. And two teaspoons—efficiency itself! Shut your eyes, Charlotte. Well, if you can't shut both, shut one, dammit! Look straight ahead, and don't cheat. Open your mouth. I'm going to place something on your tongue. Now, tell me: what is this? Good! And this? Quite right. And *this?*" He gave a grunt as she drew a blank. "Not at all bad. Might be much worse. It's as I thought—a neuritis. So cheer up, you'll be nursing Jonah through his first stroke long before your own. Now for your reflexes . . . yes, yes, yes, quite satisfactory. No, just a moment please—there is something more. Forget the out-patients gathered round. They're simply inquisitive through boredom. Lift your knee. Press it against my hand . . . no, no, harder, harder. Now, the other, up with it! Come along. Yes, as I said. Cold and the nervous excitement of that heroic dinner are to blame. Your face may recover in a week, or it may take two or three. But this is not a stroke. Thank you, Frau Winkwurth."

Panting in her eagerness to serve, the old lady drew up a chair, and set the case on it.

From his key-ring Dr. Herriot selected a key, and opened

the case. On a fitted-interior, row upon row of tiny bottles were revealed—a miniature homoeopathic dispensary.

Glancing at his watch first, Dr. Herriot then said, "Open your mouth again," and shook some granules onto her tongue. "Now lean back and rest."

Princess Sophia stood at his elbow with a sofa-rug. "Would this help?"

"The very thing; we must keep our patient warm."

Into the brooding stillness, there fell a distant, but shattering noise of broken glass.

All started violently—gazing towards the gallery and its farthest door.

"Where is François?" angrily Victoria demanded. "Sophia—you don't know? But someone must have seen him go! Dr. Herriot, until the extent of tonight's damage is known, no one should leave the hall, unless we know where they are going."

"He went upstairs," coldly Clio stared at the Princess. "Naturally he knew the kitchen quarters were safe. Hans and Charlotte had just come from there. Monsieur de Talloires *always* does the right thing—he doesn't talk about it. He's gone to see that the rest of the Château is safe for us."

Already Victoria was half-way up the stairs.

"Stop!" called the Doctor, "Princess, you're needed here, please. I'll find the Comte."

"No, no!" forcibly Frau Winkwurth caught him by the arm. "You can't go, Dr. Herriot. *You're* needed here. You mustn't leave us—even for a moment. Everything depends on you now. You're much too valuable. Let Lord Brompton go!"

"Unfortunately," began Lord Brompton, "I do not know the geography of this unhappy house."

Smiling, Prince Colonna pushed past them. Gliding up the stairs, he arrested the Princess with one word.

"Hysteria?" he murmured.

As the Prince reached the top, the Comte reappeared at the farthest door, a candle in his hand.

"Ah!" said the Prince sardonically, "felicitations! We have only to lose you to know how we love you! You are required to give an account of yourself at headquarters!"

Descending, the Comte announced: "We may congratulate ourselves. The building has stood up to this successfully so far. But I'm afraid that the top windows are also submerged. Every fireplace is choked, and all stoves. However, in some hours' time we will be better able to judge."

"Of course," interrupted Frau Winkwurth, "in daylight everything looks different. *Joy cometh in the morning,* as my dear mother used to say."

"Madame," barked Lord Brompton, "the Comte has just made it disastrously plain that there will be no such thing as daylight for *us.*"

Quickly the Comte said: "But we may hope for some subsidence. And by daylight, others more fortunately placed may see our predicament."

"*May?*" exclaimed Victoria. "Must, you mean. It's inconceivable that the village will not discover our—our predicament at once."

"François is right," said Princess Sophia. "It may not be at once. We must be prepared for that. The nearest house is over a mile away, and out of sight."

"But haven't you forgotten," Miss Storm broke in, "that three of us were expected back?"

"Of course, my dear . . ." Princess Sophia glanced gratefully at her. "This will expedite things."

"At what hour was the carriage ordered from the hotel at Springbunnen?"

"It was ordered to pick us up at eleven-thirty, Dr. Herriot."

"Then," said De Talloires, "it would leave the hotel about eleven-fifteen, possibly eleven-twenty, as he wouldn't want to keep the horse standing."

"It is now midnight," said the Doctor. "A pity none of us noticed the time of the explosion."

Calmly the Comte replied: "It was the first thing I did. The avalanche occurred at approximately eleven o'clock."

"Then, thank heaven," said Victoria, "the coachman and the horse have escaped. The worst would be over before they set out—" Suddenly she stopped, a look of horror on her face. "Hans, quick, when did Anna and Detta leave?"

"*Durchlaucht,* they are safely home. And with an hour to spare. Charlotte cleared them out when I served the *Sachertorte.* And glad to see the last of them. Trouble-makers, the pair of them."

"Oh, thank God!" for the first time Victoria sat down, breathless. "Charlotte, you've done wonders tonight."

"Feeling fletter," Charlotte prepared to rise. "Candles in the pantry."

"Electricity in some rooms, and in one or two corridors is still working, by some freak," said De Talloires, "but the central heating installation is out of order."

"What did I tell you?" cried Frau Winkwurth. "The old installation has stood up to it. It's the *new* one that has failed so dangerously."

"Sit still, Charlotte," said the Princess. "Hans will fetch the candles— What about that glass, François: we heard a smash."

"A wall mirror that I knocked down in the dark."

"Seven years' bad luck!" Miss Storm gave a singularly unmirthful laugh. "Literally you had it coming to you. And it looks as if the rest of us were going to share it!"

Sourly the Doctor said: "As a sunbeam in the home, you're miscast!"

"Well, why can't you let me have one cigarette?"

"Dr. Herriot," said Princess Sophia, "if Miss Storm needs a cigarette, surely she may smoke upstairs—in my bedroom?"

"No, Princess," he answered shortly. "Miss Storm is going to be much too busy in a few minutes to smoke anywhere. Now, listen to me, the rest of you. Go upstairs, and get into the warmest clothes you can find. The ladies ought to get into slacks if they can find them. Bring down overcoats and boots, as well as shoes. The men can carry blankets, and as many mattresses as we need. We're going to camp out here—and we're going to camp together. After the gear has been got down, persons leaving for any purpose whatsoever will report their whereabouts. Actually, there will be no need to go upstairs in an hour's time—for as most of you know quite well, there's a downstairs cloakroom through that door over there. By the time we've settled in down here—perhaps Hans will heat some soup for us. Is there an oil-stove? Good!"

"Oh, Doctor!" cried Frau Winkwurth, "you're wonderful! Napoleonic. In this way the night will pass in no time. And it's so much better for us all to keep together . . . beside our poor stricken friend here, who does look *so* bad."

Dr. Herriot, with a baleful glance in his admirer's direction, continued: "Nine of us will sleep. The other two will take a four-hour watch."

"There's twelve," unexpectedly the sleeping Albert had piped up. "You're not counting right."

"Sorry," almost imperceptibly the Doctor smiled. "Must have forgotten myself!"

"No show without Punch!" announced Miss Storm.

"Hear, hear!" endorsed the Comte.

"Is it necessary," inquired Frau Winkwurth, "to insult our best friend?"

"Alma!" said Victoria coldly, "please keep calm."

"Calm!" exclaimed Frau Winkwurth, "how dare *you* speak of calm to me—you who are responsible for everything. Yes, everything! If you hadn't gone to London last September, the Comte would never have remembered you—or put in the new installation."

"Frau Winkwurth," said Princess Sophia, "the new installation had nothing to do with the avalanche."

"How do *you* know? How do you know that it wasn't an electrical explosion that set off the avalanche?"

"Stop shouting," commanded the Doctor. "It's only too obvious that the removal of the trees on the Teplitz Ridge has laid us open to this calamity. If you can't recognize the blast from an avalanche, I can."

"Yes, Dr. Herriot, but I can also recognize the fact that if the Comte had installed this plant years ago, the trees wouldn't have been cut down for fuel. But he forgot Victoria completely till three months ago—as everyone forgot us here."

Ominously Victoria arose: "Alma, this is intolerable!"

"Intolerable is the word," the old lady was now shaking with rage. "Why should you try to protect the Comte? His indifference has been patent all along—till three months ago. But whichever way one looks at it, you're to blame for this calamity. Yes, she is, and I won't sit down till I've said my say. Years ago, we could have sold up here, and gone to rooms at Bordighera. But you wouldn't, Victoria! You preferred your beautiful Schloss regardless of the price. And now it may cost twelve lives, including your own—" her voice rose hysterically.

In an aghast silence, Albert could be heard inquiring of Clio: "Wot's she rowing at?" and Clio's reply: "Hush, dear, the poor thing's lost control . . . very, very sad."

Prince Colonna, turning to Princess Sophia, observed *sotto voce:* "A brawl was the last thing *you* expected on the doorstep of heaven—but perhaps we're heading for the other place."

"You're heading for upstairs," rejoined the Doctor. "Come along now, all of you. Cut the cackle and let's get to work. Then hot soup, and some sleep."

The guests, with the exception of their medical adviser, proceeded to file up the stairs, after their hostess.

Lord Brompton, last in the line, turned on the bottom step. "Which two will take the first watch?"

"Lots will be drawn."

Automatically the others paused, and looked back.

"But who will draw the lots . . . er, arrange all this?"

"I shall," said the Doctor. "Then the rest of you will have one person to shoot at. This will give you the consolidation you need. Hurry up now," he added irritably.

Silently they continued up the stairs, along the gallery, and out of sight.

With a sigh which he stifled as he turned away, Dr. Herriot sat down beside Charlotte.

"Better?" he asked kindly.

"Mluch mletter." She nodded. Then stiffly she looked round the dim hall, muffled in more than midnight quiet.

"Glowing vlery cold," she observed.

The paralyzed eye gazed unblinkingly at him. The sound eye wavered as it sought his.

Briefly Dr. Herriot smiled. "Colder certainly," he agreed cheerfully. . . .

INVITATION TO CONSULTATION . . .

One a.m. found an astonishing change in the assembled visitors as well as the Banner Hall.

The group, including hostess and both servants, now warmly clad in out-door clothes, were cordially drinking soup around Charlotte, who, in the face of a blackened fireplace, had become a kind of second hearth, or focal point. Although Frau Winkwurth was the only person optimistic enough to have donned a hat, of earlier hysteria there was no sign. Princess Victoria, for the third time, had suggested and Frau Winkwurth had graciously agreed that a *second* cup would be welcome—some cups holding less than others! Clio, having removed her make-up and covered her red hair with a large white linen handkerchief, now looked as dramatic as a nun on her way to martyrdom—the more so as she had assumed a long black cloak, fur-lined, which had once belonged to the late Princess Babenberg. The washing of Clio's face, and a general freshening in the ladies' appearance had provoked a storm from Dr. Herriot.

"What the devil do you mean wasting precious water like this? From now on—not another drop!"

But this had been the only squall during reunion.

Brisk from the struggle of changing into warm clothes, dragging mattresses downstairs, piling pillows and blankets, the household now crowded round the gaunt Charlotte almost snugly.

"In the name of wonder," exclaimed Miss Storm, "what did we hurry for? Anyone would imagine we were catching the night-express."

"Instead of which," Lord Brompton looked bright but bogus, "the night-express had caught us—ha, ha!"

"Honk, honk!" Albert began, but Dr. Herriot in passing absently dealt him a shrewd slap.

"The whole thing," said Frau Winkwurth in her richest, most confidential tones, "is simply a matter of time."

"The same thing, of course," said Prince Colonna, "might be said of any penal sentence."

But a playful rather than a disparaging note had entered these exchanges.

Miss Storm, dressed in clothes belonging to Princess Sophia now bore, because of this, what can only be termed a family likeness to the older woman as they sat together on the couch. Hans, who had surprisingly assumed his Sunday best, dispensed soup with a certain patronage from the centre table. Lord Brompton, engulfed in a military great-coat belonging to the late Prince Babenberg, suggested a survivor from an earlier battlefield. Prince Colonna, who had declined borrowed warmth, wore his own overcoat, and with the collar turned up, did a certain amount of pacing behind the group—very much the solitary traveller on a platform that still awaited the night train. Albert, wide-awake now, was jumping up and down in front of the Comte, who wore skiing clothes: "When are you going out?" he demanded. Dr. Herriot alone had not changed. But after rearranging the furniture in the bay, beneath the gallery, where one of the two existing lights illumined the Del Abbate picture, he got into his overcoat.

This had been thoughtfully brought downstairs for him by Frau Winkwurth, together with his scarf and gloves.

"We can't have *you* catching cold, Doctor. Of all people! I should think not. Why, what a cosy little corner you've made here with the small table and those two chairs . . . very much *tête-à-tête,* aren't they? But isn't the little clock between them rather *de trop?*"

"Precisely, Frau Winkwurth. That clock and those two chairs represent the eternal triangle. Time and the human element."

"Doctor, Doctor, you will have your little joke! But don't you think the two poor dears who sit their watch here, might at least have comfortable chairs. Such an unsympathetic *tête-à-tête,* if I may say so!"

"My dear lady, the object of this *tête-à-tête* is not that consummation which is sympathy's last word! Sleep is taboo here."

At odd moments during the soup-drinking, one or other of the group would glance from the centre table-lamp to the small light in the distant corner.

"Doctor," began Frau Winkwurth again, "it occurs to me, as I'm sure it must have occurred to you—for you think of everything—that we ought, as soon as possible, to pool *all* our information. With the night ahead of us, every little helps. And it is surprising how such things add up. Now, I for one *know* that, for people in our predicament, quiet is essential. Albert must be warned. Mountaineers have stated time and again that a shout can send an avalanche off."

The Doctor stared at her. "Madame, it has arrived."

"No doubt, Doctor, no doubt. But we don't want another, do we? Now, Princess Victoria will confirm that from our first winter here, I always deplored remaining. My actual words were: 'Then there is the question of avalanches. Quite a small one would suffice.'"

She looked across at the Princess in triumph.

"Those were your words," politely Victoria agreed. "*Quite a small one would suffice.* Every winter for seven years."

"And here it is!" In high good-humour, Frau Winkwurth nodded.

"I want to go to the W.C.," Albert announced stridently.

"All right." Curtly the Doctor nodded. "Downstairs."

"Let *me* accompany the little man," Frau Winkwurth arose. "Yes, I insist. No trouble. It will give me something to do."

"Sit down, if you please," exasperated, Dr. Herriot had arisen. "Albert is not a molly-coddle."

"*Sh'think* not!" Albert began to run to the door. "Oh, I *must* be quick!"

Prince Colonna shuddered, and resumed his pacing.

In almost no time, Albert returned. From the door he called: "I couldn't after all. It's funny."

"Come here, Albert," said Victoria gently. "Don't worry."

Albert advanced protesting, "Nothing happened—" the lack of interest in his novel experience struck him as curious. . . .

"Now then," announced Dr. Herriot, "you've all got your positions for the night. People on awakening will remember to keep quiet. Sleep is valuable for those who can get it."

"Valuable to all!" retorted Miss Storm.

"So I should have said," affirmed the Comte.

Again Dr. Herriot compressed his lips. "Princess Victoria, may I ask a question? Before this recent installation of central heating, how did you keep this hall warm? I take it that you had more than that open fireplace?"

"Yes and no, Dr. Herriot. During the first years of the war, we did not always have enough wood for that hearth. In the old days the Château was used as a summer residence. No stores had been accumulated. During the war, when the fire went out, we had a small portable electric heater in the alcove."

There was a short silence. Then Dr. Herriot said in a voice his fellow-guests had not heard before: "I have always suspected that you are a great woman. Now I know! Princess, it occurs to me that we might again try this heater, as part of the old installation is still working. It's a risk, but I think we might try it."

The portable heater, retrieved from a cupboard in the corridor, responded by glowing brightly.

The spirits of all soared instantaneously. It was suddenly obvious that rescue was simply a matter of morning light.

"Now to draw lots . . ." at the writing-table, the Doctor rapidly noted their names on some slips of paper, Albert at his elbow.

"Mine too," insisted Albert. "Is mine down? Are you shuffling me too?"

The Doctor's hesitation was infinitesimal. "Did you think I would leave you out—like the Joker in the pack? Of course you're down—on my slip."

Fleetly he mixed the slips.

The Prince had stopped pacing. The Comte, who had been seated with folded arms in the shadows for the past ten minutes, looked up alertly.

All present watched with curious intensity for the result.

Dr. Herriot then picked out two slips at random and read aloud:

"Miss Storm and Monsieur de Talloires . . . Well, you lead off the ball, with a four-hour watch—while the rest of us sleep. My condolences—the fortunes of war!"

"*Mis*-fortunes!" scoffed Miss Storm.

The Comte stood up. He looked suddenly intimidating. "Draw the next watch now."

The Doctor shook his head. "Sufficient unto the hour! Must think of the psychological effect. You shall draw them then, and awaken the two responsible. Perhaps you'll prove luckier to me than I've been to you!"

Frigidly, the Comte inquired, "Do I misunderstand you?"

"I hope not," said the Doctor promptly. "Goodnight, all!"

But as he lay down on his mattress which, as it happened, was at the coldest end of the hall, he found he was still available for consultation.

Lord Brompton, bulkier than ever in the gloom, sat down heavily on a chair beside him, and took in a cautionary breath. Was it conceivable that he was settling down for conversation? The Doctor found his bed-side manner oppressive, the more so as his lordship appeared to be edging his feet onto the mattress, out of the draught.

"Dr. Herriot, I am disquieted by a discovery I have just made."

"You're lucky—I've made more than one!"

"I feel Frau Winkwurth ought to be watched."

"Well, the avalanche is taking care of that."

"Dr. Herriot, you are pleased to be flippant."

"Flippant! You over-rate my stamina. I'm unconscious. And so should you be."

"Look here, Doctor, this won't do! I insist on bringing certain facts to your attention. That woman, Frau Winkwurth, is abnormal. I know it sounds grotesque, but during the past hour, I've watched her and I know. I repeat: she is abnormal. She is enjoying herself—positively enjoying herself. The only one who is."

"Of course she's enjoying herself. She's vindicated. She's always prophesied an avalanche. And now there is an avalanche. Cassandra has come into her own. It's quite natural."

"Do you, as a medical man, tell me that this is reasonable?"

"Not reasonable. Natural."

"Then let me inform you, sir, that I know better—that, in fact, I have proof that such behaviour *is* abnormal. And my brother-in-law, Dr. Sir Miles Lansbury can confirm it. He himself told me the following story—"

With a groan Dr. Herriot lay back.

Lord Brompton leaning weightily over him, like some uneasy confederate, hissed downwards:

"You know Ashleigh Asylum in Middlesex? Very well then. During my brother-in-law's year as Houseman there, a lunatic arrived who complained that his bedroom ceiling would come down. Each night this patient took elaborate precautions. Slept at the bottom of bed, buttressed by pillows. One week later, the ceiling *did* come down to everyone's amazement. But the lunatic was delighted. The only person who was!"

"Scarcely a bedtime story!" jeered the Doctor. "I, who resemble Frau Winkwurth in being natural rather than reasonable, would prefer my mind taken off the roof at present. Now, for God's sake, go and lie down somewhere else! The woman's asleep—or silent, which amounts to sanity in my opinion. But I warn you I won't be answerable for my own behaviour if I'm kept awake much longer."

"Sir!" began Lord Brompton, thought better of it, arose and indignantly padded away.

INVITATION TO FIRST VIGIL . . .

From the night-watch table, Miss Storm's laconic gaze followed Lord Brompton's stumbling progress to his own mattress.

"Selfish old bounder!" she muttered. "Dedicated to the Widow and the Orphan, and Christmas Dinners for the Down-and-Out! A prize hypocrite."

"We all have our weaknesses," murmured De Talloires. "Curiosity is one of mine. Long before the end, I had ceased to be of interest to you. May I ask why you troubled to hound me out here?"

Both sat with their elbows on the small table, but her hands clasped her forearms, and her chin was disdainfully raised—while his left hand shaded his brow, and his right lay inertly before him. Despite his superior strength, he appeared tired, withdrawn, beside her vitality.

She gave a soundless laugh. "Unladylike to intrude, wasn't it? No gentlewoman would have done such a thing! But even if I don't know where to draw the line, I can still draw a distinction—dear Pharisee! You know quite well why I came."

"Very well then—we'll take your devilment for granted. At least let me know how Colonna came to sponsor this. I had no idea you were on such terms."

"You knew I'd met him."

"I believe you once mentioned it. I presumed it was the merest of acquaintance."

"Too presumptuous! Unless you wished to believe it so."

"You never enlarged on the subject."

"You never inquired. But then, dear François, there were so many subjects that you did not trouble to follow up. You were simply interested in one thing, and one thing only, where I was concerned. Your pertinacity, however, on that count, completely duped me. For months on end I actually cherished the illusion that you loved me! But no, you were simply pursuing your own ends, in the business-like way that has made you what you uniquely are."

"This is scarcely the time or place for another scene."

"How wrong you are! From my point of view, it is the ideal time and place for a scene. I need not raise my voice at all. In the past, I often felt it tiring to shout you down. We singers are sometimes haunted by our throats. Here I shall not grow desperate. This is not London. It is useless for you to reach for a bowler hat and escape. The night is mine."

A smile glimmered across his reserved face. "I am in your hands," he said courteously.

"You're nothing of the sort," she retorted, "though soon you may wish you were. As Colonna would point out: like the rest of us, you're in those of Nemesis."

"Come along then," he said quietly. "I feel that Colonna opens the case for the prosecution. When did you first meet him?"

"I met him some years before I met you. I met him at isolated intervals, under curious and painful circumstances. So curious and so painful that secrecy was maintained as a matter of course. His interest in me throughout has been that of a connoisseur. I'm intelligent, of course, but he's not interested in common-sense. He simply appreciates a woman's beauty without desiring to possess it, or to destroy it. My appearance fascinates him—and the fact that there's nothing behind it to appeal to him—that reassures him. Your cousin Colonna, dear Pharisee, has a greater capacity for suffering than you would consider suitable in one of your sex. That absurd child Clio attracts him—so at once he freezes her off. She's not in the least intelligent, of course, but she's got the artist's wholesale, death-or-victory, attitude to the things he thinks important. This is the language he understands—the attitude that's furnished his life with the art which is his religion."

"I imagine," said De Talloires politely, "that your voice must mean something to him—as to all your friends."

She leant across the table and whispered: "This is where I can hardly contain my contempt—for you're genuinely musical. Yet you fob me off with a stereotyped compliment like that. What could the voice of a singer mean to that man when the singer does not possess the artist's committal?"

De Talloires glanced away.

Indifferently she continued: "No, he respects me as a person, and I know he respects few people. This appeases me for reasons that are not far to seek. For my part, I admire him as I admire no other man. Courage," she paused, "has always appealed to me."

The oppressive stillness of the darkened Banner Hall was full of tiny uneasy sounds—irregular breathing, rustling movements, spasmodic sighs. Then slowly but conclusively Lord Brompton began to snore. Across the hall, and fast asleep in her corner, Charlotte groaned.

"Continue please," said De Talloires.

"Our first two meetings were accidental, but when fate flung us together for the third time, in identical circumstances, and in yet another country, we sat up and took notice. Literally sat up—for during the luncheon rest-hour at most sanatoria, the garden verandah accommodates patients of both sexes. Once again chance had placed his chair next to mine. Yet why do I call it chance, when the only thing I believe in is destiny? We greeted each other on that occasion with the consternation of survivors—and perhaps the solicitude! Since then we've flattered each other by a certain frankness—as regards our winter plans."

"Estella, I am deeply shocked—I had no idea."

"You mean you had no interest. And that is very true. Do you remember last January I told you I was obliged to get leave from the theatre?"

"I understood that it was for a rest."

"It was. Very much so. Remember that I told you that I was going to Amonteux?"

"Yes. Yes, of course I do."

"And your reply? *Hopeless for skiing.* And my caustic retort: *I'm not interested in breaking legs or records at the moment.* And your answer, my kind friend? *Have it your own way then!* That was all. No, it wasn't! The night before I left London, your last words were: *Have a good time, darling!* Darling, I could have struck you! But that envoy of yours was actually my salvation. It finished you for me. Just as the possession of my scalp had earlier finished me for you! Yes, don't protest! I know you don't make a habit of collecting those—but neither do I. Once you had achieved me, all you wanted was a well-bred friendship petering into irresponsibility."

Stiffly he replied: "I fail to understand why an appeal to passion should invariably seem more flattering than one to reason."

"Let me enlighten you. Passion doesn't count the cost. You stand as good a chance there of going to the wall as I do. That's the answer. Reason usually resides with Number One. Now, I was *not* reasonable. What I wanted—heaven help me!—was thorough-paced love at last. Absence ardently restored by letters, telegrams, telephone-calls, sympathy on tap! This from you—of all people, who were born middle-aged! But what I detested finally in you was your *method* of escape. I didn't lose you because I demolished the situation in a rage. That's only what you *like* to think. You made your get-away on the strength of that. I never lost you because I never had you. You, dear François, belong exclusively to you. Quite senselessly I expended myself on you. That's what I resent, for I am not an extravagant woman. This I cannot forgive myself."

"Nor me, I see. However, I deserve your castigation. But at least exonerate me on one count. I am horrified to hear of your illness. If you had only given me some indication—"

"Coughed my heart out like *La Dame aux Camélias?* T.B. off-stage is much less obtrusive! But also more of an anti-climax, for I'm going to recover. Unfortunately, Prince Colonna is not. He and I are now on our way to Bergers—*not* the winter-sports hotel, but the sanatorium, where we hope to relieve each other's tedium."

"May I ask why he consented to bring you here en route?"

"Why not? I admitted to him that I had behaved abominably but I was equally truthful about you. 'Monsieur de Talloires,' I told him, 'has behaved both shabbily and sanctimoniously. It would give me the greatest satisfaction to take my last farewell of him in person. He has escaped life-imprisonment on the strength of one scene and a curt note.' To which Prince Colonna replied: 'Disgraceful! I agree he ought to pay more heavily for the inestimable privilege of freedom—especially as I dislike the combination of sanctity and shabbiness.' "

"Estella," said De Talloires quietly. "You could have seen me in London had you wished."

"By appointment?"

"Naturally, by appointment."

"At the Embassy?"

"There, or elsewhere. It could have been privately arranged."

"I dare say! But that's the point—I did not wish it privately arranged. Strange, as it may seem—now that our liaison was over I wished to meet you in the open. Socially, *cher ami*. I had set my heart on one more meeting, this time in my favour. I wished to meet you and Princess Victoria on your own ground. And I shall leave tomorrow—today—quite satisfied."

"That you have embarrassed her, and humiliated me?"

"Not at all," she said carelessly. "You're not the first people to be domestically upset, and you won't be the last. No, I leave satisfied for a very different reason. I told you I believed in destiny. Yours has you in hand. You've fallen in love with someone who resembles you as closely as any woman can resemble a man. She's quite as cold as you are, but twice as drastic. You're damn superior, François. But she's more so. I could wish you no better punishment."

"In that case," he said shortly, "the matter may now be considered at an end."

"For me?" she said cheerfully. "Yes. For you, no. With every confidence I leave the last word to *her*. . . . Look at the clock! Time to open the thermos."

As she passed him a cup of soup, he noticed that her hand was icy. Quietly he said:

"Estella, I too believe in destiny, although I have awakened belatedly to mine. Can't we talk more genially now, for the rest of the watch?"

"Why not?" again she gave that careless shrug.

"Princess Sophia is obviously very much attached to you. Your encounter here was clearly a delight to her. Won't you tell me how you met?"

For a second her face softened. She smiled reflectively. "Now that *was* romantic, if you like, and in the best sense of the word. Odd that I should have found the two most important people in my life—Colonna and Sophia—placed next me in a chair. A *fauteuil* in her case. In the late afternoon of Monday, 17th October, 1911, I was sitting alone in a Bayswater room, at the age of nineteen, wondering which was the easiest and cheapest way of committing suicide. I had exactly five shillings left in the world, and I already owed a fortnight's rent on the room. When the wherewithal had stopped coming from Ireland on my aunt's death, my operatic training automatically came to an end—two years short. But I thought myself streets ahead of any musical-comedy actress tootling her way through the West End then. I never doubted that I'd be doubling as understudy right away. Months passed and I wasn't. With my looks and voice, the chorus was a dismal certainty! But it wasn't. That's why I believe in destiny. Because of what followed. Luck's got nothing to do with it. Everything's arranged along the way. You're only free as to how you meet it. And I was thinking of suicide. More soup, François? No? Then I will. They say Royalty from force of habit never loses a chance of taking its weight off its legs. Personally, I never lose a chance of stoking. Perhaps that was why I decided quite recklessly on that date to spend half my capital in having one good meal at last. It was a listless London heat-wave dusk, with the trees hanging limply in the tepid air, and a smell of petrol predominating. But I felt better after I'd eaten, and I decided to use a ticket a journalist had given me for Covent Garden Opera House that night. My evening clothes had earlier taken the final count at the Regency Wardrobe Room. But my hearty supper at an A.B.C. had done more for me than sables, and I was the first that night to seat myself in the stalls. After that the *fauteuils* filled rapidly. The seat on my right remained empty until just before the orchestra began. Then Princess Sophia made her way towards me, bowing to me with a smile. Seated side by side, with our gaze upon each other, two complete strangers, I realized we knew each other perfectly.

"During the intervals, we talked at first of music, but I was so completely under the spell of her personality, that I did more than acquiesce in the situation, I responded to it.

"By the end of the performance, although no specific details had been given, I felt she knew everything about me, as no one but one's guardian angel could. For the first time, I was aware of another kind of existence, walking hand in hand with ordinary experience.

"The opera was *Samson and Delilah,* and as the curtain closed, she said, 'Samson's fate recalls Job's last words on the subject, doesn't it? *Though He slay me, yet will I trust Him.*'

"Rather self-consciously I replied: 'Let's hope we're not all put to Samson's test.'

"Smiling, she exclaimed: 'But of course we will be—all of us. Death is inevitable.' Yet something in the mild, almost merry way she said it comforted me inexpressibly.

"As we left the auditorium she said: 'Will you humour me? I should very much like to visit the famous Lyons Corner

House, the one that keeps open all night. We could continue our talk there.'

"By two a.m., after repeated cups of tea and numerous sandwiches, she knew those personal views and idiosyncrasies that as a rule one only admits to some fellow-traveller one shall not meet again. She had also heard something of a certain seat in Regent's Park where apprehensively that year I'd seen the seasons stalk past. And she had sighed lovingly over my statement that a penny has three sides—a discovery only made when you thumb them singly. 'Believe me,' she said, 'all you need now is a breeze at your back. Do you know those wonderful words that answer every extremity? *Sail on through the night. Your guardian god will send you a following wind.*' I shook my head, and she added: 'The quotation ends, *Her message delivered, Minerva withdrew to the heights of Olympus.* We must have faith and hold to a determined course.'

"It was three in the morning when we parted. I had some difficulty finding her a taxi. She gave an address to the driver and then turned to me:

" 'We shall meet again, I know,' and as if by contagion, her happiness was mine. I believed her implicitly. The moment was enough. It fed a hundred years.

"Through the window of the cab, she put a small leather case in my hand. 'I should like you to have this souvenir. Think of it as of sentimental value only.'

"After she'd gone, when I opened it, I found it contained twenty pounds in notes. Yet this money, which meant salvation scarcely mattered. Already I had the breeze at my back. My confidence in some larger issue had been restored.

"At the end of that week, I got my first west-end engagement. Since then, I've never looked back, financially. Indeed my success was so speedy, that in no time longing replaced confidence. I yearned to see my unknown friend again. No sooner had she disappeared than I realized my loss. Had I said one word, she would have been available. That I knew. But I had not spoken. My silence struck me as disastrous—after the amazing fashion in which we'd been drawn together. Later I actually advertised in the daily papers under *Covent Garden Fauteuil* and *A Seat in Regent's Park*. I even suggested to my lyricist that he write me a number round that last title, and another on the theme 'A Breeze at Your Back.' Two songs that were later sung and whistled throughout the country, and which increased my royalties, but brought me no other response. Until tonight—when I learnt that she had returned to Austria, the day after we met. Well, François, I think that is a prettier story than ours. Will you have your soup now?"

"Thank you," he said in a low voice. "I should be glad of it."

Both still sat with their elbows on the table, the clock between them, but an intense chill now clung more closely than the gloom. Yet De Talloires did not appear noticeably more exhausted than he had done earlier. Miss Storm's vitality, however, had ebbed in a remarkable way. Her pallor was extreme. She had burnt herself out.

"Only another ten minutes," he reminded her.

"I won't be sorry to lie down," and she lapsed into silence for a little. Then, "My God," she muttered, "what an extraordinary situation it is! Just look at this hall, how derelict it is in these shadows. When you remember it earlier, it's scarcely recognizable. You wouldn't believe that a few makeshift beds on the floor would turn it into a ruin, but it has. Lord Brompton has stopped snoring. They're as still as corpses."

"After you've slept, they'll again seem real enough."

"Of course. And it's only a question of time. That was another thing she said that first night. In time there's still time! But pretty awful if we'd actually been entombed here."

She paused.

"I agree," he said readily.

More flippantly she added, "No. That would have been too bad to be true."

"Time's up!" he announced.

"Hurrah!" mechanically she responded. Then as she turned away, she stopped.

"By the way, François, you do think we shall be rescued?"

"I have no doubt at all," he said on a carefully modulated note of surprise.

INVITATION TO FURTHER VIGIL . . .

Tap, tap, tap, tap, tap, tap . . . the Alpine Distress Signal went out in the prescribed six sharp sounds to the minute. It was repeated after an interval of one minute.

De Talloires' period for the hammer! With this tool he tapped on the raised steel fender before him. The position in the hall might vary, the procedure never. De Talloires' touch as signaller was, moreover, the most wearingly consistent. Hour after hour the din went on. Had it not been for the maddening interval of silence between each signal, the noise could long since have been assimilated and ignored. As it was—

Tap, tap, tap, tap, tap, tap . . .

The women complained that it destroyed them more than any other feature of the past three days, but the men showed a persistence in its maintainence that defeated argument.

Princess Sophia expressed impatience, Clio clamoured that it drove her mad, Frau Winkwurth who had earlier interrupted proceedings repeatedly to declare that she heard a response elsewhere in the hall, insisted that it had already unhinged the men. Miss Storm protested that she now heard the damn thing after it had ceased—which was at five o'clock, except for brief sessions until bedtime.

Victoria, alone of the women, took any interest in these

efforts to which De Talloires, the Prince, Dr. Herriot and Lord Brompton relentlessly adhered.

Occasionally she herself took a short session with the hammer. Dr. Herriot had encouraged this.

"Your signal is different from ours?" she queried. *"Tap . . . tap, tap, tap, tap . . . tap!"*

"Variety is the spice of life," he retorted. "Mine happens to be as old as antiquity. This signal was made by the Picts beyond the Roman wall. The smoke-puffs, controlled in the same way, were seen by the sentries of the legions but conveyed nothing to them."

"Let's hope," said Lord Brompton peevishly, "that *your* efforts will achieve more general recognition." And coldly the Comte confirmed that the Alpine Distress Signal was the one for the present occasion.

Thereafter Dr. Herriot threw in his lot exclusively with his forebears. Princess Victoria followed suit, to the surprise and curiosity of the other women.

Tap, tap, tap, tap, tap, tap . . .

"Only fifteen minutes more to go!" Clio called across in warning. The entire party was now watching De Talloires and his hammer with jealous resentment.

Oblivious, he continued.

In three days the hall had altered as much as its inhabitants. The flowering plants had been removed. Much of the furniture had also been stowed away. The piano had been carried downstairs from the musicians' gallery, but the Babenberg banner, which Frau Winkwurth had suggested should be removed, was still in place.

"Certainly not!" Princess Victoria declared, and surprisingly Dr. Herriot had agreed.

The mattresses ranged around the walls were as trim as a

hospital ward. The hall, though stark, was in fact, more orderly than it had ever been. The Doctor had paced it out. Morning or afternoon each guest had to walk half a mile. His word was law. None knew precisely why, although all were obscurely aware that he alone held panacea for possible disaster. His medical bag had already divided their society into two distinct classes. Those who had benefited from it, and those who had not. Of the first class, Charlotte derived a four-hourly benefit that amounted to hereditary honours. The Prince, strangely enough, had been distinguished by an unsought award, which he had received as swiftly and as silently as it had been made. Lord Brompton had no choice but to suspect collusion. But not until Albert, the third and last recipient, had been singled out upon the second afternoon, did his lordship openly denounce the donor.

"Monstrous!" he declared, when teatime silence from Albert's mattress bespoke untroubled sleep. "Here are adults, everyone of whom would be the better for a sedative, and yet you start drugging that child! A child who, from start to finish, has not shown the slightest sign that he appreciates the situation—a child who has most tiresomely romped through every hour. Such professional incompetence amounts to disqualification, in my opinion."

Dr. Herriot treated this outburst with unexpected tolerance.

"Come off it!" he said leniently. "I've been watching Albert. You haven't. *A child won't complain.* That's why one must find out, as far as one can, how things are with it."

Caustically the Prince put in: "I have always regarded them as the most vociferous of created things."

"Not in important matters. A child will accept practically any calamity without a word. It accepts the situation because it thinks it's normal. It has no standard of comparison, like an adult. Lord Brompton, you're in favour of deeds not words, and this reminds me: You've not been round the deck today. Come along! We mustn't fall behind the Continent in P.T.!"

"Bah!" said the benevolent Lord Brompton contemptuously and set off round the hall.

"Wait for me!" cried Clio. "Next to me, I think you're the unhappiest person here. I'll walk with you—I've got a suggestion to make. Nobody listens to me. But Frau Winkwurth and I both think—"

Tap, tap, tap, tap, tap, tap . . . De Talloires continued to signal. December twenty-fourth now and within ten minutes of five o'clock! Outside, darkness would again have set in, complicating rescue.

What was happening beyond their entombment, he wondered? An experienced Alpinist, he was remembering that avalanche he had once watched across the valley at Avengen, descending with the roar and rattle of a hundred express trains, sweeping farms and chalets in its white obliteration, together with some eight thousand trees . . . and coming to rest in the appalling silence from which it had first emerged. On another occasion there had been that lesser yet fatal avalanche at Yetz, when half the village had to be dug out. Once more he headed the rescue squad, saw the German shepherd dogs drawn up, the blazing torches, the fire brigade at attention . . . watched the tremendous pressure of snow bearing in . . . sensed the alarm of burst pipes . . . the dumb horror of that voiceless plea: *We shall drown!* And over all, fresh snow pouring down like milk. Where to begin? But a start made . . . twenty standing in a circle . . . the sounding line and rods pushed with difficulty through the snow. Surveying the ground by inches for hours . . . for hours by inches! The scene grey with dawn when they had put down soundings,

and taken up spades. No! hope was not given up easily or early. The human race was at its vital best on such occasions. And the first house relieved—how well he remembered the crucial fact: *They could not hear us. We could hear them.* Repeatedly he had told the Banner Hall this story. The women brushed it aside, yet tirelessly reminded one another of Hans' anecdote—of that Rencadine avalanche last winter, which had buried a stable for twenty-nine days, and from which a dog, and three goats were later got out alive.

"Twenty-nine days of *this*," swore Prince Colonna. "One would sooner be dead."

"But no tapping!" exclaimed the women. "The animals did not signal and they were got out safely."

"Those animals had hay," Hans pointed out. Custodian of local conditions, he had now achieved the importance of an oracle among the guests. "We have not food for twenty-nine days."

"We have ample food," Victoria had snapped. The Comte noticed that her poise in the past three days had been replaced by a jocular energy which her own sex found peculiarly repellent. "Three baths have been filled with drinking-water, and we have any amount of wine. We could not be more favourably placed."

A trifle hollowly Estella observed: "Our hostess defeats me: this determination of hers to make our stay as pleasant as possible!"

Tap, tap, tap, tap, tap, tap . . . another row going on in the hall! Frau Winkwurth in collision with Charlotte this time. These senseless scenes flared up as quickly as they died down, feverish as the energy that alternately mounted and fell, while the guests prepared for rescue, or further incarceration.

Tap, tap, tap, tap, tap, tap . . . all November it had snowed.

Clouds of snow lawlessly on the march, like an army of mercenaries. Then a falling temperature, a dying wind. That warm and brilliant St. Thomas' Day had been the classical preparation for just such a calamity as the present. Nor would the rider in newspaper reports differ in this case either: *Local opinion blames the alarming increase of avalanche disasters in the past two years to excessive felling of the forests.*

Tap, tap, tap—

"Time's up!" shouted Clio. "Stop it, stop it, stop it!"

In the uncanny nerve-reeling relief of sudden soundlessness, Albert shrilled: "Now, it's my turn. Play 'Rellicarry,' quick, Miss Storm."

"Estella," pleaded Princess Sophia, "can't you wean him from that tune? We've had 'El Relicario' at least twenty times in the past three days. There must be other tunes—in fact there are!"

"Albert, once only this evening. Then another, a much nicer one, after it."

Dr. Herriot glanced after the singer, as she made her way to the piano with the child. "What a change in that woman—kind, calm, comforting. She's not the same person."

Princess Sophia smiled. "Yes, she is. But the mask's off."

"I suppose it is, with all of us—although few show to her advantage."

"Come, Dr. Herriot, your patients haven't done so badly surely? None of them ever mentions the cold now. That at least they've accepted."

"I don't agree, Princess. In fact, I'm disappointed. This may go on for some time, you know."

"Don't be disappointed," she said softly. "At first people feel lost without their masks. I think you'll be surprised later."

Grimly he replied, "I only hope *you* won't be! There goes that tin-can tune again. Well, if she can stand it, I suppose we can. It's obviously Albert's cup of tea."

"And here is ours!"

Charlotte and Hans were to be seen bearing in the five o'clock brew.

The Prince rose slowly from his book beneath the Dell' Abbate picture. Clio and Lord Brompton hurried forward. Frau Winkwurth was already there. Victoria who had been counting candles at the centre table moved these aside. The Comte, advancing, proceeded to help her.

Almost precipitately the party lost itself in this absorbing activity.

"Princess!" shouted Albert. He was seen to be standing with his candle at the cloak-room door.

"Yes, what is it?" his hostess turned, her guests did likewise. Each event was momentous now.

"The plug won't work."

"Try again," said the Princess calmly.

"I have, and it won't."

"This," announced Frau Winkwurth with unction, "is the beginning of the end. Victoria, don't you realize what it means? The plumbing's out of gear!"

"God knows," Lord Brompton shot a triumphant glance at Dr. Herriot, "what ordeal is yet before us."

"Nonthence!" lisped the Prince. "We've had it. *This* is ordeal. There can be nothing more appalling than propinquity. Our present situation amounts to hell."

"Hang it all!" protested Dr. Herriot, "it might be a damn sight worse. We have food and drink. We can still move about. We have liberty to that extent."

"Without privacy," reiterated the Prince, "there is no liberty. Privacy is the only world I recognize."

Defiantly Clio exclaimed, "Well, we're all in each other's now!"

"That constitutes the ordeal."

"You don't like people, do you!" she cried hotly.

"I have told you. I like privacy." He resumed his pacing up and down before the Del Abbate picture.

"Why can't we have soup at teatime?" Albert asked. "Since there's no milk, it's not tea any more."

"Durchlaucht!" said Charlotte harshly.

Astonished the Princess turned. The guests stopped talking. Charlotte was trembling with anger.

"Durchlaucht, this hall has been turned upside down, its furniture changed, its plants gone, but still we are accursed, and with good reason. *Durchlaucht,* I warn you, you are doomed unless that heathen idol is removed—" her shaking finger pointed to Minerva. "For years I've watched those creatures—Anna, Detta, yes, and Hans, the coward—fetch her the harvest sheaf. Are we Christians, or are we not?"

The Princess looked at her. "Thank you, Charlotte," she said gravely. "I shall think over what you have said. Now may we have some more hot tea—from the kitchen?"

Charlotte, followed by Hans, went out. Albert scuttled after them.

"Amazing!" Frau Winkwurth flung up her hands, "and I assure you, Miss Storm, the woman is not even religious!"

"That's why she's superstitious," said Princess Sophia quickly. "Naturally."

"And of course she's a Protestant," the Prince reminded them. "They invariably get excited—or, shall we say sentimental—about the wrong things! Charlotte has begun to believe in Minerva. Princess Sophia, you and Swedenborg will bear me out there, will you not, that that which you believe in, you create?"

"No, Dominic, that which we believe in, we evoke."

"On your own admission then, Princess, Minerva must have prior existence!"

Sophia smiled faintly, "There are various heavens."

Startled, Clio leant forward. "Princess, do you remember what you said about heaven that night at the dinner-party, before all this happened? *I shake not the earth only, but also heaven . . . that those things which cannot be shaken may remain.* That's why *you're* here. You've been taken at your word, your belief. *We all have.*"

"Morbid, morbid!" Frau Winkwurth interrupted.

"But it's a fact. We're here because we've invited this very situation. Yes, it's true! After the first shock was over, that night on my mattress I went over the events of my life backwards, and I found everything led inevitably to this place and this hour. I *appeared* to accept Princess Victoria's invitation—but everything I'd done since birth invited *that.* And what is true for me is true for you all."

"Come, come!" said Lord Brompton testily. "A touch of egocentricity there surely! With the impulsiveness of youth, you may have precipitated yourself here. But consider the rest of us. Consider Princess Victoria, born to this house, in which she has spent years of safety. What has she done to draw down this purely fortuitous experience? Of course we know that it is of a temporary nature—but, still, an extremely unpleasant one."

"I don't know what she's done. But I tell you that she's *arranged* to be here. It's awe-inspiring, terrible, and wonderful, of course. But I just can't concentrate on its magnitude, because I'm quite frantic about another discovery I only made today."

"Your agonies fascinate me," said the Prince. "Don't hesitate to enlarge."

"Ungallant, very!" Lord Brompton shook his head.

Clio sat bold upright beside Frau Winkwurth, and faced her adversary. "No, I'll condense instead. I've lost my identity."

"Clio, Clio!" protested Victoria, "you know quite well who you are."

"I didn't say I'd lost my memory. To lose one's identity is a much more terrifying thing. Which ever way I face now is into emptiness—it's no longer solitude, for he's taken so much of me with him."

"He?" Prince Colonna raised a derisive eyebrow.

"Yes, of course. Abbey is my identity, and I didn't know this till life was threatened. Till the shaking of heaven and earth began."

There was an embarrassed silence.

"At least," observed the Prince, stopping short in his pacing, "you know now."

"But it means my whole life has been sheer waste so far. How do I know I'll get another chance? Abbey of all people too! The last person. I'm in love with the wrong man."

"Cheer up!" said Dr. Herriot. "One invariably is, at your age."

She gave him a blighting look. "Of course you don't understand. I didn't expect you to. But if I don't speak I'll scream. The *other* was the wrong person too. Yet I enjoyed him—although nothing could have come of it. But I'm not enjoying being in love with Abbey. This misery's quite different. . . . Florence and everything seem so wonderful looking back. I can't realize it really happened to me. I tremble to think I had that happiness, and did not realize it! The Albergo Toscano in a heat-wave! Shall I ever smell dust again, and garlic and feel a road bake my feet? Those dinners we used to have at the Pompeii, garish with light, the music rather rowdy, but somehow satisfactory, and the food delicious. Abbey's conversation caustic, but full of information. That's what I miss here. You're all highly educated, or most of you. But Abbey was for ever turning his knowledge to practical purposes. He was creative. I see that now. Whereas none of you are doing anything with your knowledge—except brooding on it."

"At this stage of our career," again it was the Prince who spoke, "we can scarcely be blamed for that."

"No, but even before the avalanche, I felt this about you. What I admired in the Comte was his air of authority. I've been blind, blind, blind."

"Well, dear," began Frau Winkwurth, "you're certainly blind no longer."

"Nor dumb," put in the Doctor.

Fiercely she turned upon him. "There you go, all of you—showing me up in all my awfulness! Oh, I know I've learnt a lot from you—all of it sobering. But haven't any of you learnt something from me?"

"Strange," murmured the Prince, "this passion to instruct!"

"Only strange to *you*, alone in your world of one!"

"Pay no attention to Prince Colonna," Frau Winkwurth said. "But tell us more, dear. It's all most interesting. Has Mr. Abbey declared himself?"

"No," said Clio sombrely. "I have given him literally no encouragement. I see that, looking back. But the affinity has declared itself in other, inescapable ways. At moments he's nearer me here than he ever was at Florence. Then this tomb becomes heaven. But the moment passes—and I'm alone with you again. Ghastly!"

"What a time Charlotte's being with that tea," began the Princess. "François, do you think anything has happened? No, perhaps it's better not to fuss them."

Again anxiety became a ferment with them all, later to flare into the usual tiff or quarrel. An antagonism that would as swiftly subside, but anything—Dr. Herriot reflected—was better than inertia. The symptom that he most disliked was a growing tendency for the group to act in concert at the slightest sound. In this perpetual gloom, the ear dominated awareness.

Did you hear anything?

Thought I did . . .

Must have been imagination!

Just for a minute . . . did you again?

The two servants were coming down the hall, carrying the tea, and more hot water.

"Better late than never!" briskly Frau Winkwurth admonished them.

Charlotte turned her twisted face, Medusa-like upon her, but Hans stopped short, and in a fury said:

"Serene Highness, it is understood that the oil-stove takes time."

"Very well, Hans. It is understood." Victoria was alarmed by his incensed expression. What on earth was the matter with him?

"Serene Highness, it is also understood that in future the child does not follow us to the kitchen."

Coldly she replied: "It is understood."

But the Comte had risen. Quietly he laid his hand on Hans's shoulder. "Come," he said, "don't waste time. Be frank with us. Why are you and Charlotte soaking wet?"

On an indrawn breath, Hans's rage was seen to expire as a balloon deflates—with a gasp. He averted his head.

"Monsieur le Comte," he said in a low voice, "since morning water has been oozing into the kitchen from above. We fear part of the roof has collapsed. The place is flooding, but we have opened the cellars. Monsieur le Comte . . . We can conceal from you no longer that the tanks have burst."

In a stunned silence Princess Victoria put down the tea-pot.

Automatically Charlotte lifted it, and began to pour out second cups. . . .

INVITATION TO REVELATION . . .

Two hours later the oil-stove, the oil-drum, kitchen utensils and stores had been set up in the Banner Hall. The need for speed had dissipated shock, and activity had bred a spurious cheerfulness once this latest manoeuvre was successfully executed.

"It will certainly be cosier in here now," affirmed Frau Winkworth.

"The fumes, if not the odours, will add to the gaiety of nations," observed the Prince.

"I'd forgotten them," Frau Winkwurth shook her head. "Dear me, Victoria, who would guess that this is your beautiful Banner Hall!"

"You might," said the Princess crisply. "Dr. Herriot, I feel that there should be some change now in our planned routine —in case we are not rescued early tomorrow."

"I agree with my niece. Even if it be a temporary alteration."

"Yes," said the Comte, "routine might well be broken every second day."

"Every second day!" wrathfully Clio turned upon him. "You speak as if we were here indefinitely. It's sheer defeatism!"

"Hush-sh-sh!" Victoria glanced across at Albert's mattress.

"No, it's realism," said Estella Storm. "Simply futile getting shrill about it, Clio. What we're trying to say, Dr. Herriot, is that this particular routine has become revolting to us. There ought to be a change."

"A change? Good God!" expostulated the Doctor, "if you can think of another, go ahead."

Victoria smiled wanly. "I sympathize. But the fact is you've legislated for us *en masse*. Women need more breaks, a different rhythm. Let's arrange to make tomorrow brighter at all costs. This perpetual gloom is getting us down. We'll have more candles tomorrow. I know it seems extravagant—"

"Have it your own way then! You're not planning a dinner-dance are you?"

"No," retorted Miss Storm, "but we may give a concert if you and the other men stop that devil's tattoo for an hour."

" 'Pon my soul," Lord Brompton shuffled over to the electric fire, "you ladies are wonderful. An example to us men. This organized misery has gone on long enough. I've always said so. And I say it again. What is more: there ought to be readjustment all round. This afternoon those tanks burst. It's obvious that the roof is affected. Anything may happen to me—or to *you*," he nodded to Dr. Herriot. "Now, in the case of an accident, we ought to be prepared. You should leave the rest of us instructions about your—er, medical supplies."

"Thanks for your solicitude. I don't intend to pass out yet."

"I should think not!" cried Frau Winkwurth. "Don't depress us, Lord Brompton. Dr. Herriot is our life-line. He can't die."

"He might," insisted Lord Brompton. "If, for instance, the tower fell on the roof here, he might be the very one to go."

"So might you," the Doctor said. "And if we're hit together, you'll still go first. In all cases of official calamity, the elder is always most sensibly presumed to have died first. So, legally, I outlive you, even if we go out hand in hand."

"Sir," Lord Brompton's rich voice shook with anger, "your flippancy is in poor taste."

"So is your persistence where my medicine-chest is concerned. And this goes for others present. Nobody's going to get a thing unless it's essential. The fact is: the general pulse is as steady as an eight-day clock. If I'd had to choose a set of physiques for this occurrence, I couldn't have picked a likelier lot. It's your concerted attitude that is pathological." He rose and began to drum his feet warm. "You're sick of my schedule, you say? Let me tell you that I'm bored to death by you—and the way you have again begun to bleat about the cold. Scarcely a remark that hasn't got a rider to this effect: It's so cold! Colder than ever! Cold, isn't it?"

Passionately Clio broke in, "Here's a change then! It's no longer cold. Let's have the truth. It's clammy now. We might be buried at the bottom of a well."

Victoria, for once sunk in an armchair, her face hidden by her hand, listened. How often had this squabbling conversation taken place, or one exactly like it? Times without number, surely. François had just gone upstairs with a candle on yet another tour of inspection. Why was it always left to him? Of course he knew the house better than the other men, and it was not suitable that Hans, a servant, should take this risk. But the Doctor or Brompton ought to go with him. Colonna alone showed annoyance when he declined assistance. She had begun to wonder if François were deliberately doing this to harrow her? His inspections were taking longer and longer, as he attempted to open windows, to test doors and chimneys. Twice lately in desperation, she had begun to climb the stairs herself, but in the gloom had luckily been able to slip back, unseen by him, as he reappeared on the gallery again. Quite hideously he was getting on her nerves. For no length of time did he seem able to remain in the hall, unless he were signalling. And when he did sit, as one of the group, he had become as much an onlooker, a background figure as Sophia used to be. But with this difference—Sophia's withdrawal had been meditative, François was uncomfortably vigilant. Dr. Herriot might be nominally in charge, but the Comte's brooding silence was off-set by a curious alertness that hourly increased her uneasiness. He appeared to be watching and waiting for some crisis other than rescue—a *dénouement* he seemed to expect any moment within the group.

Tante Sophia and Miss Storm were entering the hurly-burly of Clio's conversation with Dr. Herriot! Her aunt and that woman did everything together now. It was all part of the present nightmare. Albert, too, had drawn apart from her since the *débâcle*—he was forever with the singer. First François, then Sophia and Albert—Miss Storm had captured them all. Dr. Herriot would probably be the next to succumb although, to do her justice, the lady certainly did not set out to captivate. She took less than no trouble! She was, as far as Victoria could judge, devoid of charm which, of course, made her supremacy more disconcerting!

"It's preposterous," Lord Brompton had burst forth again, "yes, preposterous that we should be left so long submerged in a building of this size! What are the people of Springbrunnen, Bergers, and Gautz thinking of?"

"Hang it all," said the Doctor, "the road may also be cut off! The Château isn't the only focal point in the neighbourhood. Admittedly Springbrunnen is safe enough from avalanche, but the park around us may be completely blocked.

We don't even know what the weather conditions are. There may be a dozen reasons for delay. And another thing—when the rescue squad does reach us, it may be by the other end of the building."

"I refuse to believe that the clock tower can be covered. That must be visible for miles around. The entire civilized world must know of our predicament now. This is 1921. I myself am on the board of the two air-way companies. This inertia is inexplicable."

At this stage Victoria again roused herself to reassert that avalanches were almost unknown locally, but that, of course, there were often other disasters—fires . . . floods . . . and lost climbers.

"When rescue occurs," she assured her guests, "the villagers signal the other hamlets, across the valley, by ringing on hand-bells."

"Hand-bells!" groaned Lord Brompton.

"For generations," his hostess explained, "that has been our custom. The villagers are highly proficient with these bells. In groups they can actually ring out certain tunes."

The Doctor nodded. "Yes, I've heard the blind do that at hospital concerts—it's quite effective."

"Effective—bah!" Lord Brompton could scarcely contain his ire.

"Here we toll the Town-Hall bell for disaster," Victoria continued, "and ring the Church bell for rejoicing—but no rescue party of any size is ever complete without its own group of hand-bells." She paused. "On the return from any rescue they always ring the same tune: *"Nun danket alle Gott."*

She glanced up.

François had reappeared on the gallery. The inspection

was over for the night. He was coming downstairs, looking precisely as he would have done on the most ordinary occasion. After all, what could happen to him up there, that could not as easily happen down here?

Below her breath Miss Storm was confiding to Princess Sophia: "Extraordinary, isn't it, but Prince Colonna has altered less than anyone. I think he's also behaved better, don't you?"

"M'yes," Sophia was reflective.

"François has become as shadowy as a cipher. Odd to see him playing second-fiddle to Dr. Herriot like this."

"François is an ambassador, my dear. Unmask a diplomat, and reveal a lawyer. Unmask a lawyer, and disclose a judge. Remember our ordeal is not yet over. Surely you don't imagine that any present have fully declared themselves?"

"Ladies," announced the Comte. "I hope you will forgive me if I put through signals for ten minutes now."

"No!" shouted Clio. Springing to her feet, she faced him. "you heard what Princess Victoria said, after we spoke to her. The routine must be broken. It's night outside. Dr. Herriot says the park may be cut off. Why should we be driven crazy by your hammering? It's senseless. A man ought to act constructively in a crisis. Sit *down,* Dr. Herriot—we're not going to be dragooned any longer. We're sick to death of men. Nothing's happened for three days, except you bossing us around. And nothing's going to happen—" Her voice rose in a scream, "It's *hellish!*"

A crack like a revolver shot rang out behind her.

Flying glass from the narrow balcony window, in a shower of daggers, stabbed the gloom, and crashed between the guests and the statue of Minerva. An icy breath, colder than their stagnant tomb, now lanced the Banner Hall.

For a second the group stood paralyzed, then swiftly the Comte passed up the stairs, along the gallery, through the musicians' golden cage, to the narrow balcony window facing south, the only one without a shutter.

"Bring the storm-lamp!" he called to the Doctor.

Silently both surveyed the naked snow sealing them in, white as milk, hard as iron. Cold leapt from it in an icy flame that licked the skin.

"Close it up quickly!" shouted Lord Brompton. "Every moment's valuable. Think of the ladies."

"He's right," muttered Dr. Herriot, "but how on earth—"

"A wooden shelf—" began the Comte.

"Too narrow; and it takes time to cut a shelf down!" Leaning over the balcony he ordered: "Bring that narrow table upstairs. Ah, thank you, Princess, you thought of that too!"

Staggering with the table, Victoria, Prince Colonna and Clio edged it along the balcony.

"Useless," pronounced the Comte. "Too wide, too short."

"Search must be made," declared Lord Brompton. "At least bring down a precise measurement, Dr. Herriot."

A further few minutes were lost in measuring the embrasure. Already the temperature had dropped noticeably.

"Nothing else for it," said the Doctor, "we must ram the embrasure with cushions."

"That will have to be done in any case," began the Comte.

"No, I have it!" cried the Doctor pointing to the Del Abbate picture. "That will do—yes, I believe it's just about the size."

Turning the guests stared. No one grasped at first to what he referred. Advancing below the light which illumined it, Dr. Herriot exclaimed:

"This ought to fill the bill. Yes, I'm right, it will! Or as near as doesn't matter—"

"Stop!" ordered the Prince. Again all present turned, including the Doctor. His languid patient was unrecognizable. "Under no circumstances is that picture to be touched. It is a masterpiece, an heirloom. I forbid it."

"Good lord," said Dr. Herriot, "I daresay they're all heirlooms. What of it? This happens to be the one that fits, so its number is up. Stand back now, this is no time for sentiment."

"I should think not!" cried Frau Winkwurth. "We may all die of pneumonia, while you're quarreling. I call it providential."

But Prince Colonna did not stand back. He maintained his position in front of the Del Abbate, his eyes, beneath their hooded lids, flickering with venom:

"Princess Victoria, be good enough to inform these vandals that this picture is my property."

The Princess moistened her dry lips. "Dr. Herriot," she said, "this picture belongs to Prince Colonna. We cannot touch it."

"Princess, I don't care to whom it belongs! This is a matter involving life itself."

"This is still my house, Dr. Herriot. That picture is my guest's property."

"D'you mean to tell me that you are prepared to lose life—" began the Doctor, but calmly the Comte cut in:

"Don't let us lose our heads first! Colonna, you can have no objection to the canvas being removed. Dr. Herriot, frame, glass, and boarding will afford all the support required, without Del Abbate's canvas."

The Prince frowned. "I have no objection—" he glanced

towards Clio—"if Miss Tubbs helps me to remove it. I have reason to think that she knows how to handle pictures."

Clio's chin trembled. "Let's have that fiendish hammer," she held out her hand to the Comte.

Without a word, the group watched as she and the Prince took down the Dell' Abbate, and together turned it over.

Kneeling on the floor, she worked on the back of the frame with the speed and ease of an expert, knocking back wedges, taking out pegs.

"We won't roll it yet," she told the Prince. He and she might have been the only people left in the universe. "Push back that *credenza* against the wall, and we'll prop the picture upon it, below where it was before. Now, we can still see it. It'll do us both good. There's your beastly frame," she turned to the Doctor. "Pick it up, before you put your foot through it."

Again without a word the Comte and Dr. Herriot carried away the frame. And as silently came downstairs again, when the aperture was sealed.

Hans having swept up the broken glass, hostess and guests were drinking some mulled wine, their conversation still subdued. At the moment, Hans and Charlotte sat by themselves, a little apart, beside the cooking stove, slowly savouring their Burgundy.

The Comte and Dr. Herriot approached the centre table, and, in their turn, proceeded to drink the wine awaiting them in the lamp-light there.

Then, setting down his beaker, the Comte addressed the Prince.

"Be good enough, Colonna, to explain that statement, publicly given, twenty minutes ago, that the Del Abbate picture is your property?"

"Be good enough, De Talloires, to tell me why I should inform you?"

"You compelled Princess Victoria to remove the picture. I found your attitude oppressive."

"The fact that you are Princess Victoria's fiancé, De Talloires, gives you at present no jurisdiction over her business affairs."

"Admittedly it does not. But neither does it prevent me from protecting my own interests."

"Believe me, Victoria is well able to look after herself."

"I refer to my business interests, Colonna."

"There you have not done so badly after all. Your future wife has lost you the Del Abbate masterpiece, but she has netted a small fortune. She already holds my cheque. I have my picture. Come, De Talloires, enough of this nonsense. I have paid *silently* and handsomely for the canvas—which, I would remind you, I need not have done."

Trembling, the Princess arose. "Exactly what do you mean by that?"

"I repeat: I have paid *silently* and handsomely for the picture. You would both be well advised to let it go at that. I regard this cross-examination as an affront."

"I must ask you to explain the word silently," said the Princess.

"Look here," the Doctor broke in, "would you like the rest of us to go over there, beside the servants?"

"Certainly not," said the Princess coldly. "Prince Colonna, having made such a statement before you all, must explain it."

"Assuredly he must," the Comte confirmed.

Languidly the Prince sat down. "What impertinence!" he murmured. Then in a louder voice: "You were warned—

Very well then, face the consequences! Princess Babenberg's daughter has taken upon herself to sell the Del Abbate picture. But I need not have dealt with her at all. I might have dealt with Prince and Princess Babenberg's *son*."

Smoothly the Princess said: "But this picture belonged to my mother, Prince Colonna. It was given her by her step-sister Geneviève. Did you not know? Ah, I see you did not!"

"It is open to question if legally you are entitled to any family property."

The Princess no longer trembled. Perfectly poised, she gave a cool little laugh:

"Do you, at this date, question my legitimacy?"

"Legitimacy, my dear lady, is not so much a matter of time as of parentage. Any scientist will bear me out there—" he leant forward, "even a *botanist!* Need I go further?"

"Monstrous!" Lord Brompton attempted to rise. " 'Pon my soul, Colonna, you must be out of your mind—" but the Comte put out a restraining hand.

"Prince Colonna shall go as far as he pleases. But no further here. Please sit down, Victoria. There is something I must make plain to you both, and which Augustus could have at once confirmed. The Del Abbate picture was indeed presented to Princess Babenberg by my mother years ago. But only for her lifetime. Your masterpiece, Colonna, belongs to me."

This time Victoria's cool little laugh shook slightly:

"Does this mean I have been trying to sell your property?"

"I'm afraid you have, my dear. If this is a shock to you, I'm sorry. You must get into the habit of consulting me for the future. Needless to say I shall not issue a writ against you, if you still wish to sell it! Everything rests with you."

There was a silence electric with implication.

Solitary beneath the second light the Del Abbate canvas continued to bloom in its own beauty, a self-contained sanctuary, yet open to all who had eyes to see.

"In which case," said the Prince harshly, "I regret my precipitancy."

"As you will certainly regret its consequences," said the Comte. "These will be costly, as I intend to sue you for your insult to Princess Victoria."

"My dear François, there I am, unfortunately for you, on sounder ground."

"You will have ample opportunity to prove this in open court. In any case, the result will be costly to you, as a slander remains a slander, even if based on truth."

The Prince's eyes narrowed. "May I also remind you that slander is not actionable unless pecuniary damage can be proven."

"Come, Colonna, you are not at your best tonight! Princess Victoria will certainly suffer financial loss in not being able to deal with the rest of her property until her legitimacy is confirmed—as confirmed it will be."

"Such publicity cannot fail to affect the Princess' prestige."

"Much less disastrously than it will affect your pocket."

The Prince's sallow skin had paled. "Yours also."

"In the interests of justice—" the Comte's smile was satirical—"I am prepared to mortgage Vermontaine and d'Annecy to the last acre. You, Colonna, will, of course, have your *objets d'art* to draw upon. A Frenchman does not lightly sacrifice his acres, but we are a tenacious people."

Stiffly the Prince arose, bowed slightly, and walked across to his mattress.

"Victoria," boomed Lord Brompton, "we ought to apologize for having heard such . . . such innuendos! I know I speak for all when I say that every word will be dismissed—forgotten. Attribute such ravings to the present disaster, the strain, the damp. Aspersions cannot exist in connection with your dear mother. Our lovely and legendary Princess Babenberg—one of whose greatest charms in the eyes of her admirers was that no scandal could touch her or them. Her discretion was proverbial. She tired of all her adorers long before they ceased to worship—and *what* security this affords to all concerned. A unique virtue, in one of your sex, if I may say so. No complications, no unpleasantness, no aftermath. A woman in a million!"

Had he been wearing a hat, he would, Victoria felt certain, have uncovered then, but, "Thank you, Lord Brompton," she said soberly, and crossed the hall to where the sleeping Albert lay.

De Talloires picked up his hammer. "Ten minutes, ladies, before bed." He was polite yet peremptory.

"*God!*" muttered Miss Storm, and closed her eyes.

Dr. Herriot, in the adjoining chair, stretched out his legs, and also shut his eyes. Oddly enough, he was beginning to find Miss Storm's expletives restful.

Princess Sophia silently opened her book, and in the circle of lamp-light began to read.

Lord Brompton tiptoed to the decanter.

On the sofa Frau Winkwurth drew closer to Clio:

"My dear, what a shocking scene! But how interesting! The only thing that impressed me in Prince Colonna's outrageous statement was that reference to a botanist."

"A botanist?"

"Yes, a botanist. Now . . . *why* a botanist? Why not a biologist? That botanist occurring as he did in the Prince's accusation struck me forcibly. If you come to think of it, one hardly ever meets a botanist. Of course one may see them and not know, poking about in fields, or on the mountains—that's more romantic. Yes, perhaps Beatrice Babenberg met him collecting specimens on these very alps, a warm spring day—and not a soul in sight. In this district, I assure you, there need never be a soul in sight. It might go on for months. In such circumstances days pass like hours!"

"A botanist," repeated Clio.

"You must admit a botanist is unusual. Now that teeny-weeny detail did smack of truth to me. You'll agree a botanist is an unlikely person to think up. I've never met a botanist. One doesn't—unless by arrangement."

"Well, I have," said Clio. "Quite recently. A Mr. Garett Phelps. He's quite famous in his own line too. He—" she paused frowning. She was fumbling her way among unspoken implications, such as his introduction to Princess Victoria—unable to understand her own reticence as she left her sentence unfinished. "What Prince Colonna suggested was really horrible, Frau Winkwurth, for it might mean that the Château itself didn't belong to the Princess, that nothing did. Why! Princess Victoria herself wouldn't be royal after all—or only half."

"You needn't worry about *that*. It won't make any difference to *her*. She's her mother's daughter, and the Beauharnais consider themselves superior to Royalty. And of course by the time she's married Monsieur de Talloires, she's as good as doubled the original dose!"

"When—if—"

"Yes, yes, for a moment I'd forgtten. Here we are. Why did you remind me? It had been quite fascinating. In fact, I was so carried away by the Prince's insults and the Comte's threats that I quite forgot to look around and see how the Babenbergs took it."

"The servants must have heard."

"That wouldn't make any difference to *them* or the servants. No, it's one's friends who are the danger."

Said Clio sepulchrally: "Here we are, on the verge of eternity—cutting each other's throats, *and* behind their backs!"

"Speak for yourself," said the other tartly. "None could be sorrier than I for the *situation*. Speak for yourself, my dear."

"For you too. Everything I say now is true—" the girl's voice held a note of wonder. "How strange that is! It's almost a relief. Abbey used to say I was the liar of the ages. How surprised he'd be— I must leave you now."

"Leave me? Why? Where can you go?"

"The Comte has stopped hammering. That means it's eleven o'clock. I always sit by myself at eleven o'clock."

"You're going to say your prayers perhaps? How nice! Shall we say them together?"

"Oh, *no!*" Clio shrank back. "Please excuse me—I just couldn't!"

Rising, she almost ran towards her mattress.

The old woman stared after her into the gloom for as long as she could. Curiosity draining out of her face left it oddly vacant.

Slowly uncertainty invaded her as she gazed into the swollen shadows of the hall. Existence itself was ebbing away in this endless gloom. Colour, heat, light, all had drained away now. Before her very eyes, ruin was enacted. Inertly enacted. The familiar had lost its form in this no-man's-land.

Suddenly she recognized it for what it was. The phantom frontier between life and death.

Choking, she raised her hand to her throat, but as her eyes rolled up, she caught sight of a dim outline in the darkness, and hysteria abated.

The Babenberg ensign-armorial was still recognizable from the abyss, the banner which from the year 976 had marked the true birth of Austria. It was under the Babenbergs, after all, that Austria had begun its long and steady rise to power. That was as much a fact as the present nightmare. More so. Austria and the Babenbergs had certainly gone on longer!

Silently she continued to stare at this last token of authority; hungrily, thirstily feeding herself on that rigid symbol of survival—the Mark or Boundary, *Crowned,* and was unaware that, for the first time in her indebtedness, she had identified herself fully with her benefactors.

INVITATION TO AFTERMATH . . .

One hour later, Dr. Herriot, taking the storm-lamp, approached the statue of Minerva. The Prince's mattress lay to the right of the goddess. Across the hall, Colonna in his chair, was still discernible to the long line of lowly beds beneath the gallery.

Dr. Herriot stopped a pace away, and flashed his light. The Prince continued to lie limply in the chair, his chin dropped, his skin leaden. Was the man dead?

Dr. Herriot set his lamp on a stool, with the light full on the unconscious figure. Then he bent down and took his pulse. Rapidly he loosened the scarf at the Prince's throat. Colonna, unlike the other men, still wore a collar. True, it was one of the Comte's, and too large for him, but it was, undeniably, a collar. Dr. Herriot removed this also, and, in doing so, saw a dire sight.

Bending closer, although his gaze flashed impassively over this revelation, the Doctor clucked with exasperation.

In the folds of Prince Colonna's neck the pale skin was startlingly stained. Suprarenal pigmentation had him literally by the throat. This accounted for his languor—all the symptoms of increasing exhaustion which Dr. Herriot had already observed.

Slowly the Prince opened his eyes.

Silently the Doctor took out his brandy flask. Holding a

tot to his patient's mouth, he saw the Prince swallow, and after a minute or two revive as calmly as if he had just been asleep.

Folding the scarf loosely around the exposed neck, the Doctor removed the lamp from the stool, and sat down. He had determined on his course of action.

His first words were calculated to surprise.

"What the devil do you mean," he asked, "by not turning up at Bergers Sanatorium on the date Dr. Daelker arranged?"

"Are you the man from London?" Prince Colonna attempted to get his bearings.

"I should think I am. Admittedly you weren't the only case Daelker wished me to see, but from my point of view you were the most interesting. Now I shall have to shuttle back to Bergers with you. What do you think I am? A boomerang?"

A faint smile twitched the pale lips.

"One thousand apologies. My friend Miss Storm particularly wished to make this call, at this date, before she too went to Dr. Daelker's."

"Miss Storm—what's she doing at Bergers?"

"As you intend to return there—which I much appreciate—I may as well be frank. Miss Storm is returning to complete her cure. I hope, for her sake, it may prove her last visit," his voice trailed off. With some effort, he added: "I have a high regard for her."

"To return," said the Doctor grimly, "to your own case: Dr. Daelker did not give me your name. He simply referred to you as his Florentine Prince. No need to look pained! He's prodigiously proud of you. Hope I'm going to be the same! But it wasn't till I saw your neck that the bell rang."

"My *neck?*"

There was a sharp silence. Then easily the Doctor said: "Yes, there's a trace of pigmentation—but that will scarcely surprise you. And now that we know where we are, we can tackle the situation." He spoke with zest.

"Addison's disease," mocked the Prince, "apparently holds no terrors for *you.*"

"I should hope not!" retorted the Doctor. "But from now on I expect some co-operation from you. This condition is one I intend to deal with, so oblige me by ceasing to label it. You may yet die under very different indications than those of Dr. Addison!"

"Interment here, for instance, below the Babenberg eagle?"

"Good lord! What a set you are. Individually, most of you fighting fit, but positively no team spirit!"

His vigour was contagious. The Prince sat up on his chair.

"Another tot?" suggested Dr. Herriot.

Unassisted, Prince Colonna drank.

"Now, get to bed," his physician ordered.

"Who's taking the first watch tonight?"

"The two plaintiffs—for their sins," said the Doctor.

"Plaintiffs?"

"In that *cause célèbre* Babenberg *versus* Perugia. The Comte drew his own name and that of the Princess tonight. I suspect him of cheating, but don't mention the fact. He might sue me too. Good night."

"Good night, Dr. Herriot. As regards Babenberg *versus* Perugia, I should value your indications on that case also."

"By the time we're dug out of here, Prince Colonna," said Dr. Herriot cryptically, "you can take it from me that more than the hatchet will be buried."

Oddly cheered, his patient turned on his side and slept.

INVITATION TO MIDNIGHT WATCH . . .

A few minutes later the watch took up its position, one on either side of the small table, the clock between them—the Comte calmly, the Princess with sang-froid.

Considerable sang-froid, the Comte decided, in view of the Del Abbate canvas which rested on the adjoining *credenza,* against the wall.

Princess Victoria faced the gallery. Behind her the Comte could just discern, across the hall, the figure of Minerva, but the Horae, in their wreaths, framing the narrow balcony window above, tapered into impenetrable night.

Slim as a girl, Victoria, in a ski-tunic, sat upright. The tunic was extremely shabby, but it had been designed by Boeckl of Vienna, and its style was still sprightly. Bareheaded by day in the perennial dusk of the past three days, she wore for the increasing cold of a sedentary watch, a loose riding coat, and a small round Cossack cap. The well-known statement that a Viennese woman has never been a fashion-plate, but always a lady of fashion, struck the Frenchman afresh in these wholly incongruous circumstances, where none had washed for three days. In this drab predicament, the blond beauty of Estella Storm had suffered a natural eclipse, but the dirtier Victoria Babenberg's face became, the better looking she grew. In this respect, she was rather like a Russian, he reflected. But then, of course, on her mother's side there was Russian as well as French blood—and the Cossack cap alertly fitting the small skull emphasized the Slav cheekbone. The patrician element was certainly enlivened by this Tartar indication! His increasing anxiety over every worsening phase in their entombment was for a moment forgotten. He found her an exhilarating sight as she coolly out-faced him now, completely oblivious that her hand was trembling on the table!

He permitted himself to smile. "Good evening," he said pleasantly. "Quite a time since we have met."

Suavely she replied, "Surely not as long as that?"

"The 30th September, to be exact," he said. "Two a.m. at Claridge's, before you caught the train some hours later from Victoria for the Stromberg—" he paused. "Since then, of course, you have again departed from Victoria. This time in my absence."

"How time flies!" she commented, but had the grace to drop her gaze. "François, it's so unlike you to increase embarrassment. The crumpled rose-leaf is your especial grace. Can't you see I'm floundering? This is quandary!"

"To one of your resource? What can the dilemma be?"

"Surely it shouts to heaven? How does one return a cheque to a man living night and day in the same room with one? Oh! for that blessed face-saver—the daily postman! After all, there is Colonna's purchase, standing on that table!"

Imperturbably he watched the merriment in her eyes, blue-black in this light—the lower lip caught by the flash of her white teeth.

"I can scarcely tear up the Prince's cheque, François. That would, of course, be the simplest way. He must know that it's safe in that respect. But I suppose one has to return it?"

"It is, I think, the custom?"

"I suspected as much! Failing deliverance by registered mail, I presume I must hand Colonna the cheque myself?"

"I believe it is the usage of polite society! Of course the situation bristles with other niceties. There, as you say, is his purchase! I do not know what view an international court would take of the problem. Many countries hold that a penny down is a bargain closed. But when the goods sold are not one's own to sell, all courts, I believe, are agreed as to culpability! Now, had you sold my picture, as the Comtesse de Talloires et d'Annecy, I might actually have had difficulty in proving that I had not given you permission to dispose of my property. In fact, it would hardly have been worth my while to summon you publicly—whatever I might have said privately at Vermontaine, where, I understand, the picture originally looked remarkably well."

"François," she said suddenly, "forgive me! I'm in sackcloth and ashes."

He did not reply.

"And of course," she amplified, "I shall never do anything like this again."

"That I can well believe. But the first apology is surely due to Colonna."

She hesitated, then half-ruefully added, "I agree. He was willing not only to pay a small fortune for the picture, but to swallow his detestation of me to get it."

"And why should Colonna detest you?"

She shook her head. "I am Maman's daughter—but it baffles me what her crime can have been. Yet he still hates her, although she's dead. Tante Sophia might know, of course."

"Do sisters-in-law usually confide in one another?"

"Sophia and Maman adored each other. Maman herself

told me that she wished Tante Sophia had married Emile. And no brother was ever dearer than he was to Maman—" she broke off. "That may have had something to do with Colonna's resentment."

"Well, Sophia married neither Émile nor Colonna."

"That's true," said the Princess thoughtfully, "she married neither. Perhaps it might be wiser not to inquire further."

Imperceptibly he smiled. "What a wife for an ambassador! Only once does discretion seem to have failed you—on that last visit to Florence."

"Florence? How did you find out?"

"The wife of the military attaché there saw you in the street. Captain Dubost himself told me. You and I were there together on that Monday night. Strange. But he did not mention Professor Drury. Perhaps, like you, he thought this inadvisable."

"Oliver? Why should he mention him?"

"As I entered my hotel in Florence that night, Professor Drury left it. That could scarcely be coincidence."

She stared at him. "François," she said astonished, "it was coincidence. I had no idea Oliver was in Florence. I did not see him. I went for one purpose only, to dispose of my—of your picture through Guerini and Abbey. I had a brief meeting with Colonna about this—and an unexpected encounter with Garett Phelps. Then I hurried home. This, of course, accounts for your lack of cordiality since."

"My lack of confidence—for you can do nothing to alter my love, Viccy, nor can I!"

Swiftly, almost defiantly, she raised her chin. "I want to be happy with you. I want to believe in your love. But I cannot."

Dryly he replied. "You are obliged to punish me, you mean. Deservedly."

She gave an uneasy laugh. "That scarcely explains why I should suffer myself."

"Because we are one," he replied. "You cannot escape your own wound. From my own pain, I can assure you that this is also mortal for you."

Flushing, she turned away her head.

Across the table, he took her hands. "Our roots go back a long way together. Help me to restore Eden—you who love a garden."

"This is scarcely the place."

"Why not? We have been three days and nights in present darkness! Light appeared on the fourth day, according to Genesis."

Amused, she glanced up again. "*Eh bien!* Which shall it be? We have seen any number of gardens together. The pines and cypresses of the Villa d'Este . . . a sunstruck hour watching the lizards zigzagging on the balustrade, so hot beneath our hand? Somehow the fountains del Nettuno do not appeal so much tonight! I was sixteen, you were twenty-eight on that hurried visit. How bored you were—in what haste to leave the family party! Or would you rather have the full glare of the Crimean Riviera? The lilies and roses of the Romanowsky villa, blooming in tumultuous confusion against a still blue sea? You were too strenuous in those days to linger in a garden. Sailing, swimming, polo, what-not—I hardly ever saw you! The twelve years' difference in our age added immensely to your prestige. I worshipped from afar—manoeuvring next my hero when I could! I remember at Dulber a certain lovely lady who would gladly have pushed me from the crags behind the Grand Duke Nicholas' palace. Almost the only occasion when you could be said to have encouraged my suit! But then if I was too young in those days, perhaps she was not young enough! But lovely all the same. And how heartily I loathed her. The name was Manuela. Surely you have not forgotten? Her dark hair hung heavily; her skin was the colour and the texture of a tea-rose; a high-bridged nose held guard over a foolish full mouth, but she had an obstinate chin, and long, pale plump hands. No wonder you were nervous!"

"Victoria, I understood that we were looking for a garden!"

"Nearer home then? Shall we ransack the Babenberg grounds, Wien? But that was more of a park than a pleasance, wasn't it? And a sparse park at that! Dusty in summer when the horses cantered through . . . the *cour d'honneur* was sandy, even in springtime. Perhaps you didn't notice? You were invariably riding in or out. And once dismounted, in rapid circulation elsewhere! I used to watch you from a certain window above. If you went back, you'd find your initials scrolled there by a diamond borrowed, unbeknown to her, from Maman. Such a majestical *F* for François—a double-banked frigate of an *F,* all sail set against the sky. Old glass —so your bluest sky was always faintly tinged with green, your whitest clouds curving with the rigour of bronze.

"But in the gardens at Schönbrunn you were forced to weigh anchor! Often for hours on end. Yet even at Court, François, you still set your own distance. Yes, shall we return to Schönbrunn with its avenues and hedges clipped with French formality, and the Gloriette another aloof ecstasy? You were ever *there* rather than *here*. But by that time, alas, you had become obsession!"

"*Incroyable!*" he murmured. "May I hear how you recovered? Shall we, as you suggest, move still nearer home—to the summer of 1911, and another celebrated garden? Or is that one at Kew sacrosanct to you and Professor Drury? You were, I imagine, very much in love, before permitting yourself to take the step you did."

"Very much in love, François. And very much annoyed with you."

"Seriously, did I ever cross your mind then?"

"Like the Gloriette—at an appropriate distance. Yes, I must admit it—when Oliver appeared, I was able, more resignedly, to contemplate your distant charm! But to one loss I was never reconciled." Again she smiled. "I know it sounds absurd—"

"Continue, please."

"It's the story of another garden, even nearer home, yet much farther away! As a child, I fell in love with its picture on a wine-bottle. In gold leaf graceful chimneys trace a Renaissance sky. There is a winged court with a shallow centre fountain. The first ducklings have been known to trespass in that low, open basin. Smooth sward, habitually deserted, runs surprisingly into hayfields east and west. All the life of the place lies in the farm buildings beyond, and on a sloping vineyard due south. Minutely the white-burgundy label indicates one of the giant sycamores which earn the seat its ancient name: *Fevilles Vermontaine*. There is an autumnal fall in the very words, and something of the fountain's trickle! Yet it's with summer's whisper hot upon it that I love it most. On the wine label, above the sycamore, halfway between heaven and earth, is a coat of arms, showing shield and crested helm, with a powdering of heraldice dots that I once believed must be snow in summer. Snow—" she broke off, and gazed suddenly aghast into the stagnant dark.

He laid his hand upon hers. "Continue," he repeated.

Slowly her gaze travelled to his face. Uncertainly she smiled, but said calmly enough: "The sycamore is the sacred solitary tree, isn't it? The legendary one that stands in the vault of heaven, between the rising and the setting sun. Doesn't one of Rameses III's inscriptions run: *I give thee great gardens planted with trees and vines . . . I grant thee groves and copses . . . and flowers of all lands for thy beautiful face.*"

"For *thy* beautiful face," gently he corrected her.

"To return to Vermontaine," she began.

"To return." Silently he kissed her hand.

Absently she continued: "I was seven when I first saw the picture, nine when I arrived by coach there, lurching in a leisurely way through its pastoral landscape. After the Babenberg Palast, after the Hofburg, after Schönbrunn, can you imagine what it meant to a child to find itself in a garden that had no end and no beginning in the open, ambling countryside?

"The house was full of summer sun and silence that first evening; the doors wide, and the bees in final frenzy among the honeysuckle.

"I had been sent to Tante Geneviève, as I showed signs of listlessness—a growing child's anaemia. All that evening I kept running in and out alone, with arms outstretched as if I were about to fly! You hadn't happened then, François. I didn't see you till the week spent in the little lodge on the edge of the forest. Do you remember, it was called the Wood-Cutter's Well? No one knew why. It just held four of us, Tante Geneviève, you and me, and old Bette who cooked for us—the only one to find drawbacks in heaven!

"I recollect that you went fishing by the hour but, at that stage of your career, had time for us as well. There were long lazy afternoons too bright to cast a fly, in which you did your best to amuse me. The open country was as flat as the floor. Another cottage, a mile off, stood out like an event in history. The fields in front stretched to eternity! There, colossal cows chewed the cud endlessly! The sky came right down to the road. The light was so pure that every daisy dazzled. My tiny bedroom was upstairs, and when a load of hay passed, it was as if the world came to an end in a tidal wave of clover! The window opened right on to my pillow. Waking at dawn, the bland, simple scene had all the innocence of a nursery-rhyme that's come to life. For the first time I began to *see*. I discovered that there's nothing so eerily alive as the beady black eye of the white moth, sharing the same blanket! I saw the first flower that you gave me, as I have never seen another since—a dandelion in full blow. Breathless, the gossamer hood clung to its stem, and in this airy nebula, through its star-tweaked tracery, one saw the knotted stamens, fresh and green from that other sphere—the earth! You laughed when I refused to blow out my universe!"

"Beloved," he replied.

Again she did not seem to hear. "Then there was the church," she told him, "gaunt as a cathedral. All the villagers were there on Sunday, and yet the building still seemed empty, its great bulk sunk in that water meadow."

Indulgently the Comte took up the tale: "Stone pillars, whitewashed walls; the shields of Granvelle and Vermontaine; the scarlet flowers and gold vestments of Whitsun."

"Yes, remember how guilty we felt when the bell-ringer stopped ringing in the nave the minute we arrived! Then he walked up the aisle behind us, stepped into an empty pew beyond the pulpit, and automatically became the entire choir! The pews were covered with bird-droppings, too, from the sparrows flying gaily in and out. Will you ever forget the chatter of the starlings above the west window? So incessant that the priest's voice had to strive against this! Then the occasional lulls in the service when the burbling of the wood-pigeons could be heard in peace."

"I remember the missal we shared, Viccy—so small that we hardly saw the page, far less the type. What eyesight our grandparents must have had!"

The Princess nodded. "We could not read a word, but like the pigeons made appropriate crooning noises, and watched bees plundering the altar flowers."

Musing, the Comte continued: "The priest alone laboured under any sense of urgency that day. He did his best for us, but he was too late—the summer's day had already imposed its own benediction." He paused, and added irrelevantly, "My dear heart."

Reflectively she shook her head. "Then those long light evenings when we played draughts by the hour. One of the men was missing—do you remember?—and we used a chocolate, which periodically I ate to your annoyance. All this while Tante Geneviève stitched her way through a chalice veil and burse for the convent at Annecy. We sat in the window, to the sound of crickets chirping, while the tiny room grew dark and huge behind us, and moths flitted, lighter than ash—"

"Until the lamp was lit, when they blundered round us as big as bats!"

"Then your mother would exclaim: 'The grasshopper has become a burden, bed and oblivion are best!' I can remember, too, that she began to embroider a cushion-cover while we were there—which she promised should be mine on marriage. How elated I was! Crimson and lilac polyanthus on white brocade, and a hymeneal torch bound together with the motto *Do Not Divide Us.* Which reminds me, François, what happened to that cushion?"

"My dear child, I have no idea."

"Odd," her brow puckered. "Hardly the sort of thing that a bachelor would later present to the convent at Annecy. It must be somewhere."

"To return to Vermontaine . . ."

"Ah, yes. After the Wood-Cutter's Well, to return to Vermontaine was to find its countrified garden the height of cultivation, its mossy lawns velvet, its roses damask—" for the first time she faltered. "François, what time is it *now?*"

"Early morning, and our first alone. A memorable occasion! December twenty-fifth, 1921. All those gardens, Viccy, and not a single souvenir!"

"What is it to be then?" but now she spoke with a certain effort. "A *boutonnière* for a diplomat? Vervain, of course. Worn of old by all ambassadors."

"Aren't you being a little grim, my dear? It's also the herb of sacrifice."

She hesitated. "I'll take it back then. I need it myself." She shivered slightly.

"What's the matter?"

"A sick spasm. The truth comes over me in waves that, as hostess, I'm responsible for nearly every person's presence in this house."

"You heard what Clio said. It was Minerva's invitation. Not yours."

"To what will it lead in the end, I wonder?"

"Let's hope to the Innsbruck express, then Zurich, Basle and Paris."

"Paris!" she exclaimed, as if the name itself were restoration. "As I may not keep Colonna's cheque, I warn you I must have one from you! It need not be as large however! Yes, Paris for my trousseau—solely because I am marrying a Frenchman, for of course Vienna remains my arbiter of elegance. Still, Paris does well enough upon occasion! Paris by all means, François. Moreover, there I shall not be so tempted to extravagance! Nor will we need a fashionable honeymoon. That can come later when we are a jaded elderly couple! No, for the present let us return to Vermontaine—if only to secure my cushion cover!"

"Home then!" He smiled. "Pleasant to plan ahead." His voice altered. "Do you know, you are the only woman here who hasn't taken me aside to ask privately what our rescue chances are?"

Rallied, she cupped her chin upon her palms and winked: "Why should I tempt the soul of rectitude to prevaricate?" Again she hesitated. "In my less robust moments I feel our chances have become about fifty-fifty."

His eye gleamed in answer. She could feel his strength, adequate as virtue, available for any issue, in silent reserve.

"Pessimist!" he said softly. "Now give me a flower for the rest of the way."

"François!" suddenly she covered her face with her hands, in an admission of despair. "I've tried to explain. There's too much at present between us."

"How true," he muttered, and with an abrupt movement bodily lifted the table to one side. The forgotten thermos flask rolled off and crashed to the floor.

All round the hall, the sleeping guests sat up in consternation and with exclamations:

"What's happened?"

"What is it?"

"What's that?"

"Go to sleep," De Talloires genially replied. "Morning watch has just begun. *Darling,*" he added incomprehensibly.

Through the darkness Lord Brompton could be heard expostulating, "Sounds more like the Changing of the Guard to me! Devilish inconsiderate . . ."

INVITATION TO ECLIPSE . . .

Two days later in the damps and dark of the Banner Hall, odours of cooking and paraffin were no longer apparent. Cold had become paramount.

The water used for hot-water bottles had been so often reheated that most of it had evaporated. The warmth from the solitary electric heater amounted to mockery. But the light from the two electric lamps remained invariable and was now regarded with the confidence accorded to a natural force, the guests repeatedly complaining that the beams did not reach farther.

The Doctor was finding it increasingly difficult to get his charges out of bed.

Cowering under rugs and blankets, each resisted the preliminary attempts made by him and the Comte to get them onto their feet. Constantly they complained of earache. But acidly Dr. Herriot insisted that all arise for the repetitive meals of hot gruel, dried figs, and Burgundy, and what they had once blightingly and now listlessly termed recreation. But he was forced to recognize that the apathy of the Banner Hall now indicated a stuporous condition. And he did not like it.

Once more he and De Talloires shook them up for tea.

Methodically the Doctor next went through his afternoon's examination of Charlotte. More loudly than usual he announced his findings:

"Face practically normal." He handed her a mirror. "No longer interesting except to me, as an unusually speedy recovery."

Charlotte smiled and mouthed into the glass. Then she sat down the better to enjoy this spectacle of a normal face. She alone appeared indifferent to the fact that she was hourly now in a worse plight than before.

"Just look, Herr Doktor, at last I frown with ease! And the smile—no trouble at all! Then the nose, it too can be used. But my eye is the prodigy . . . open—shut, open—shut, as slick as a snuff-box. When I think of my anxiety! There was in particular one night—"

"Quite so!" The exuberance of convalescence was upon her, and he had scant patience with the reminiscent stage. "Keep out of draughts," he quoted, for he was equally intolerant of relapses, which he regarded as a personal reflection.

Oblivious of all but her appearance, Charlotte continued to study each feature with enthusiasm.

"At such a time," pronounced Lord Brompton, "her satisfaction is idiotic!"

Impatiently Clio and Frau Winkwurth agreed.

With approval Dr. Herriot listened to these signs of reaction. Earlier he could not have believed that his music-hall trio, as he dubbed Winkwurth, Brompton and Tubbs, would vindicate themselves as they had done. Did egoists, after all, put up a better fight than the disciplined? At least once a day, Wynken, Blynken and Nod could be counted upon to rally afresh with their views and their Planchette. These *séances* had in fact become the salvation of the situation. Prince Colonna and Miss Storm might be ribald on the subject, but they too pricked up their ears. And Princess Sophia had lent undoubted prestige to the proceedings by remaining, as she put it, "open to conversion" while Victoria and the Comte, amicably sceptical, had afforded the three occultists exactly the same indulgence they would have accorded Bridge addicts during a wet week-end.

At the moment Clio had again fallen asleep on the couch. It was time to awaken her, and yet the Doctor hesitated. Weakness! Albert too was sound asleep. Once Clio was alert, he'd get the boy stirring.

Princess Sophia continued to sit as usual with her book in the circle of lamp-light. Present yet absent, he thought dryly. De Talloires and Victoria were two other escapists. Flagrant the way their joy in one another now conveyed itself at each glance! It dated, of course, from that night they had smashed the only thermos, confound them!

Frowning, Dr. Herriot glanced across the hall to where, beneath the gallery, the patient who exercised his mind most could be seen slowly arising.

Estella Storm, candle in hand, next groped her way to the centre table, her fair face smudged with fatigue, her past hardihood lost in a growing but unexpressed dismay. She was fading off the scene quicker than any of them. He ought to feel a professional impatience, instead he was angry and alarmed. Her dumb acquiescence was wholly unexpected.

As Hans set down tea, Lord Brompton busied himself by borrowing the Prince's gold pencil. Planchette had now exhausted the lead in all others.

"I hope you realize," Dr. Herriot gibed, "that you've added a thirteenth personality to our company," he pointed to the small circular board, "by that infernal machine. But perhaps you aren't superstitious?"

Lord Brompton merely grunted. Planchette had come to stay—and the Doctor knew it. Everybody knew it. Its function was now as assured as that of any meteorological office. You could take it or leave it; its fiats went forth. And had done so with authority for three days—since the advent of Guerini, in fact. The late senior partner of Guerini & Abbey was now in complete control of the board—a characteristic any of his directors would at once have recognized. Tidings, often of an irascible nature, proceeded and continued to come through from Guerini with the celerity of a tickertape machine. In their excitement Planchette's three scribes had quite shamelessly admitted that previously they might have given the board a push at times—or, as they termed it, encouraged it—but for such there was now no need. This was *possession,* dynamic, undeniable.

And certainly Guerini's first announcement had gripped converts and unbelievers alike. For four days, he stated, rescue squads, in unprecedented conditions, had been digging.

"Why not six?" Lord Brompton insisted.

At this point Hans, fascinated despite himself, had interrupted, "There is equipment at Bergers, also at Gautz. Such has to be assembled. This takes time. The spirit may be right enough."

Thereafter the assembled company had settled down to Planchette as attentively as persons awaiting a trans-Atlantic call . . . or the uninitiated watching the manipulations of a wireless operator in a radio-room.

Guerini might then be said to have got into his stride.

To their satisfaction, the guests next learnt that if the human element had been slow in getting off the mark locally, this had not been the case further afield. The world-press, they were assured, was hourly dominated by bulletins of their plight. Prayers were being offered in every capital. America had despatched dollars. Practically every Alpine resort had offered advice. In Florence Rosa, a maid at the Albergo Toscano, had been interviewed by the press, Rosa owning the melancholy distinction of having dreamt of the disaster on the actual night of occurrence. In Canada woollen comforters were being knitted.

At this stage Lord Brompton had again lost patience, but Frau Winkwurth had advised him not to interrupt the flow.

Guerini, pressed for reasons of his own solicitude, had tersely replied. "Must get Abbey back to business."

"Oh, *darlings!*" Clio turned, her face radiant, "If you only knew how typical that is of Guerini! Not that I *need* further proof—I *know*. I will admit I felt dashed on reading that Rosa had dreamt the disaster. It ought to have been Abbey. But as you've heard since, it's been Abbey first, last, and all the time behind our rescue."

"Our *what?*" intoned the Prince.

"Well, each time we ask Guerini where Abbey is, he says *Springbrunnen.* Each time I ask Guerini how Abbey feels now he knows that I'm in danger, he writes *Desperate.* It's too, too wonderful, although I can quite understand it. After all, Abbey literally hounded me into the Château. It's only natural he should be practically prostrate now."

The two Princesses, exchanging smiles at this point, had been startled a moment later by the disclosure that Guerini was stepping back to allow Louise to speak! Urged to reveal her whereabouts, Louise hastened to add that she too had arrived!

Lord Brompton, whose spirits had risen to unreasonable heights with this announcement, recklessly whooped with delight, "Good old Louise, *now* they'll have to hustle!"

"A most successful *séance,* certainly," commented Prince Colonna.

"*Séance?*" protested Clio. "This isn't a *séance*— How can you! This is prayer in action."

"An unusually successful prayer meeting then," the Prince agreed.

"After all," cried Clio, "there's nothing so *very* unusual in getting in touch with the dead. It's getting in touch with the living, like this, that is the test. So many distractions. That's how I first knew I loved Abbey. Our communion in absence was perfect."

Yes, Dr. Herriot welcomed these brief outbreaks which died off all too soon.

Now, he challenged Miss Storm. "You're not a reader like your bosom friend?" he indicated the elderly Princess by the lamp, still intent on her page.

The singer sighed as she sat down. "No—and one feels one's limitations at such times."

He smiled. "That reminds me of my window-cleaner in London, a thin little lad, with an eager face which has had a good deal of plastic surgery done to it since the war. He confessed to me that he was a bit of a reader. Cosmology, he added, was his subject. As I searched for a suitable book for him, I asked him, 'Are you also interested in philosophy?' 'No,' he said apologetically, 'only in the Cosmos—I like something I can handle.' Nothing like a man who knows his limitations!"

And, leaning forward, Dr. Herriot awakened first Clio, then Albert.

Princess Sophia laid aside her book; and, grouped around the centre table, the guests began to drink tea. Then conversation, animated for a few minutes, flagged as abruptly.

"Are we buried?" said Albert suddenly.

Aghast they stared.

"Are we buried?" said Albert again. "Are we down below? Are we dead?" His gaze came to rest on the large, pale gentleman, with the rich voice.

"Poor child," said Lord Brompton, "you don't know what you're talking about."

"Yes, I do," Albert's voice rose. "When you're dead you're put in a hole in the ground with a stone on top, to keep you from getting out. And sometimes it's a cross."

"Gruesome!" Lord Brompton repressed a shudder.

"Come, Albert," said Princess Victoria, "that is not the whole story. What were you taught in Sunday School?"

"When you die, you go to heaven. With the angels. This isn't heaven," Albert insisted. "People's bodies is put in the ground. In the cemetery. This isn't the cemetery either."

"Of course it isn't," said Dr. Herriot briefly. "It's the Château Maria Sophia, and we've been caught in the snow. They're doing their best to dig us out, but it's taking a damn long time, and we've just got to be patient."

"Albert," the Comte rose, "I'm going to send out signals now. You may come with me and tap. It's time you did your share."

"Before they begin," said Princess Victoria, "I wish to apologize, Cousin Colonna, for that unfortunate business transaction of mine. François and I have a suggestion to make. When we leave here—yes, when we leave here, we hope that you will take the Del Abbate on life-loan. I no longer feel that it belongs to me, for I was willing to sell it. And François would like you to have it. With you, the picture came before anything. It—it has cost you also this perilous visit here."

There was a strange dry silence. Then the Prince said stiffly: "Your generosity puts me to shame. I deeply regret my recent effrontery. I can only hope, on your part, for what Homer calls a deed of oblivion."

Smiling, the Princess quoted: *"With an act of oblivion on our part—* What could be fairer? You have chosen a perfect passage, Cousin Colonna. It ends, doesn't it? *And let peace and plenty prevail!"*

"Charming!" declared Frau Winkwurth.

"Most gratifying," endorsed Lord Brompton.

"The devil take it!" exclaimed Dr. Herriot, "will you look at that?"

Clio had again fallen asleep on the couch.

Roughly he shook her.

She came out of her doze in a rage. "Stop it, will you? Leave me alone. . . . And now they've begun to signal! I tell you, I'll stand no more. This is hell! *It couldn't be worse—"*

As she spoke, both lights and the electric stove suddenly went out.

The Banner Hall was plunged into final darkness.

INVITATION TO DEAD RECKONING . . .

Long into the early hours of morning, De Talloires lay awake, tirelessly examining possibilities, endlessly weighing probabilities.

In his opinion, and he was the most experienced person present, the outlook was black indeed.

On the fourth day at latest, effort, he considered, should have been effective. And this was the seventh. . . .

There were, of course, at least half a dozen explanations why rescue had not yet been accomplished. Sedulously he went through these again—to rediscover burial as the only answer.

A paragraph from an official textbook imposed itself repeatedly on his attention now: Avalanche—*deriving from the French avaler—the original meaning of which is to descend to earth. . . . A snow avalanche ensues when a snow mass, pent up on a mountainside, loses it hold, and is discharged. This sounds a very simple operation, but when it is realized that the hold itself is brought about in several ways, and that it is released in several other ways, the matter becomes more complex.*

It certainly did, he decided wryly, especially when he remembered that of those human beings present, some had come with love, some in hate, some like the servants from duty, others for sanctuary, or like the innocent Albert for health.

None had come for death, yet that might be what each would find here.

It was too bad, he concluded coldly, his heart appalled. . . .

INVITATION TO STYX . . .

Across the hall, pin-pricked by two candles, Prince Colonna and Clio seated themselves for the first night-watch they had shared.

To the girl's surprise, the Prince did not sit as he usually did, collar turned up, chin sunk on breast. His attitude was alert, his expression for once tolerant.

"A game of draughts?" he suggested.

She shook her head. "No, thank you. The fact is, I must talk to you. It's a heaven-sent opportunity really—getting you alone." She glanced over her shoulder. "As alone as anyone can be here."

"You terrify me," said the Prince. "Elucidate."

Leaning forward, Clio lowered her voice. "It is thought that you are the one for the step now to be taken. It is considered that you are the right person—in fact the only one—to handle Dr. Herriot."

"Indeed? Who, may I ask, has been dwelling on me so purposefully?"

"The ladies. At least the bulk of them. The Comte we feel is not elastic enough by nature. Then, too, he is almost host here. That might cramp his style. Lord Brompton is impossible. Far too inflammable. From the start he's rubbed the Doctor the wrong way. But Dr. Herriot seems to like you. It's really quite extraordinary. I mean to say: he seems to like so few people."

"And how do the ladies suggest I reward him for this favour? My popularity here has not been marked. I cling to my raft."

"Yes, I know," she hesitated. "It's not going to be pleasant for you. But it's got to be faced. So we feel. That is to say, the majority of us."

"May this majority be more clearly defined?"

"I'd rather make the *position* plainer, Prince Colonna—then you won't feel fussed about detail. The situation really speaks for itself. Even the toughest women, despatched as spies into enemy country, are always given a lethal pellet to save them in the event of final calamity. Husbands abroad often protect their wives in this way, when the natives threaten. Anything might happen to Dr. Herriot at any moment, and none of us would know our way about his medicine chest. Now, if you will ask him to give us, right away, a final dose, to hold in readinesss, it would add to confidence all round."

"Not to Dr. Herriot's, I imagine. As to the ladies, they have already adjusted themselves to calamity in the most high-handed fashion. At no time have the natives had a chance. On behalf of the latter, I can assure you that all I now desire is a hot bath and solitary confinement for life."

"That's facetious!" Clio nodded. "But we shall be truly grateful if you'll tackle him after breakfast."

"Do you seriously suggest that I ask Dr. Herriot in his professional capacity to assist members of this household to commit suicide, in event of a crisis?"

"Baldly put, yes."

"Then baldly put, no. I have heard myself in this hall described as a pagan, but this is the first time I have been mistaken for a barbarian. Upon occasion I have found it possible and practicable to insult friends and relatives, but I should be quite incapable of such a breach of taste as this you propose. Even on my own behalf. And, as you will have noticed, my neighbours mean still less to me."

"You refuse to help us?"

"I decline to take such a gauche and irrational step."

"Irrational!"

"To imagine that Dr. Herriot would comply before occasion demanded."

"But if occasion arrives when Dr. Herriot can no longer help?"

"Then it will no longer be his responsibility. That's all he is interested in, you will find."

"You mean his patients don't come first with him?"

"I mean that his profession comes before his patients. He observes the rules of his game. You could not, for your present purpose, have fallen into more ruthless hands. Moreover, the gentleman does not believe in immortality. His aim-all and end-all is to prolong life here. You may take it from me that in each case he will contend with Nature itself to prevent quietus. Resentfully contend."

"You won't help! This is too frightful." She stared at him.

"You exaggerate. As our experience enlarges, strange frontiers buffet us—" he shrugged—"there is no other word for it. But why should any experience daunt you? You are an artist, after all."

"What's that got to do with it?"

"To the artist, frontiers are thresholds."

She hesitated. "As an idea, that's well enough."

"I assure you, it's the only reason why the rest of us put up with you. Artists have a way of surviving."

"You're plausible," reluctantly she made a stand. "And of course I know that millions of people have died in terrible ways since the beginning of time. But that doesn't make me feel any braver. After all, when the pressure is put on, what can I care for others. I'm only interested in *me*."

"Profoundly true," murmured the Prince.

"What I mean is: I only *know* about me. It's quite enough. More would kill me. Princess Victoria is my ideal. Perfect poise. That is my dream for myself—complete calm, endless tranquillity."

"Amazing! One would never guess this from the energy of your personality."

"Oh, I don't know. I have moments when I achieve something of all this. But the Princess has it all the time."

Curtly he said, "She is vested with an ancient authority. This complicates her personality in daily life, but simplifies it in a crisis. She will behave according to principle—as a principle—to the end."

"To the *end?*" Clio's face paled. "Then you think this will be the end? Yet you won't speak to Dr. Herriot for us? How ghastly!"

"Not at all," he said lightly. "The situation is quite simple. You must bind yourself by a stronger oath than his Hippocratic one. The great oath of the Gods remains for any ambitious soul. Bind yourself to silence by Styx—and when the appointed hour comes (here or elsewhere) go without a word."

"Styx—" She shivered. "Cold, cold, cold . . ."

"Cold?" the Prince looked bored. "The children of Styx were Power, Zeal and Victory."

"It's—it's an idea," again she agreed mechanically.

The Prince leant forward. With his thin, dry finger he

tapped imperatively on the table. "Achilles was dipped early in Styx; only his heel escaped immersion. It alone remained vulnerable. Remember?"

Dubiously she smiled. "You are very kind."

"Tell me something I can more readily believe!"

"Of course I do realize," she took in a long breath, "that if we *are* rescued, it proves nothing. Far finer people have had faith and perished."

"I could not agree with you more."

"If there's a meaning, Prince Colonna, it must be beyond this event itself. This event must be secondary. *Gracious,* think of a thing like this being secondary!"

"A first-rate idea on your part. Come, let us dismiss the agony column for a little, and speak of matters that delight."

Heavily she said: "Look at the Del Abbate, then. Let's talk of that."

He glanced across at her. The girl was actually learning how to behave!

"Signorina," he said softly to the swollen face confronting him, "you may yet end by humanizing me! By all means let us speak of the Del Abbate. Of course, neither of us can see the picture clearly now."

Both turned to where it stood upon the Spanish *credenza,* propped against the wall—the canvas which had again changed hands, and yet remained exclusively in Del Abbate's own.

"But," the Prince affirmed, "one can always talk about it, for this picture tells a story, yet would satisfy any purist as a formal harmony. Amiel has said: *a landscape is a state of consciousness,* and this canvas instantly conveys that fact. It is the most impressive thing about it. Move the candle closer, and you will see what I mean! That luminous horizon of land, sea, and sky, that momentous foreground heightens intuition.

Here are trees, static yet tumultuous as thunderclouds; and the aspiring symbols of cities, towns, and villages, harbours and hamlets—civic monuments and temples . . . buildings, you will note, from which life has mysteriously withdrawn at that moment when the heights are transformed, and the storm abates in serenity.

"It is, in fact, more than a picture. It is a window in the wall, Signorina, through which we may watch not only the world and his wife, but the universe beyond them. And as it is a Renaissance window, the figures in the foreground are those of classical antiquity."

"Go on," said Clio, somewhat drowsily. "I could listen to you all night."

The Prince shot her a sharp look, but continued with his lullaby. "Foremost lies the dead Eurydice, aureoled in an unearthly twilight, the loveliness of her naked form chastening at a glance. At her feet Proteus, the God of Change, in his customary place, the seashore, pours the libation to the Kingdom of the Dead upon the ground, as was the antique way. And at this vital moment of dying, there leaps to life around the fallen figure the vivid events of her earthly life, in a simultaneous vision. Here is the headlong haste and the serpent that destroyed the nymph as she flies from the unwelcome arms of Aristaeus. You see, Signorina, there are dangers also in flying from the other man! Time and again there is her beloved husband, Orpheus himself. The mourner will at once recognize him, in the circle of the bereaved, surrounded only by the animal kingdom, for when a man tastes death, he finds his kind no longer inhabits the same world. They have become spectres. The dead may be seen and handled daily, but only the bereaved can know death—" he paused. "Eurydice, in dying, has experienced something quite different."

Clio, her head resting on her outstretched arms upon the table, replied a little thickly: "Funny to hear you say that. Sort of thing Princess Sophia would have said. Go on, all the same."

"And so, Signorina, the conclusion is irresistibly borne in upon us that the gloom and terror of the Greek Plutonic region is that of man's own mind when in eclipse. Fear, after all, is one of the experiences that we are counselled to forego. And as we watch Orpheus consulting the Sibyl, we have a shrewd idea that she is warning him as the Cumaean Sibyl warned Aeneas that only a few children of the Gods have made the journey to Hades safely, for it is the return from Hell, Signorina, which is the crux! Orpheus did not forget his promise to Pluto. He had drunk of the Well of Remembrance before entering the Kingdom of the Dead. He broke his promise. Princess Sophia would of course point out that his failure was one of faith. His fear that the God had broken his promise, that Eurydice was not with him on the journey back, was simply the projection of his own weakness on the divine. The promise cannot be broken, Signorina. The individual's integrity must respond to that of the Cosmos, which, as its name indicates, is order, harmony, perfection—" again he paused.

"Order, harmony—perfection," she repeated drowsily, "lovely—just what I say."

Smoothly he continued: "Gazing upon this—er, scene before me, beauty disarms criticism. The transformation of that precise horizon is felicity itself. The traditional handling of the subject is informed with poetry."

Glancing across his shoulder at the picture, dim but bewitching in candle-light, he added half to himself—as if his final conclusions surprised him, "Del Abbate's landscape discloses no golden age that will pass away with its season, but a glimpse of the abiding order of the universe as, inexorably, it declares and disposes of evil, and as infallibly maintains divinity, with its eternal assurance that throughout the temporal, this sanctuary is also secure."

He turned back to Miss Tubbs.

The watch was fast asleep.

He sat for another two hours in silence. Once or twice the trapped fume from the oil-stove threatened him with drowsiness, but the prevailing chill of the hall, and his own thin blood reduced this temptation to a trifling inconvenience.

At 3.45 a.m. he arose, and quietly heated some soup, prodding Miss Tubbs with her own spoon before he sat down again.

"Four o'clock," he announced. "You will now awaken Princess Sophia."

Clio, blinking, said charitably, "Can it be that time already? Passed quicker than usual, hasn't it? Poor Princess Sophia! I don't like to shorten anyone's sleep, but if you say so, I'll get her up."

INVITATION TO LAST VIGIL . . .

"Since when, I wonder," asked Princess Sophia, "has the middle-watch become the morning-watch?"

"Since it incorporated with Nemesis! Sit down, mine enemy. The stove smells less from this angle. Some soup? There you are! Yes—when your death was reported to me after the war, I little thought you would yet live to be buried with me!"

Stirring the soup, she smiled. "Preposterous, isn't it? Remembering, too, how you have treated my niece, I am surprised that I can bring myself to speak to you—even in the same tomb!"

"Remembering how you have treated her cousin, you mean!"

"That old story. Can't you forgive and forget?"

"Trite, Sophia. You are certainly at a loss tonight! If it gives you any satisfaction, I regret that disclosure about Victoria. It was given under duress—for in the Family circle I suffer no arrogance but my own. Then, also, the stresses to which I have submitted since burial have un-nerved me. I had counted upon the comfort of finality after interment. Instead of which, I find myself entombed with eleven other persons—ten of them extremely ill-chosen. You appreciate my predicament?"

"Yes, but I also feel for Viccy's."

"On the whole I do too. Victoria, as hostess, has certainly earned the more strenuous of Minerva's titles—worker and warrior among men. But some less pleasing also. As Athena Apaturia I find her ruthlessly devoted to her own clan. Possibly you derive benefit there, but let me remind you of the stage which precedes this cult of the Family. As Athena Tritogeneia, she is water-born—the stormcloud split by lightning. Reduce her temperature to dangerous levels and we meet the lady later in snow, and are finally buried by her."

"As like draws like, Dominic, I would much rather think of her as Nikephoros—in her own name Victoria!"

Touched, despite himself, he held out his hand. "And I do not forget that the Athenians looked upon her as their Kore! For your sake most of all, I hope she does indeed prove our Persephone."

After a moment's silence, "Your hand is surprisingly warm," he said. "But then you have been asleep. And for how many years! But of what were we talking? Ah, Minerva!"

"Dominic, duress had nothing to do with your wretched attack on Viccy's mother at the dinner-party. Why did you label her in that way?"

"I might have called Beatrice Babenberg a much less flattering name than Front-Line Minerva. As you well know. But at that stage, I was still subject to the proprieties. My incarceration had not yet begun—with its invitation to freedom. Semele the Subterranean would be a more accurate description of the lady's activities."

"Why punish Viccy for this?"

"I am still rancorous."

Sharply she sighed. "Circumstances were too much for Beatrice. In the end they dominated."

"You still deceive yourself?" impatiently he discarded her hand. "That woman was dominated by one thing only throughout her career—her objective. I repeat: Aristotle's definition alone disposes of her satisfactorily: a political animal."

In a low voice Sophia said: "When did you discover the truth?"

"Less than a year before Victoria's birth."

The Princess started. "You don't say so!"

"And in the strangest, yet simplest way. Both she and Garett Phelps played their parts to perfection. They were betrayed by an infinitesimal detail. I might almost say by that which has position but not magnitude. I am nothing if not observant, as you know."

Rather haggardly she stared at him. "Then you knew everything, all the time?"

Acidly he replied: "The whole time, my dear innocent!"

Faintly she said, "How did that happen?"

"Romantically. On a May morning in 1886, as I approached the Château Maria Sophia on foot! I was then an impecunious man of thirty—fortunately fond of walking. On my rare visits to the Château, I invariably tramped in by the Garten-Girlande. Prince Babenberg was, I knew, in Russia for three months. I had not announced my arrival, but it was not a household that stood on ceremony with its welcome.

"I like the southern aspect, with that absurd temple of Minerva, between its oak-trees, commanding the approach to Italy. There was a low stone seat inside, on which I used to rest, facing the open pass with its superb vista upon my country.

"But on this occasion, as I came in, on the right, my tread noiseless on the thick turf, I perceived that I was not alone with the Goddess. Two persons were seated there: Beatrice Babenberg and a man I later discovered to be Garett Phelps, the botanist.

"I could swear they had not heard me—and yet instinctively they knew of my approach, a second before sight disclosed us to each other. The extraordinary *lifelessness* of their attitude confirmed this. They were seated as correctly but as inertly as two dolls.

"Then the Princess smiled, and at once the entire naturalness of the situation declared itself, as introduction was effected.

"I should merely have thought that I had stumbled upon a passing flirtation had it not been for two things—that dead second of time as I entered. Destiny might have hung on it! And something I noticed as together the three of us passed out of the temple. The sun, defining that which has position but scarcely magnitude, caught a golden hair twisted across the breast of this dapper gentleman's jacket.

"This souvenir intrigued me, occurring when and where it did. Beatrice, as you know, was discretion itself. Yet not for one instant did I connect it with the full force of that dead second, when a kingdom might have fallen! And it was precisely this failure to correlate that exercised my curiosity.

"At once I proceeded to discipline conjecture with fact! Any study of Garett Phelps' scholarly career will at once reveal a globe-trotting propensity. In search of elusive Flora, he was, I discovered, indefatigable. He had, moreover, taken part in several important government expeditions. He was a man seasoned by hardship—to whom, in my opinion, an exacting love affair with a celebrated beauty would mean less than most. I put him down as a practical man, quite as practical as the lady. I could not understand what they were doing in each other's picture. I bought Mr. Phelps' books. These confirmed my view of the gentleman. I got out a map of the world, and traced in Indian ink such journeys as he mentioned. This net was instructive, but not conclusive, and at this stage I might have lost interest had I not again been forcibly reminded of our botanist some months later. In February, 1887, to be exact. Then Beatrice, with customary aplomb, announced the arrival of Victoria as the birth of a seven-month child! As Frederick did not return from Moscow till August, this proclamation did not deceive me. It certainly cannot have deceïved Frederick. By now, I was more than interested. I was fascinated. Neither Beatrice nor Phelps was the type to risk anything for love, far less all. But I concluded that both might be of those who will safeguard a stronger interest with all that circumstance can offer. And Victoria was assuredly a guarantee of good faith, on the lady's part. In short, I regarded those two hardheaded persons as business-partners, who later found themselves in closer personal bondage than they had originally bargained for."

"*Business*-partners?" protested Sophia, in a low voice. "That element never entered the situation with either, I am certain."

He shrugged. "Political partners may be a more accurate description, but to an unsympathetic outsider, with a distaste for professional espionage, the alliance was a business one. As I have ever been suspicious of disinterested activity, these two persons aroused first my curiosity, and then my contempt. I might, at a pinch, die for my country. I certainly would not spy for it. I cannot therefore credit them with the selfless intentions that you have done."

Princess Sophia gave a short laugh. "You really had no proof at all. What effrontery!"

"I had all I required. I drew out all I needed."

"Why did you do it?"

"Because Beatrice Babenberg interfered three times in my life, with disastrous results."

"Dominic, don't blame her for that first occasion in Florence. She genuinely forgot to give me your message."

"Strange that she should have offered to deliver it—should herself have taken the letter from Max, to whom it had been entrusted. In the neatest way in the world, she intercepted it."

"I blame myself. Had we not earlier had those misunderstandings—"

"Misunderstandings?" He laughed soundlessly. "You and I understood each other only too well. That was the trouble. From the beginning a wordless communion linked us. At any distance our moments coincided. Space did not exist if I wished to look into your mind, or you mine. It was this very participation that you could not forgive. I was the last man you wished to love . . . the most unsuitable for charming Saint Sophia who had a weakness for general rather than particular benevolence. If love were inevitable, you preferred an individual whom you could make your own by bell, book and candle—through the accepted stages. Instead of which, you found to your alarm that you were precipitately one with me—before you loved at all—and in the way most sacred to that fastidious soul of yours. Never shall I forget your startled look when first I quoted the actual thoughts you were bestowing on that scene before us. Later in Rome, when time and again I met you, without appointment, in public park, or gallery, or theatre, alarm was gradually replaced by pleasure. That girl Clio and her Abbey have awakened to a similar affinity. Watching the young, one catches one's own youth on the wing again—and with fresh awareness. I had almost said *first*

awareness! Blurting out the truth of their telepathy, as she did the other day, with no sense of the fitting—I too almost betrayed myself."

"That, Colonna, I can scarcely believe!"

"Now, you have become dignified! Yes, almost I found it in my heart to warn her that—should she be rescued—never to see that man again."

"You feel that Clio and Abbey would be better parted—as we were."

"Before they make too many memories together, and become resentful of division, as I have done. You, Sophia, with your gift of loving your enemies are in another class. I might define a martyr as one who loves a saint. Unfitted as I am for this heroic rôle, I resent it also. Above all, I resent you."

"And I do not wonder!" impulsively she leant forward and laid both hands upon his cold one. "Nor do I forgive Beatrice for the advice she gave me, when that belated letter was finally mine. But this I will say: I believe my dismay frightened her. Till then she had not guessed how much I loved you."

"She certainly took the speediest way of curing you! Curious, wasn't it, that she remembered to deliver the letter on the very night I gave that farewell party? How did you later describe it? The worst of everything in the best of taste! An apt description of my prodigal companions! But how natural that she should say to you, as I'm sure she did: 'Don't agonize over this unfortunate delay. I appreciate that your silence may have conveyed indifference. Go round and see him *now*. It is barely ten. It's unconventional—still, you need not wait!' But you did wait, Sophia. You were the life and soul of my wild party, and how I hated you for it! It wasn't till two in the morning—you left at one with that infernal Bragance—that I got the truth out of Carola Selm. Something *might* have been said to Beatrice that morning on the Via Tornabuoni—of the festive departure planned for me that night. That was good enough for me—or shall we say, bad enough?"

To his surprise, the Princess began to laugh. Silently but unmistakably she was shaking before him. "Dominic, never shall I forget your fury next day. Outraged virtue could not have been more indignant. I was left suing for forgiveness, and indeed I still am!"

Soberly he replied, "Can you forgive yourself, or even explain the third mishap? True, it was twenty-two years later. I was over fifty at Viccy's coming-of-age ball at Florence, you were forty-six. But something of life remained then, and my inheritance was at last in sight."

"No," she replied, "I cannot forgive myself. But there were facts connected with the episode which you never understood. At the time I could not explain. Nor did I believe that your anger and your—your—"

"Arrogance?"

"Yes, arrogance could part us over such a trifling failure. Not till that day when I arranged to meet you at the gates beyond Fiesole, did I suspect that Beatrice was involved with Garett Phelps, or that he was a British agent. The night before, he had turned up at the ball, as you know. It was apparently the first time they had met for years. I believe now that she could not resist the temptation to show him Viccy—at a distance. But Frederick not only returned next morning, he also informed Beatrice that he knew the other was in Florence. Dominic, I was actually on my way to meet you—by the side stairs—when she and Frederick met me on the entresol. 'Here she is!' Beatrice exclaimed. 'As I told you, Frederick, we are now off to luncheon at the Lanzi.' I tell you, I was as helpless under those circumstances, as if I had been bound, hand and foot. Frederick did not leave us until late afternoon, when she was forced to tell me something of the situation. It was her idea that we took that *carrozzella.*"

"Was it her idea that you took the Fiesole road?"

"She gave the driver the instructions. How was I to guess that you would still be waiting there, after five hours? Mercifully she did not see you."

"But I saw her. It was enough."

"I telephoned. I telegraphed. I called. But you had gone. You did not answer when I wrote that I could explain."

"Naturally I did not. I tell you, I saw her. I repeat: it was enough."

"Dominic, do you really believe that two appointments I failed to keep, and one which I contrived, were the cause of our separation?"

"They were, at any rate, three misfortunes from which we never recovered."

"I'm afraid," she said slowly, "that Lucifer, not Beatrice, was to blame. I confess that, for me at least, the widening gulf was charted 'Proper Pride.' "

"Very different from the ambient plains on which we first so satisfactorily met, those illimitable Russian steppes."

"No, Dominic, we met before that! Or have you forgotten? You joined the train at Königsberg. Peering out, I saw Frederick greet you in the windy dark. Visibility was poor, but I knew you instantly! Then you too looked, saw me, smiled."

"Bland yet astonished—a dazzlingly fair face through a wet window—then your own breath blotted it out. Wretch! My first glimpse of my own heart, and you ruined this as well."

"But what an idyllic morning lay ahead, Dominic, for that wedding party on its way to Moscow! Petrograd came first of course. Those memorable palaces . . . repositories of treasure

—statuary, tapestries, bronzes, china, every conceivable *objet d'art*."

"Yet no pictures, Sophia."

"Yes, few pictures. I too felt that lack. But what an experience those interiors were. Disconcerting as a dream that is faintly tinged with nightmare—grandiose twi-lit corridors, haunted by the odour of vegetable water. Noble vestibules reminiscent of museums in which caretakers have cooked their evening meal, and omitted to air out afterwards!"

"Not unlike our present situation," he observed ironically. "Yet you remain untroubled in extremity. You always did."

"Each of us has his own difficulties," she began. "Mine have always been peremptory, but then I have a passionate nature."

"Passionate, Princess?" he said acidly. "Surely not."

"Passionate, exclusive, possessive," she calmly replied. "With these attendant devils in dignified occupation, I have known most fears—every tremor known to desire, and each dread that humiliation can devise. But at the height of my anguish, judge of my surprise to discover that this tortured failure had achieved one flawless contact. I found I loved God. I have been rejoicing ever since."

"Curious," he said glibly, "that in our different spheres we are both subject to the same frailty, the passion for perfection. You in life and I in art."

Steadily she faced him. "Is there anything else you wish to know?"

"No," he replied harshly. "In humiliation you were not alone. But in this we differed—I failed to find mine instructive."

"Perhaps your case called for love, Dominic. And on reflection, you may find that this was yours always."

"Sophia, your words should warm me, but at this age they merely agitate me. Shall we have some more soup."

"Soup would certainly be a diversion," she agreed, "although I am now a little tired of this particular bean."

He lifted the saucepan from the stove. "The entertainment is scarcely what one would expect from Minerva. But if we live to write our bread-and-butter letter, no doubt we shall be grateful."

Together they drank. As he replaced his cup, he smiled for the first time, and his spectral face leapt fitfully to liveliness.

Benignly she faced him in the still light painted by the candle on their gloom.

"Sophia," he said, "what are we thinking of, at this moment?"

"Moscow, 1883," she said promptly, "fragrant, unforgettable with lilac. We are driving in our first droshky together, that smallest possible victoria, with the largest imaginable driver ahead, padded presumably to keep out the heat!"

"How the immensity of the Russian sky subdued to beauty the garish element in those towns."

"Now you're back in St. Petersburg! Moscow was sheer perfection. But because you were twenty-eight, and I was twenty-two, I suppose the hurly-burly of state coaches, caparisoned horses, parades, processions, all the trappings of Court ceremonial made the most immediate impression."

"Yes, it was our first experience of Eastern splendour. But we were just sophisticated enough to be surprised by the mildness of the fairy tale in its oriental setting. Culture is always genial."

"Ah, Dominic, you ought to have fallen in love with a pagan goddess."

"Our circle certainly held several," he agreed.

"Carola Selm perhaps?"

"Instead of a blue stocking more at home with Erasmus and John Colet—a disconcerting siren who disturbed our flying moment with imitations of immortality."

"No, Dominic, more at home with Russia, as you were then! We adored the Russian people—and the astounding yet indulgent perception that was theirs."

"I adored you. Now that we are dead and buried I may safely confess this. In those first spring days you wore, I can remember, a double-breasted olive coat, with a small round sable hat. I remember also that you found my formal Italian title for you touching. *Touching!* That struck me as odd. 'Illustrious and Most Noble Princess.' "

"And the return journey, Dominic, through swift, short summer— Glorious! A continent of sunflowers and rye, still rivers, placid lakes. Peasants intimately at home in this vast expanse, with their cattle, sheep and goats. People with all day to live."

"Well—for a little we shared that illusion."

Silence fell between them, in the clammy gloom of the Babenberg hall—sudden as a stone into a pond.

The clock ticked loudly, its beat laboured, each second an obstacle overcome.

"And now where are we, Madame?"

"Moscow still, of course. A wedding in the Church of the Assumption, its iconostas sparkling with light. Men in full dress uniform, and women with the diamond *kakoshnik* springing from their heads like halos, are simply a background, like the dim Byzantine interior for the ecstatic fact that we are together!"

"And now?"

"A summer evening window. And Moscow is a hilly skyscape of domes and watch-towers; of gold and silver roofs. Five hundred guests are festively milling at a safe distance in the white marble Throne Room, already drowsy with roses from the Sulkowski hothouses. But in this wan, cold corridor we have Moscow to ourselves. Far and wide through the window, from hundreds of churches thousands of bells are pealing as no other bells have ever done."

"So far, so good. But at this present deplorable moment of what am I thinking?"

"Of the brazen clatter we long most to hear from the church of the present moment, Springbrunnen! What time on the clock now, Dominic?"

"Seven a.m.," he said shortly. "But our watch is over. I intend to waken the house an hour before its time—to its fury! The fact is: you and I can sleep at last. Let the world muster. This is reveille!"

INVITATION TO DELIVERANCE . . .

Tap . . . tap . . . tap . . . inertly they listened as the Comte tapped on.

The Prince, who had slept for four hours since his watch, once more sat on the outskirts of the group. The abyssmal dark of the hall was pricked in three places only by candles. The guests bulked like unsteady stones in this sea of shadows.

Perfunctorily Charlotte swilled out soiled cups in a pail of dirty water.

Mechanically Hans swept the floor below the gallery.

Albert's mattress lay in the middle of the hall. The Doctor had finally agreed that it might be drawn there. All had emphasized that it would make a change.

"Not many more we *can* make," pleaded Miss Storm.

"We can move it back," Dr. Herriot had at first retorted.

"Don't!" she said faintly. And Albert continued fitfully to preen himself, as centre of attraction. Princess Sophia had since read him a story. In the pitch blackness, Miss Storm had twice rattled forth "El Relicario."

Once she stopped, and struck the same note twice, addressing Princess Sophia: "Worse today, isn't it?"

"Yet not so bad as it might be, all things considered."

"Perhaps not . . ."

Obdurately Frau Winkwurth continued to play Patience

by the light of one of the candles, under the desultory gaze of Lord Brompton. Clio nodded on the couch. Deftly Princess Victoria proceeded to halve each candle of their dwindling stock.

A remarkable change had taken place in each since the final electrical eclipse—a certain solicitude, a compliant attitude was now in evidence that Dr. Herriot did not like at all. As the temperature of the hall continued to drop, no comment was made, although hitherto as a topic of complaint the cold had served in place of the weather. Dr. Herriot regarded this restraint as his patients' crowning feat, and it left him most uneasy. From the time that the light failed, moreover, he and the Comte had actually achieved a modicum of cordiality towards each other. *Hand in hand, heavenward,* he perceived, seriously disquieted.

Princess Victoria finished counting the candles.

"I'm sorry to say," she announced, "that our allowance must now be one at a time." Her voice was flat, listless.

Her guests looked up, listened—depressed by her unusual lifelessness as they had never been by each other's. What was the matter with her? Then this resentment of theirs also petered out.

Dr. Herriot sat down with a grunt.

"As bad as all that?" said Sophia softly.

He grimaced. "As full of pains and aches as any hypochondriac! To be buried before your time is an instructive experience. But my quarrel with you, Princess, is that you are still unchanged or, rather, unenlightened! You still ignore calamity!"

She laughed. "I don't ignore it, Dr. Herriot. But I do not think it is our greatest danger."

"I know, I know!" brusquely he broke in. "*I shake not the*

earth only, but also heaven . . . that those things which cannot be shaken may remain. And having written off death in immortality, and calamity in its own chaos—I'd like to know how you dispose of evil, before we part."

"Evil disposes of itself, Dr. Herriot."

"At considerable expense!" he taunted.

Slightly astonished, she replied, "Yes, the expense is considerable but not ruinous. You see, Dr. Herriot, I believe that one cannot commit lasting evil on another. Corruption, like salvation, has its corresponding response."

"But what of the perpetrator, Princess? How do you dispose of the active agent?"

"For him also there must be a further stage. Despair. In his ultimate identification with misery, he finds his own level—and escape."

"An extremely unpleasant form of purgation!" commented the Prince.

"Consoling for the enlightened, perhaps."

"Scarcely, Dr. Herriot, as Princess Sophia blames the elect, persons like yourself, for our general lack of headway!"

"I beg your pardon—" began Dr. Herriot.

"No, no." She smiled. "I simply feel that exceptional men will have to reach a far higher stage of devotion before the average can advance with confidence."

"So, of course, Dr. Herriot, she lays retrogression at your own feet."

Together they laughed—the Doctor uneasily, the others pleasantly.

"Come, Dr. Herriot—" smiled the Princess—"if evil is its own death, and calamity but a process, won't you yield an inch elsewhere? Here we have seen the best and the worst of one another, and in every case have retained respect. That at least has not been shaken. None of us has earned laurels, but won't you concede an immortelle?"

"A deathless respect?" he queried dryly. "This certainly has been earned, yet how can brief breath support it? However, if I seem boorish, let me at least admit that you have mine—as long as memory lasts."

"Reckless creature!" said the Prince. "That is all this siren wants, for if memory be immortality, as the ancients held, hereafter you are lost to reason, although distinguished by your friends! Meantime, let us be thankful for the temporal. Repeatedly I have warned the Princess that we fail to exploit the present if we persist in plundering the future. Were our moments not fleeting, were our hold on existence not transitory, we should perish hourly from anxiety, grief—yes, and joy."

Meantime the Comte continued to tap the signal.

As the energy of the party ebbed through inaction, De Talloires' unaccountably increased. Occasionally now his companions looked at him askance, some with dislike.

"I'll damn well see he stops at eleven-thirty," Lord Brompton rose, struck his shin, and sat down in disgust. "Outrageous that we should endure this till midday. He ought to be making his rounds of inspection now. Lunacy to leave those till noon."

"You know quite well why he waits till then," Princess Victoria retorted.

"An able-bodied man of his age," muttered Lord Brompton, "playing about with a hammer."

"Puerile," said Frau Winkwurth mechanically.

"In five minutes," declared his lordship, "I shall take action. I've had enough. We all have—"

He broke off. The frame, boarding-up the lancet window had fallen, as it sometimes did, onto the balcony again.

"All right!" Victoria said irritably. "I've got the lantern. Come along, Doctor."

Hurriedly both disappeared upstairs.

But the party by the table did not trouble to follow these movements. They remained motionless. They alone had glanced up at the crash. They alone had seen.

Staring upwards, each now sat paralyzed.

From the lancet window a glimmer streaked the hall. It was not light, but neither was it darkness. It was a phantom blade stabbing the gloom.

The Comte's signalling had abruptly ceased. He was already half-way along the balcony.

Stupefied the guests sat on.

Their unnatural silence awakened Clio. Alarmed she cried: "What's happened?"

Then she too turned.

Victoria from the balcony was calling down.

Her voice was clear, but none could follow what she said.

"Louder!" called Frau Winkwurth weakly. "Louder, louder!"

"It *is* the light!" Victoria was calling. "François, where are you? It is the light!"

For a further second the guests remained stricken—then as one they stampeded up the stairs. Stumbling as they went, they charged towards the window.

"Gently!" shouted Dr. Herriot. "This balcony is not the gallery, d'you want to bring it down? One at a time now, one at a time!"

Trembling they gazed. Cold grey air was welling in upon them. As each stared in turn through the narrow aperture, there could be seen a dismal light with, in the distance, the gaunt branch of a tree. No sky showed, and all else above, below the branch was formless white.

Lord Brompton was the first to recover. "Monstrous!" he exploded. "Where the devil is everyone? Deliverance after a week, and no one here to take advantage of the subsidence. Outrageous! *Have we to rescue ourselves?"*

This climax of absurdity hot-haste on calamity produced anti-climax. Hysterically guests and servants began to shout with laughter as they tore downstairs again. Dr. Herriot could do nothing with them. They collapsed on chairs, they rolled upon the sofa, they lurched across the floor in transports of mirth. Prince Colonna himself shook vehemently, tears of derision running down his face. Clio and Albert blindly racing the full length of the hall, ran into the stove.

Momentarily sobered, the assembly collected its wits. All spoke at once. Nobody listened. Every few minutes, however, one or other of the party hurried upstairs for yet another glimpse of this shining miracle—a dull day outside.

For half an hour it was to the women a delirium of relief.

Hurriedly the men examined the windows on the ground floor. Each was hermetically sealed by snow. Upstairs, search revealed every aperture clogged as usual.

Gravely they announced this.

The women brushed such nonsense aside, for as Clio next peered through the embrasure, sunlight struck the distant branch.

"The sun—the sun!" she cried.

Sobbing with joy, she flung her arms around the nearest neck, which chanced to be the Doctor's.

Craning out in turn, Victoria announced: "I can see the

path. Positively I can! Only a small section is visible, but I can see it."

"Monstrous!" Lord Brompton had begun again.

"Good God, man!" Dr. Herriot exclaimed, "can't you realize that the park may still be submerged? A subsidence like this can clear the way in hours where days of digging may fail. We don't begin to know their problems."

Furiously, Lord Brompton shouted, "Oh, we don't, don't we? *You* haven't begun to grasp ours. Why, there may be *more* snow! Think of the need for speed. Anything may happen. Someone should drop out of this window while they can."

"Into twenty feet of snow?" suggested the Comte.

Dr. Herriot was staring out now. "Scarcely as bad as that—if one managed to jump clear of the stuff banked against the wall. The path is certainly visible ahead—for the few yards one can see."

"Nothing," announced the Comte, "shall be done hastily."

"Hastily!" screamed Frau Winkwurth. "And you call yourselves men? Why, it's daylight outside. What are you waiting for? We ladies have been entombed for days. If there is a man among you, he'll jump down right away, and investigate. The snow will break his fall."

"It can't be more than a drop of eighteen feet," Victoria was leaning farther out. "And onto snow . . . really as safe as houses! I believe that I could do it."

"Anyone could," Frau Winkwurth cried. "Once in the snow, all one has to do is to use a swimming movement, such as guides advocate. And you will achieve the path."

"Were this aperture wide enough," said the Comte, "which it is not, that leap would still be dangerous. Moreover, the path is probably completely blocked beyond that clearance. It would be madness."

"No man," agreed Lord Brompton, "could get through that aperture in any case. As you say, De Talloires, we must await the rescue squad. I had hoped to expedite matters. But I doubt if a child could negotiate this opening."

"Nonsense!" Princess Victoria again knelt on the low sill. "I once climbed out as a girl to help an injured bird—along that coping."

"As a girl?" his lordship demurred. "Possibly. But no woman could now pass that space. Just look at it."

To the astonishment of all, the Princess began to laugh: "What a challenge to my figure! I simply can't resist it. Who knows? In the end I may become what every woman longs to be—a legend."

"Viccy!" said De Talloires ominously, "this nonsense has gone on long enough. That snow is banked for fifteen feet at least."

"But, François, one could jump clear of it, if one took care, as Dr. Herriot says. And it's pretty solid. You said so yourself. Look what happened a minute ago when we flung out that log! Part of the path *is* clear. Round the corner, it may be easier still."

Distastefully he stared at her. She was quite serious. She too was drunk with impatience. It was deplorable.

But Lord Brompton had now peered farther out.

"Don't be idiotic, Viccy—" he began. Then he too saw the sun, and in his turn was vanquished. "'Pon my soul, just look at that—the *sun!* If this window were a reasonable size, we'd all be out in five minutes. I can see the path myself as the dear girl says!"

"You can see a portion of the path," said De Talloires.

"Ahead one might quite easily be buried. If the path *is* open round the bend, our rescue from outside can only be a matter now of hours. If it is not open—then why, at this stage, trifle with impossibilities?"

"For the simple reason, my dear fellow, that a unique chance has now offered itself. How are we to know that there won't be a further submersion? Already I fear we have been given up for lost, disgraceful as that is. But if one of us could escape and make contact with the outside world—"

"In the form of another snowdrift?"

"Should that prove to be the case, then our prospecting member would simply return—and re-enter the Château."

"Climbing the face of the building with their teeth, I presume?"

"Sarcasm will get us nowhere, De Talloires."

"Of course it won't!" Victoria said swiftly. "We've got eight pairs of full-length window curtains in the hall. You could knot a rope, and I could be hauled back. But to get out it would, of course, be much easier to jump."

"There's your chance, La Coraggiosa!" the Doctor gave Clio a friendly nudge. "Do you fancy suicide at this stage of your career?"

Brusquely she shook him off. "Princess," she said, "I'll do it, and be glad to—if only to get even with myself. And there's the sun. *I'd like to!*"

"Dear Clio," said the Princess gently, "it is out of the question. You're thinner than I am, but your bones are larger. Even sideways you could not edge through. You've quite a formidable skull, you know. Mine is much smaller. And my hips—I rejoice to think that, possibly, my hips are unique!"

"That will do," said the Comte icily. "Be good enough to go downstairs, ladies."

"If the Princess is going to break her neck," said Prince Colonna, "I agree with De Talloires. She should not do it in a hurry. By all means let us study the subject from every angle first. Cherish the lady a little longer."

Back in the body of the hall, Hans and Charlotte were discovered stolidly ladling out the midday soup, six candles recklessly alight.

The merest pretence was made at a meal.

"Patience," began the Comte.

"Patience!" chorused the guests indignantly. "Something should be done at once . . . something ought to be done . . . something must be done!"

"If we are marooned," Lord Brompton amplified, "as well as buried—where, I ask, are the planes? Not a sound can be heard through that window. If I've told you once, I've told you a hundred times, I, myself, am on the board of two airway companies. Deplorable is the word for the present failure to co-operate. Abject, the only description of the general public's efforts."

"If we're going to act," said Victoria, "it ought to be while the sun is out. As Lord Brompton says: I can easily scuttle back, if the road's blocked."

"There's a girl!" cried Frau Winkwurth. "Hans will be waiting to haul you back. We all will—won't we, Hans?"

But Hans's response was dogmatic. With the best will in the world, he asserted, the Princess could not get through the window. Her backside, he explained, would prevent this.

At this point the Comte abruptly left the family circle, striding into the outer darkness of the hall. Throughout a lifetime he had rarely been so angry. To his chagrin, Victoria had displayed less sense than the undisciplined Clio.

Pacing back, he was just in time to hear Dr. Herriot say:

"Then as a start, Princess, I'll take down the curtains. The sooner we get busy on that rope the better."

"Sit down!" ordered the Comte peremptorily.

"François!" the Princess sounded pained, yet placatory.

"Enough of this foolery," said De Talloires. "Dr. Herriot you amaze me."

"You don't amaze me," snapped the Doctor, "but you annoy me. Princess Victoria, do you wish to take down your curtains?"

In the strident silence that followed, Hans could be heard breathing busily near the Comte.

"Not at the moment," said the Princess, after a pause, "but thank you, Dr. Herriot. . . ."

INVITATION TO THE FUTURE . . .

"In fact, Dr. Herriot," provocatively the Comte pursued his point, "your irresponsibility does more than amaze me, it astounds me."

"My what-was-that?" unexpectedly Dr. Herriot had stepped up to De Talloires.

"Your irresponsibility. It's only too apparent that the Princess might break a leg, an arm, even her neck if she took this absurd step."

"I don't consider it an absurd step. There's little risk, if she can get through the window. And some good might be effected. At the worst, she can come back."

"Who says so?"

"Well, it's obvious."

The Comte smiled disagreeably. "There spoke ignorance."

In protest, the other guests mistakenly laughed.

The Doctor loured. "Withdraw that remark!"

"No, I believe it to be true. And no man worth his salt would let a woman take this risk."

"Repeat that, will you?"

Disdainfully the Comte looked down. "No man worth his salt—" he began, when the Doctor's fist shot out.

To the onlookers' consternation, De Talloires' head jerked back. He had received a telling cut upon his chin.

Unhappily for Dr. Herriot, this success was fleeting. The Comte was a head taller. His retaliation sent the Doctor reeling. But only for a second. Dr. Herriot was stockily built. Once more he closed in.

Petrified, the others stared. It was incredible that such a thing should happen.

"Disgraceful!" Frau Winkwurth craned forward.

"Barbarous," muttered the Prince.

"Remember the ladies!" Lord Brompton arose.

"Watch the stove!" yelled Clio and Albert.

Victoria had reached the stairs. This at any rate would stop them. Swiftly she ran along the gallery.

Downstairs the Doctor, lunging, slipped and fell. The fight was over.

"Look!" shouted Albert, pointing to the balcony.

Dimly they saw her poised there, crouched in the embrasure, in the attitude of a sprinter about to take off—saw her leap and vanish.

"Frightful!" La Coraggiosa sank back on the couch.

"Quick, Doctor, Clio's fainted."

The Comte alone achieved the balcony in time to see his betrothed flounder out of sight, in waist-deep snow. At the corner, she turned once and valiantly waved.

Thereafter, followed by Hans, he made his infuriated way to the front entrance. Nor was he again to enter the Banner Hall, where an appalled and guilty silence prevailed.

Dr. Herriot issued a tot of brandy all round.

"Dear, brave girl!" Frau Winkwurth addressed space. "None of us will ever forget that sight."

Albert began to cry.

"Oh, I can't bear this." Clio shook them off, and again stumbled up the stairs.

The splash of sunshine had disappeared. Through the hole in the snow, no sky showed. The stricken branch still hung lifeless in the dismal light. All else, above, below, was formless white. It was not silence. It was stupor.

Staring, she saw nothing else, but suddenly in her own ears, delusively, sound rushed in to fill this vacuum. Harsh, discordant noises, all the medley of beleaguered desire—handbells, whistles, voices in fevered illusion.

Trembling she drew back from the blank, the lifeless scene.

"Listen!" she called. "Listen . . . listen! Can you hear it? Do you hear it?"

Deceptively distant, some confused commotion assailed them. "Bells . . . bells . . . bells!" they cried.

Leaning into the embrasure, Dr. Herriot was the last to hear the nearing uproar. But he heard it more distinctly as, critically, he listened. Many persons, hidden for the moment, were on their way out there.

"Someone should tell the dear Comte," Frau Winkwurth insisted. "You go, Doctor." She spoke with scant ceremony. The tide had turned, the old order was re-established.

But in the entrance hall, Dr. Herriot hesitated. It was the strangest scene of many he had witnessed there.

The Comte and Hans were frenziedly digging down the compacted snow, rigid behind the open door. A guttering candle stuck in an empty bottle lit the cavernous doorway from a wall recess. Their tools were a coal-cellar grape and shovel. Both men were bleeding at the nose from the pressure they had exerted. They did not once glance in his direction. They made no sign that they had heard his news—nor could the Doctor find it in his heart to blame them, as he turned away.

Alone with Hans, De Talloires laboured on . . . the snow

of ordeal flying over his shoulder—as in the end it was through this door that she must return, and through the same that she would finally leave with him, en route for Innsbruck . . . Zurich . . . Paris—then Dijon for Burgundy, Vermontaine . . . and home.

Behind him, ludicrously enough, the other guests were prematurely and hastily bidding each other goodbye, with the enthusiasm of those too long together.

"Only she could have done it. Elegance itself!" concluded Frau Winkwurth. "Doctor, we ought to have a second tot. We need it. We have much to reproach ourselves with. You, perhaps, more than anyone. Thank you, Lord Brompton . . . you perhaps less. What was it that she said again? *Who knows? In the end I may become what every woman longs to be—a legend.* Do stop snivelling, Albert. Think what you have to remember! Not the Princess who couldn't sleep on a pea, but the Princess who passed through a needle."

The End

The Author acknowledges with gratitude the information so fully and freely afforded her by the Institut für Schnee und Lawinenforschung, Weissfluhjoch, Davos, Schweiz.